ADVANCE PRAISE FOR

ONLY BECAUSE IT'S YOU

"A fresh take on friends-to-lovers, *Only Because It's You*
proves that sometimes the best relationships are the ones you
never see coming. A modern romance, a love letter to
Toronto and Addis Ababa, and full of humour and
heartwarming moments—Rebecca delivers pure joy!"

CHANTEL GUERTIN, bestselling author
of *It Happened One Christmas*

"Smart, witty and full of heart. A refreshing take on
the well-loved marriage of convenience trope."

BAL KHABRA, *USA Today* bestselling author of *Collide*

"Rebecca Fisseha's *Only Because It's You* is a masterful blend of
humour and vulnerability that will leave you breathless. Miz
and Kal's romance will fill your heart long after the last page!"

AMY LEA, internationally bestselling author of *The Catch*

ONLY BECAUSE
IT'S YOU

ALSO BY REBECCA FISSEHA

Daughters of Silence

Only Because It's You

REBECCA FISSEHA

DOUBLEDAY CANADA

Doubleday Canada and colophon are registered trademarks of Penguin Random House Canada Limited

Library and Archives Canada Cataloguing in Publication

Title: Only because it's you: a novel / Rebecca Fisseha.
Other titles: Only because it is you
Names: Fisseha, Rebecca, 1980- author.
Identifiers: Canadiana (print) 20240380754 | Canadiana (ebook) 20240394577 |
ISBN 9780385688512 (softcover) | ISBN 9780385688529 (EPUB)
Subjects: LCGFT: Romance fiction. | LCGFT: Novels.
Classification: LCC PS8611.I8525 O55 2025 | DDC C813/.6—dc23

Cover, text and map design by Talia Abramson
Illustrations by Talia Abramson, (skylines) based on images by Serhii / Adobe Stock
Map by FourLeafLover / Adobe Stock
Typeset in Bembo by Sean Tai
Printed in the USA

The authorized representative in the EU for product safety and compliance is Penguin Random House Ireland, Morrison Chambers, 32 Nassau Street, Dublin D02 YH68, Ireland. https://eu-contact.penguin.ie

Published in Canada by Doubleday Canada,
a division of Penguin Random House Canada Limited,
320 Front Street West, Suite 1400, Toronto, Ontario, M5V 3B6, Canada.
Distributed in the United States by Penguin Random House LLC.

penguinrandomhouse.ca

1st Printing

Penguin
Random House
DOUBLEDAY CANADA

To Mesi & Serkie

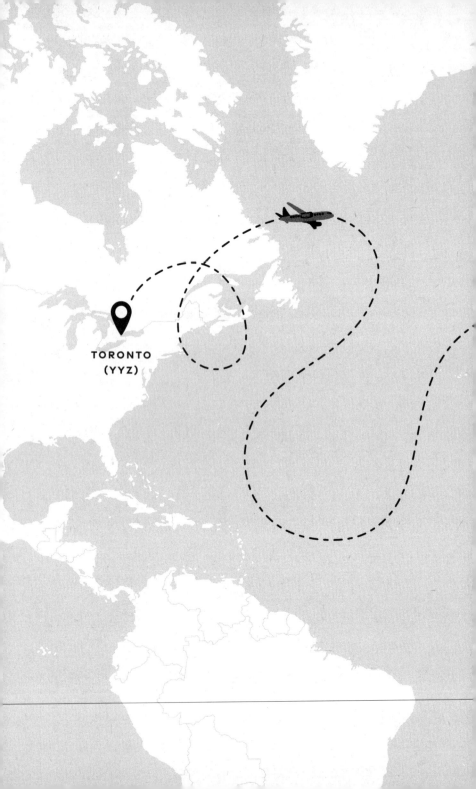

TORONTO
(YYZ)

ADDIS ABABA
(ADD)

1

MIZ

*B*ecause *somebody* doesn't return what they've borrowed, here I am, crouched on my bedroom floor, decked out in my running gear, rummaging through Daniel's gym bag looking for my AirPods. I should already be at Union Station, meeting Aimé for our run. But I refuse to go out, especially in this August heat, without my afternoon playlist.

"Come on," I growl, feeling around and peering in the bag. I wrinkle my nose. What does Daniel have in here, a dead animal? I mean *a bit* of funk can be sexy, but something of his is in desperate need of a wash. I'm not about to put any guy's crap in the laundry though. From there, it's all downhill to wifey-town. No, thank you.

My phone chimes from the armband strapped to my biceps. I know who it'll be even as I take it out to look.

Aimé: I'm here.

Shit. Hoping she won't check my location and catch me lying, I text back:

Me: Sorry, omw.

After months of trying to convince her, she's finally agreed to meet me for a trial run, starting at Union Station—a quick 2 k from my place—and working our way down to the waterfront. I have to get to the station.

I put my phone aside and shake the bag's opening, hoping to see my earbuds in the contents. Instead, a small black box tumbles into view. I reach for the velvet cube and flip it open without a thought. Almost immediately, my breath catches in my throat.

I freeze, staring at what's carefully nestled in the small black box. "What the . . ." My mind spins, as if it's buffering.

Finally, my brain catches up to what I'm seeing, and heat rushes up my entire body. "Oh shit!" I whisper to myself.

I snap the box shut, hurl it back in the bag, and scuttle backward on my butt, one hand slapped over my mouth, eyes so wide they feel as if they'll pop out of my head. I take a deep breath and then make the sign of the cross, like my mama. *This is not happening.* I whip my head around my apartment as if I'm expecting to see a hidden camera, my heart speeding as fast as one of Rophnan's EDM tracks. Inhaling deeply, I take the box out of the bag again. Cradling it in my shaky palms, summoning all my courage, I lift the lid of the box by a teensy fraction. My heart sinks. Nope. It's still an engagement ring. With a sigh, I open the lid fully. Undeniable— it's an engagement ring, a one-carat square-cut diamond, sparkling in the golden late afternoon sunlight. I grip the box, in breathless awe at the ring's almost holy artistry. I collapse in on myself as the shining proof that Daniel wants to *marry* me hits me like a ton of bricks. The question is *why.*

It's the same question that I'd had when I was fourteen and I'd

spotted Dad's wedding ring still on his finger, for reasons unex-
plained, and when I'd found Mom's rolling around in the back of
her bathroom drawer two years later. As I stare at the glittering
ring, panic starts to shorten my breath and I begin feeling light-
headed. I close my eyes and try to focus on breathing. *Inhale two
three four, hold two three four, exhale three two one. Whoosah.* Then, as if
I am handling a grenade, I stand up and gently place the open box
on my dresser. Tiptoeing backward, I pick up my phone and sink
down on the edge of my ancient, back-pain-inducing mattress.

First things first: Aimé.

> **Me: I'm going to be late. Warm up without me. I'll
> catch up.**

Then I put my phone on silent. Figuring out my next steps
will require complete concentration. I march out from my bedroom to the living room's floor-to-ceiling windows and look
down at the spot where Daniel usually parks. He's supposed to
come over tonight, to celebrate the sale of his biggest property
to date, and until a few minutes ago, I had been looking forward
to our night together, and to a morning of me trying to quietly
ease out of bed for my dawn run, but inevitably tickling his early-
riser with the bedsheets and waking the rest of him up too, ready
to get busy. I feel my body warm at the thought.

Focus, girlie! I do one lap of my one-bedroom apartment—
through the living room to the kitchen island, into the bathroom
on the opposite side, and then through the walk-in closet, ending
up back at the entrance to my bedroom, all the while hyperalert
to all evidence of Daniel: size thirteen FILA slides, a giant jar of
whey powder, Old Spice shower gel and deodorant, a beard

trimmer, his boxers in my laundry hamper. I frown. Bro's been getting comfortable.

But marriage-level comfortable? Really? "What planet are you on, Daniel?" I mutter as I grab my headband and shove it on my head, messing up my side plaits. To say that Daniel and I have never talked about marriage, or any other major life subject, would be an overstatement. Talking isn't our priority when we hook up. Hooking up is.

"Who tries to marry a one-night stand?" I ask nobody, adjusting the straps of my racerback tank that feels suddenly too tight. I walk over to Daniel's bag and kick it—but I know that this is my fault. I got greedy. I ignored the terms and conditions of a one-night stand, which are right in its name: one night. Instead, I let that one night repeat for the better part of two years. On again, off again, on again. And here I am now, freaking out because my *one-night stand* bought me an *engagement ring*. I groan. *Now what do I do?*

"Think, Miz, think," I squeak, pressing the heels of my hands into my eyes. *I must contain the situation. But how?* I squat low until I end up on the floor again, legs wide, and flop forward, leaning on my elbows. I almost laugh. I'm so stressed I'm stretching. Kal would be proud. It does relieve the knot in my back that's formed from just that half-minute of sitting on my mattress a moment ago. I lean into the stretch for a few moments, my hands almost reaching my Asics, and slowly feel my breathing regulate and my heart stop racing. I sigh. Okay, I am all brain now. *What am I going to do?*

Option One: I put the ring back in the bag, let Daniel propose. He'll probably do it tonight—a double celebration, he thinks. My breath becomes shallow again, and I close my eyes and inhale slowly through my nose, spreading and lowering my palms to settle my energy. "Come on, Miz, just play the scenario out. It's not gonna kill you. He proposes. Then what?"

How to turn him down gently? How? Get sick? No, I can't do that. Then it hits me. I clap my hands and sit cross-legged in triumph. I'll ask Daniel if he's sent a *shimagile* posse of family elders to Mom. He won't have. Mom doesn't know of his existence, or that of any guy I've been involved with since I was fourteen. Hell, *I* forget Daniel's existence until he pings me.

So make Daniel do proper asking, the *tiyeka*. Because I surely can't give him an answer until he's asked my parents for my hand first. He must formally send his people all the way from Calgary here to Toronto to seek Mom's blessing. I pause. *But then what? What would Mom do?* I have no idea. I only know what she *did* do, twenty-two years ago, the last and only time she found out I was dating: she pulled me out of school in April and sent me to stay with Dad in Ethiopia for a long summer break. *That* had been a nightmare. The only silver lining—besides meeting my dad for the first time—was that I made a lifelong friend in Kal.

Dad is safer. I would tell Daniel to send his people to Dad all the way in Ethiopia. Dad would be forced to ask me about this guy, and I'd tell him that Daniel is some joker I barely know. Dad would refuse his blessing, and I'd be off the hook, baby! I pump my fist and do a little dance in place.

I take out my phone to call Dad and give him a heads-up. But when I open my mouth to sound out what I would say, the words get stuck in my throat. I can't do it. Between my parents, Dad is the reasonable one, but I still can't go there. I've never talked to them about anything like this. Something tells me that my plan will no doubt backfire, somehow. When it comes to my love life, I've kept my parents on a need-to-*never*-know basis ever since I was fourteen. It's worked brilliantly, so why mess with a good thing? Not to mention that this is a fair thing too; they've kept me on the same basis my whole life about whatever caused their estrangement. My parents are the last people to go to about anything related to marriage.

I stretch out on my back and hug my knees to my chest, rocking side to side. The motion is soothing, and that ache in my back really dissolves now, but my mind keeps racing. *Who can say no to Daniel for me?* I mull, though I already know the answer: no one. Not Kal, who tried to sell me on marriage even as far back as when we were teenagers; and not Aimé, who's been engaged to her college boo for years now; and obviously not my mom and dad. I have to do it my own damn self. I sit up, still hugging my knees, and force myself to visualize Daniel proposing and me saying no, the ring box in my peripheral vision. But hard as I try, I just cannot see myself being so brutal. I may not want to marry him, but I don't want to hurt him either.

So then what? That leaves me with only one other option: I have to avert the proposal before it can happen. I straighten my now-fluid back. Yes, this could work. I can't let the proposal happen, period. When Daniel comes over, I will send him on his way, for good, before he drops to a knee. I'll tell him we're through. He may be upset, but I know it won't be for long; his big sale will be consolation enough.

I jump up, suddenly happy again. I have to meet Aimé. This first run has been months in the making, and I can't just not show up when it was my idea. I'll just keep the run super short—she won't complain—and then get back to my condo before Daniel shows up. I check my phone and see a series of texts from Aimé.

Aimé: It's summer I'm already warm.

Aimé: Wheere the f rrrr u???

Aimé: You're still at home?!

Aimé: Hello! You better be putting out a fire or something!

You could say that, I think. I edge up to the ring, which is sitting on my dresser, commanding the space despite its size. Before putting it back in Daniel's gym bag, I gingerly pluck it out of the box and take a photo of it to show Aimé. I study the shot as I would an X-ray of a complex injury at the clinic. On the screen, the ring looks so minuscule. Harmless. A mere photograph really doesn't do justice to this catastrophic moment. *When is something like this ever going to come around again? Exactly never.* No, Aims needs to behold this historic horror show in full 3-D. I drop the ring in the teeny waistband pocket of my shorts, then I snap the box shut, toss it in the gym bag, pull the zipper tight, and head out the front door. Leaving everything exactly as it was, more or less.

2

MIZ

Minutes later, despite being weighed down by the three meals and two snacks I've had today, plus the ordeal I've just endured, I fly out of the elevators and through the lobby, barely acknowledging Everest, the concierge, on the way. Once outside in the bright sunshine, I dash past Daniel's usual parking spot, taking the side streets to Union Station until I get stopped by a light at University Avenue. Belatedly, I squat and tent the fingers of my right hand on the ground between my feet—a pre-run ritual for luck that I've had since I first started running when I was fourteen, when I first went to Ethiopia, when Dad, at a loss as to what to do with me, had plonked me in a kids' running camp.

I inhale the clammy downtown Toronto air infused with the pungency of hot, wet garbage and let the din of traffic, sirens and jangling streetcars wash over me like spa Muzak to a city girl. My phone pings again. *Jeez, relax, Aimé.* I don't even bother to read her text. I just check her location. Sure enough, her dot is still at Union.

The light changes, and I strap my phone back on and am off again, barrelling down University, weaving through students, office workers, shoppers and tourists as if I'm navigating an obstacle course. At Queen, held up by another light, I hop in place in time to the busker hammering away with sticks on overturned plastic buckets, the scattered beat fitting for my discombobulated state. From then on, I sail through four green lights in a row, through the financial district's tunnel of skyscrapers, my aches and pains that are so much a part of me dropping in to say hi like old friends.

I make it to the meet-up point in nine minutes, record time even for me, emerging out of the congestion of downtown into the wide plaza in front of the station, under the expansive sky, thick with the aroma of grilling street meat and pulsing with a mix of commuters headed home and suburbanites coming into town for whatever game or concert is on tonight.

I see Aimé sunning herself at the base of one of the rows of giant columns fronting the station entrance and immediately feel proud of her for just having made it this far today. Months ago, I had proposed—ugh, that word should be banned! I had *suggested*—the idea of us doing a race together with the hope that it would get her out of her life slump. Aimé had been on the Olympic track as a pro sprinter until the grind got too much, so she'd switched to a job as a hearing aid specialist. After some cajoling, which included promising to do the Big Chop haircut with her in solidarity so she can start going natural, she had finally agreed to do a 10 k with me. I pick up my pace as I run past a row of taxis and toward my best friend of seventeen years, startling a flock of pigeons in front of me. When she spots me, Aimé takes her time standing up, leisurely wiping dust off her butt, sipping on an iced drink. I laugh as I take her in. *Of course* she's jazzed up as if we are going to be trailed by photographers for a sports magazine. From specialty running socks to sweat-wicking head- and wristbands, Aimé has chosen high-priced brand names for every part of her running outfit, claiming craftsmanship impacts performance. I say only practice impacts performance. I couldn't care less what I run in as long as I can move in it—and ideally without a diamond ring snug in my waistband pocket. I feel sick. *Why did I think it was a good idea to bring this thing out with me?*

Aimé squints at me with suspicion, and I feel as though she can see the ring pressing into my flesh. "What's going on?"

"Hmm?" I say, hands on my waist, kicking at the heel of one shoe with the foot of the other, avoiding her eyes. I feel her waiting.

"Why are you being weird?" she asks, studying me. After nearly two decades of friendship, she knows me well. I *am* being weird.

I sigh. "Okay, brace yourself," I say finally, and stick my hand in my pocket and pull out the ring. I hold it out in my palm for her to see, careful to keep my fingers curled in just in case a pigeon swoops for it. The pigeons in this city are rude like that. "Look what I found."

Aimé's eyes widen, and she leans in. "Miz," she says carefully. "Em, what am I looking at?" Her confused eyes meet mine.

"I'd say it speaks for itself." I let her take the ring in for another moment before I slip it back into the safety of my waistband pocket and begin to walk. Aimé falls into step with me, looking dazed. "Miz, 'splain."

"I found it in Daniel's gym bag," I say flatly.

Aimé stops right on a subway grate, and I halt alongside her. She looks bewildered. "For you?"

I nod.

She shakes her head. "Why would Daniel have a ring for *you*?"

"Exactly!" I feel almost relieved. I'm not crazy—even Aimé knows that Daniel and I weren't *that* serious. Suddenly, I feel worn out, the weight of this situation exhausting me in a way that sprinting all the way from my condo to downtown hadn't. I plop down on the edge of a black concrete planter, and Aimé sits beside me.

"Zang!" she says. "This is nuts."

"Mm-hmm." For a few moments, we just stare blankly at the giant Scotiabank arena screen at the far end of the street, as if we're at home, zoned out in front of the TV.

"But . . . you guys just mess around," Aimé mumbles, chewing on her straw. "Like, the math just ain't math-ing."

I keep my eyes on the screen as I respond. "I know. I'm racking my brain, trying to figure out what the fuck he's thinking." I finally break my eyes away and stare at Aimé. "Make it make sense."

She glances at my belly suggestively. "Hey, who wouldn't want to lock you down?"

I roll my eyes. "I'm not pregnant." I scowl at her. "Say something helpful, please."

She finds her sentence carefully. "Uh, maybe he's . . . holding it for a friend?"

My eyes bug out with hope. "Yeah?"

Aimé flinches and sucks in air through her teeth. "You said to say something helpful, not true."

I throw up my hands. "Oh god. Why him? Why me? How? It just doesn't add up!" But the evidence was right there, on my phone, in my shorts, burned into my retinas.

"When do you think he's going to do it?"

I tug at my tiny waistband zipper. "He's not. I'm making sure of that."

"Meaning?" Aimé draws out the word as if she's sensing trouble.

I avoid her eyes. "I'm going to handle it," I say simply.

"Handle it how—" Her mouth falls open in dread. "Miz! *What* are you going to do with that ring?" When I don't answer her, she grabs me by the shoulders and forces brutal eye contact. "Miz! You *have* to put the ring back where you found it."

I shake her off. "I know! I'm not a thief! I just wanted you to see it." Aimé looks doubtful, but I ignore her. "When I get home, I'll put it back in his gym bag. Then, when he comes by later tonight, I'll break it off with him. That way, I don't have to say no when he actually proposes." I extract myself from my friend's tight grip and stand up. "It's kinder."

She looks at me quizzically. "Why can't you just say no? Aren't you sassy Miss I-Don't-Do-Marriage? You've been saying no to marriage all your life, even though ain't nobody ever asked you. But now shit's getting real, and you're too scared to say one little word?"

I deflate, mollified, mortified, mummified by this unflattering truth about myself I've been forced to face this afternoon; reality scares the shit out of me.

"Yeah," I say in a tiny, sad voice.

My naked admission softens her. "It's funny," she says gently. "Isn't being a couple a prerequisite for breaking up?"

I kick at a cigarette butt on the ground. "But I don't see what else I can do. I've got to break it off."

Aimé points up at me. "*After* you return the ring."

As if I want to keep this thing. "Obviously. When I get home, I will put the ring back, all slick and undetected. *Then* I'll end things. He'll be none the wiser." I let out a long breath, close my eyes, and turn my face up toward the bright sunlight. "Phew, I feel lighter already."

Aimé stands up and pats me on the back. "I'm glad."

"But right now, we train," I say, hopping up and down, windmilling my arms. "Let's go!" I shout like an overhyped coach, turning back the way I came and breaking into a run. "Come on!" I holler over my shoulder, turning my head around just in time to run straight into a nasty cloud of cigarette smoke.

She comes up in my peripheral vision, doing something between a fast walk and a trot. "But . . ." She pants, the ice in her plastic cup clattering as she scrambles to catch up. "No pep talk? No speech?"

"No way. No other way but to dive right in! Remember, sip, sip, exhale, exhale!" I slow slightly at the intersection to turn south in the direction of the lake, but then, at the slightest taste of that breeze from the open water, I gun it like a cheetah chasing dinner (or escaping a wannabe fiancé, same thing), through an underpass. I suddenly hear Aimé yelling my name.

I stop and look back to see her bent over, heaving. I return to her guiltily.

"What is with you?" she snaps at me, her breathing clipped. "Might I remind you I'm retired from sprinting?" She finishes all the lemonade left in her cup. "This is not what I signed up for, Miz. Forget this." She turns around. "I'm going home."

"No, no!" I say hastily, grabbing her arm. "I'm sorry." I move us to the side, out of the path of a couple struggling to wheel their suitcases across the cracked concrete. "My bad. I'm just in a rush to get back home so I can put this thing away." I suddenly feel deeply stupid for having brought the ring with me, for dragging Aimé into this disaster.

"Well, I'm not about to die today because of that," Aimé retorts, a hand on her hip. Seeing my expression, she softens and pulls me into a hug with a sigh. "Don't worry about the run." She pulls back and pushes me in the direction of my condo. "Go home and deal with Daniel."

I smile at her gratefully and pull her in for another hug. "Thank you."

"Just go home," she says sternly. "You know how you do. You say you're going to do five k and then end up doing eight. Today's not the day for that. You go straight home, no detours, you put the ring back. You got it?"

"Oh, believe me, I do," I say. It's a known fact that if I could have one superpower, it would be to be able to run forever. "I'm beelining it home. *Bzzz.*" I give her a wave before I push off in the direction of my place, motivated, if not by beats bouncing, by time ticking. As I run home, I mentally replay the loop of Derartu winning for Ethiopia in '92—a three-minute YouTube clip that gets me emotional within the first thirty seconds. *Straight home. No detours.* As my breath and stride fall into perfect sync, a sense of calm comes over me.

3

MIZ

What's one extra kilometre? was what I had said to my-self ten minutes ago when I let my legs take a slight detour on the way "straight home." Quitting the bliss is too hard, man. Especially when I had already been itching for a run before the *incident*, having missed my usual dawn run thanks to Daniel. I turn the corner to my street in the fading light and come to a screeching halt. Daniel's car. *Noooo!* I look up at my tenth-floor window, my mind already imagining Daniel up there, staging an elaborate proposal scene, then opening his gym bag to get the ring out, then not finding it, then . . . ahhh!

I hurry into my lobby, where, thankfully, Everest is not at his desk to catch me in his usual fatherly chit-chat. I see he's let Daniel leave his business cards on the counter again, and I scowl. When did those two get so buddy-buddy? The elevator takes for-freaking-ever, as usual, but finally, I make it to my door, bracing for the worst—balloons, roses, Daniel on bended knee holding out a twist-tie in place of a ring because for some reason he's *that* determined to propose tonight.

I quietly let myself inside. Daniel is perched on a stool at my kitchen island, talking shop on the phone, his defined latissimus dorsi spread taut on either side of the backrest. I hang my keys on a hook on the wall-mounted key rack, next to the spare set that Daniel borrows on mornings when he leaves after me. He extends his arm out to me, and that's when I see it, on the floor at his feet.

The gym bag. *Mama, no.*

I reluctantly take one long step from the door, bringing myself within his reach, my brain already whirring through a million possible strategies for how to get him away from the island long enough to slip the ring back in the box in his gym bag. He pulls me in for a hug and quiet kiss while he listens on the phone. I recognize his co-agent Naomi's voice on the other line. On the countertop is paperwork and a notepad scrawled with offers and counteroffers in the seven digits.

"Unexpected developments," he whispers into my ear.

You and me both, I think, making sure his hands don't go anywhere near my waistband. I peel myself off him. The only thing I can think of right now is putting the ring back and then cutting Daniel loose, because I am who I am: always a bridesmaid, but dear God, never a bride.

Despite having been a dope bridesmaid at every one of the six weddings I was asked to grace with my flyness and unabashed party spirit, never have I ever believed myself to be one of those "next in line," like in that song "Ale Gena." No matter how loudly I bellowed the refrain with the crowd at the end of weddings to usher the newlyweds into their matrimonial future, I was not going to be a bride. Hell, I'm the only Ethiopian female in existence whose own parents have never, ever asked her about when she's getting married.

I saunter over to the sink and pour myself a glass of water, then stand leaning against the kitchen island, drinking and watching him talk. I'm trying to calm the anxiety in me and appear casual, cool, chill.

When Daniel finishes the call, he pulls me in over the top of the kitchen island for a deep kiss that almost wipes out my recollection of recent events, were it not for the hardness of the ring cutting into my skin against the counter.

"How was your day?" he says into my mouth.

Before I can answer, his phone chimes. We both look down at the caller ID. It's Naomi again. "Damn, y'all are on fire today," I say, sliding my finger across the screen. "I just want to say hi," I say to Daniel. I like Naomi a lot. She's like a cool older aunt slash mentor who convinced Daniel to leave Calgary and relicense to work in the Toronto real estate market.

But before I have a chance to say a word, a breathy female voice fills the air. "Tell me again what you're gonna do to me tonight, baby."

My jaw drops, and I look up at Daniel, stunned. His hand is frozen, reaching for the phone on the counter, and he looks just as shocked as me. After a few seconds of dead air, I inhale sharply, as if to speak. I don't even know what I'm going to say, but then I start coughing uncontrollably.

Daniel quickly takes the phone off speaker and slaps it to his ear. "Hello?" he says urgently. He looks at the screen, his face full of sheer panic.

"I guess she hung up?" I say hoarsely, finding my voice between coughs. "What the fuck, Daniel? That is so nasty." I stare at him. I am so mad, but it's entirely on principle. This guy is fixing to *propose* to me, but he has a side piece . . . who is *Naomi*?

Or should I say sugar mama? It's so gross . . . but also kind of perfect. This makes breaking up with him a million times easier. Relief fills me, and I suddenly feel lighter. Sure, the fact that Daniel is sleeping with her hurts a bit, but a bruised ego is a small price to pay to have a breakup excuse served to me on a silver platter. "I can't believe you!" I say, trying to make myself sound as devastated as possible. "Unbelievable!" Without waiting for him to respond, I dramatically storm off to my bedroom.

When I realize he isn't following me, I whirl around and see him sweeping his papers off the counter and into his shoulder bag. Then I watch as he picks up his gym bag and heads for the door without saying a word. I, and my shattered trust, could not matter less to him.

"What're you doing?" I say, my voice coming out as an unintended squeak. "Are you actually *leaving*, Daniel?"

"I gotta go." He glances at me before he steps out the door, but his face is completely blank.

"Excuse me?" I yell, now angry. I hurry after him, grabbing the door before it slams and following him out to the hallway. I'm not an expert on proposals, but I'm pretty sure this is not how the lead-up is supposed to go. And besides, *I'm* the one who's supposed to throw *him* out. That was the plan, after I put that ring back.

While he jabs at the Down elevator button, I say the only thing I can think of, trying not to barf as I say it. "You leave now, you can consider us over!"

Daniel finally looks at me, and when he does, it's as though I've just spoken gibberish. "*Us*? When has there ever been an 'us,' Miz?"

The player is stealing all my lines! "Seriously, Daniel?" I sputter. I don't know what else to say. Everything is happening so fast. I've completely lost my bearings. I've lost control of the situation. The elevator arrives and dings open, already filled with a few people. Daniel all but dives in and starts pushing at the button to close the doors.

"Wait!" I call out feebly, but I don't make a move to follow him in. I'm not trying to broadcast my business out to the elevator, lobby or beyond. As the doors slide shut, he's not even looking at me, but down at his phone, redialling Naomi. "What the . . . *what?*" I hiss to an empty hallway. I grab my phone out of my armband and call Daniel. He immediately declines my call. How ironic. I'm supposed to be declining him—*no, goodbye, we're through*—and he's supposed to beg for forgiveness, scramble to explain, try to win me back. Instead, he bounces? *He* leaves *me?*

I stomp back to my apartment angrily, wounded. In the kitchen, I toss my phone on the countertop and rush to the windows. Daniel is pacing outside his car, talking on the phone. Judging from his frantic gestures, I'm sure he's talking to *Naomi.* I watch him pace for a few moments, then he hangs up, gets into the driver's side and peels off like an F1 racer.

I throw my hands out. "Uh, okay! See you later, I guess?" I suddenly remember the ring and extract it from my waistband and stare at it. *What now?* What was I going to do with this thing now? I didn't want this in my condo. I shuffle over to my bedroom and open my nightstand drawer. With one final glance at the sparkling stone, I tuck the ring in the back corner of the drawer. "This is temporary," I say to it, as if it has feelings about being abandoned in the dark.

I straighten up, and as I do, I see, at the base of my bedside lamp, my AirPods. *Of course that's where Daniel left them.* I scowl at them—they started this whole mess in the first place. I scoop up the white case and plop down on my lumpy mattress, sighing as I examine them. Clogged with Daniel's earwax, of course. Gross. *Can't even respect my property, but you thought I would marry you?* I roll the edge of a tissue to a point and start cleaning them. Something nags at me. Something's *off*. In fact, multiple somethings are off. Why would Daniel plan to propose to me but have someone on the side? And why would he haul ass to do damage control with her instead of salvaging what he has with me? Why, in all the time we dated and he borrowed my AirPods, had he never cleaned the damn things *ever*, like, not even once? It's the least a guy could do for the woman he's planning to wife up!

Oh. Oh, Miz, you sweet idiot.

I drop my hands to my lap, sending the AirPods to the floor.

Why? Because the ring wasn't meant for *you, Miz*. It was meant for *her*.

I get very still. *I'm* the side action? Then I unravel, sliding down to the floor with relief. *Thank you, baby Christos.* I knew the ring didn't make sense. I *knew* that what Daniel and I were doing wasn't *that* serious.

But then my relief dissipates as I realize that I've not only sto-len—let's call it what it is—Daniel's property, but I'm blocking another woman's happiness. I groan. Even if I may personally think I'm doing Naomi a favour, this is bad. Really bad.

I pull the drawer open slowly and peer in. The diamond twinkles at me from its dark corner like a sad little alien. "I'll get you back to him," I promise it. Or rather, to his gym bag. I don't know how I'll manage that, but somehow, I'll make this right. I close the drawer again, this time with solemnity, feeling heavy with this burden that could have been so easily avoided, if for once in my life I had stopped running when I was supposed to.

4

KAL

I'm relaxing on an old sofa on our rooftop terrace, luxuriating in the memory of another exquisite sunrise that my housemates slept through, when a text comes in from Miz.

Miz: NEED to meet up tomorrow!

I sit up and quickly start typing back.

Me: Agree! It's been a while—

I'm about to suggest SanRemo, our usual café, the closest thing I've found in Toronto to our teenage haunts in Addis, when a call from Donna, our company stage manager, interrupts my typing. I freeze. In three years, Donna has only ever called me once, when my family back home was urgently trying to reach me. Now, two thoughts clash in my head. Either something has happened in Addis again. Or something has happened with my papers. I take a deep breath and answer.

"Donna?" I say.

"Are you sitting down?" she asks sharply.

I lean forward and grip the railing. "Yes?"

"Your moment is here, Kalkidan."

"My moment?"

Donna takes a deep breath. "You're going on tonight."

"What?" I'm not sure I've heard her correctly.

"For the next eight nights," she continues. "The rest of the show's run." Before I can collect myself enough to ask how this could be happening, she goes on to explain that last night, Grant, the lead actor who plays Antony in our production of *Antony and Cleopatra*, was involved in a serious car accident that left him with a concussion. My heart seizes reflexively but I try to focus so that I don't miss anything.

"So you need to come in much earlier today," Donna is saying. "You know, to go over everything with Oliver and wardrobe and props, and I'll need you for the cue to cue. Provided all goes well, you can come in at your usual call times after today." She sounds upbeat and businesslike, but I sense a tinge of apprehension in her voice. I stand up slowly, not trusting myself to let go of the railing.

"You good, Kalkidan? Hello?"

I want to say *No! I'm not ready for this. Give the part to someone else!* But I have ingested the role of Antony like none other, so much of the story, the love dynamic, familiar to me. Understudying the part, never expecting that I would be called on to share it with the world, has been an incredibly organic and cathartic experience. To say that I wasn't ready would be an out-right lie.

"Thank you very much, Donna," I manage to croak. The cascade of children's laughter from somewhere nearby suddenly cuts through the air. It should be joyous but, in that moment, sounds ominous to me, as if saying *But can you* really *handle this?*

"Don't thank me. I'm just the messenger," she responds briskly. "I'm rooting for ya! We all are. Call time for just you and Maeve is one o'clock. Gives you two enough time to rehearse and have a dinner break. And remember, keep yourself available going forward, just in case."

"Got it. I'm there," I say, forcing confidence into my voice. But when I get off the call, I can't physically move. I'm frozen, like a statue. I don't know how long I'm standing there until I hear a noise below and look down to see Silvio, the only other early bird in our household of five actors, locking his bike to the railing of the front steps.

"I'm up tonight," I say hoarsely. He doesn't hear me. "Donna just called me," I say, louder this time.

He looks up, unclipping his bike helmet. "And?"

"Grant's out for the rest of the run. Some kind of accident."

"You serious?!" Silvio says, understanding what that implies. I nod, and he beams at me. "That's incredible, bro!"

"For the rest of the run," I say softly to myself again, as if it's for the rest of my life.

Silvio disappears from view as he goes into the house. Moments later, he barges onto the rooftop, hooting, hollering, and slapping my back.

"It doesn't feel real," I say to him. "Am I dreaming?" I run my hand back and forth over my bare scalp, my head shaved for the role I've been playing as Cleopatra's so-called "attendant" since June. Now what? A wig?

"No, you look very awake to me!" Silvio says with a grin. "That sponsorship is as good as done! They were really cutting it close."

"You're telling me!" There are six months and thirteen days left on my current work permit, which expires at the end of February, but I've been promised that the company will sponsor my permanent residence. That I've managed to go from post-graduation permit to regular work permit (twice renewed) since arriving in Canada eight years ago is more than I could ever have dreamed. When I first told my family my plan to pursue becoming a stage actor in Toronto, abdicating my growing responsibilities in the family business, they had seen it as a more extreme version of coping with the heartbreak of the split with Muna. They'd been waiting for me to come to my senses and return home, where they could keep a closer eye on me.

"If I'm being honest, I was starting to get worried," I admit.

"Nah. Oliver's always looking out for you, man! And once they see you tear up this part? Forget about it."

A part I would never have got anywhere near as a new African immigrant Black actor, had it not been for Oliver, a Black-British, Lagos-based director who took me under his wing after he saw me in my theatre school's final year showcase, claiming that he had found this generation's Wegayehu, the legendary Ethiopian actor. I know it was pure chance that Oliver, with this deep knowledge of African theatre trivia, should come along at such a critical moment in my time in Canada.

I follow Silvio inside the house to start getting ready. One p.m. is hours away. I can do a full read-through of my scenes by then. "I have to tell Miz," I say, as we cross through my bedroom. No one but Miz will be as happy for me as I feel for myself, not even my housemates, whose congrats will understandably be tinged with envy. They know how rare it is to be called up as the understudy to a lead part—and not just any part, but Antony in *Antony and Cleopatra*, one of the greatest love stories of all time.

Miz has been my biggest cheerleader from the moment we reconnected in Toronto when I moved here. Since then, she's supported me so matter-of-factly, as if I was born to be onstage. She did not tell me to go get my head checked or insist that I was overreacting to heartbreak—the usual responses I got from everyone back home when they learned I was leaving a legacy family business, a city-wide chain of bakeries in Addis Ababa, to go study acting in Canada.

"Or," Silvio says, excitedly tapping my script, which I've picked up from my desk, "you could just let her show up and get the surprise of her life."

I take a moment to let that scenario play out in my mind. "You know what," I say, warming to it, "I like that. Who knows when I'm going to have a moment like this again, right?" Silvio gives me a thumbs-up. Yes, I will wait until Miz comes to closing night, as she always does. I open my text to her and delete what I'd been writing.

Me: Sorry, I can't.

Miz: Sunday?

There aren't any shows on Sunday, but just to be on the safe side . . .

Me: No Sunday's also out.

Miz: But Sundays you're off.

I frown. Miz is usually pretty easygoing—it's not like her to be so insistent. The reason I chose Canada and not the US or Europe, where I have plenty of friends and family, was exactly to avoid people who would be a drain on my time and energy, a distraction. Here I knew no one other than Miz, who has stayed as breezy and carefree as she was at fourteen.

"It's going to kill me keeping this to myself the rest of the week though," I admit to Silvio. "I have to tell somebody!"

"What am I, chopped liver?" Silvio says in mock offence.

I wave the script at him. "You know what I mean, man."

He scoffs at me and heads out of my room. I pull up WhatsApp and dial Eske. "Hey, Sister-of-Kalkidan," I say, when she picks up. I move around packing the necessities for rehearsal: script, clothes, snacks.

"Costs you a US dollar every time you call me that, you know," she retorts, her always-a-decibel-too-loud voice slicing through the city noise. "I'm invoicing you when you come home." Being older than me, even if only by eleven months, Eske is very touchy about being referred to in a way that prioritizes me. As the latecomer babies of a family of five kids, we might as well be twins. We have been equal partners in crime since day one, taking the fall together no matter whose bad idea it was that got us busted. And it was usually for something involving the house—almost burning it down, crashing the car into it, flooding it. Eske is my buddy, the part of my Addis life I miss the most.

"Oh, it's worth it," I say, laughing at her reaction. I share the good news about the lead part.

When I finish telling her, she responds, "You're still coming home for the anniversary, right?"

I scoff. No matter what I say about life here, with Eske, all roads lead back to when I'm coming home next. She took it hardest when I broke ranks and left the bakery eight years ago, and has never lost hope that I will get over my "life crisis" and return for good, not just for visits. I've only been back to Addis twice since my move—once for a regular visit and once for the funeral. She knows that if it weren't for our parents' wedding-anniversary party in January, five months from now, I would stay put in Toronto until my papers were finalized.

"Eske, I'm not even going to answer that," I snap. I am the last person whose presence should be doubted. I was the only one who supported our father when he insisted the party go forward as planned even though Emay was gone. The celebration was originally meant to have been seven years ago, for my parents' fortieth anniversary, at a lakeside resort in Bishoftu, but kept getting pushed back year after year because of delays in the resort's renovation. And then Emay died, and everyone in the family thought my father had lost his mind when he announced two years ago that he wanted to have the party. To him, though a ruptured brain aneurysm had stilled his wife's presence in body, her presence in spirit remained vibrant. I had never been prouder to be a Son-of-Legesse than in that moment. Forget Shakespeare, my father was living his love in the purest, time-space-defying way.

She may be gone to you all, I remember Abay saying, when my siblings tried to reason with him to cancel the party. *Not to me.*

Oh, how we talk. You would envy our conversations. He was dismayed that his own children believed mere death dissolved love. I didn't say so, but I felt I knew, by a lesser fraction of course, what my father felt. After Muna had ended our relationship, it had taken me a long time to stop having conversations with her in my mind. I can only imagine how much more intense that attachment would have been had we married.

"Good. Because nobody gets to skip that," Eske says, always having the last word even when no one is arguing with her.

"But Eske, did you hear me? I got a lead part! I am Mark Antony!" I reiterate, taking myself downstairs to the kitchen where I begin filling up my water bottle, phone pressed between my ear and shoulder. It does sting that she's ignoring the most exceptional news I've had in years. Is it too much to ask for a little enthusiasm?

"Obviously, you are Antony," Eske says. "Who else are you going to be, his horse?"

"In nothing less than the greatest true love story in history," I add, on purpose. After Emay and Abay's, of course. And what, once upon a time, I had thought was Muna's and mine.

"Excuse me?" Eske says, her pitch rising to take the bait. I smirk. Now we're even. "How about Atse Tewodros and Tiruwerk, Makeda and Solomon, Seble and Bezabeh. Do those sound familiar to your ears? Or have the Agents Smith washed them all out of your brain, *Matrix*-style?"

"Impossible, dear sister of mine," I mollify. "They are tattooed on my soul." I hear a text coming in. "Hold on."

Miz: Hello?? Sos WHEN?

She sent the message with Echo effect, so that dozens of the same message bubble up and disperse across my screen.

"Got to go," I say to Eske. I disconnect while Eske's still saying, "I better see you in January, Antony!" then I type a response to Miz, all while I throw my water bottle into my backpack and zip it up.

Me: I can't. Sorry. Work stuff.

I hate avoiding her, but she'll understand soon enough.

5

MIZ

I am wrapping up my shift at the clinic on Monday, completing charts and updating my patients' treatment plans, when Omar, the RMT, pops his head into my treatment room. "Your boyfriend is here," he says to me, his eyes twinkling with glee.

I freeze, my pen in mid-air, panic washing over me. Daniel's been trying to get in touch with me since he bounced on Friday night, calling and messaging me so much I almost thought about blocking him. I wouldn't put it past him to show up at my work unannounced—he's done that before. Two years ago, one fall afternoon, he popped up here out of the blue, months after our hookup at the soccer games that July, when he had told me he was born and raised in Calgary. What he'd failed to mention was that he was planning to move to Toronto in a few months.

But the light in Omar's eyes now tells me he means Kal. Of course. All weekend, while ignoring Daniel, I had been hounding Kal until he finally agreed to meet me today after work. I place a hand over my pounding heart. Phew. I return to my paperwork.

Every time Kal swings by the clinic, we get teased. I can only imagine what Eve, the receptionist, is putting him through. "Omar, you know perfectly well that Kal is not my boyfriend."

But Omar's not one to miss a tense muscle, whether he has his hands on it or not. "So why the freaked-out face?"

"What freaked-out face?" I flatten my expression. He knows damn well I've known Kal since I was in grade nine. "For the last time, Kal is my boy. Period. Friend. Period. Huge difference between that and *boyfriend*. Language matters."

Omar whips me a talk-to-the-hand gesture and unleashes a torrent of salty Moroccan French laced with Arabic as he retreats. I only catch *fausse immigrante*, but I get the gist. "Who you calling fake!" I clap back, even though by then he's gone. *Show-off.* So what if I only know English and barely any Amharic? So what if I came here when I was two for a surgery, and so what if Mom and I never went back home? I still consider myself an immigrant.

"I'll be right there," I call out loudly enough to be heard in the lobby.

"Got it," Kal yells all the way from the waiting room.

Good thing the boss isn't here. We're yelling as if we're in my apartment. I hear subdued murmurs as he and Eve make small talk. When I see her heading for the bathroom, I hurriedly stuff my lunch container into my backpack and rush to reception so that Kal and I can make our exit without any more innuendoes.

When I round the corner, Kal glances up from his phone and does a very unsubtle double take. I hold out my pointer finger in warning. "Shut up. Not a word. I know."

I look like crap today, and I know it, dressed in my first blue scrubs as if I graduated from physio school yesterday. My go-to hairstyle for work is moisturized curls pushed back by a colourful scarf, but today I'm wearing my hair in a lazy ponytail that still shows the lines from my overnight plaits. The halo of frizz around my hairline makes me look like a stranger to edging gel. Earrings? Brow liner? What are those? Luckily, my clients have bigger concerns, like trying to regain their lost mobility and functionality, and don't care what I look like.

Kal raises his hands in surrender, biting back a smile. "No word from me," he says. "I do love to see our women taking care of themselves, but once in a while, everyone just needs to, you know, let their hair down." He, on the other hand, looks as if he's on his way to a first date. Pressed long shorts and polo shirt, freshly shaven, the nails of all ten fingers and toes perfectly trimmed, elbows lotioned. His leather sandals are even polished. I go in for a hug, taking in the scent of shoe polish, more quintessentially Kal than any cologne. Only his bald head still catches me off guard.

I scowl at him. "I had a rough weekend, okay? No thanks to you abandoning me." I begin walking toward the door. Kal being unavailable all weekend had seriously thrown me for another loop.

"Well, I'm here now," he says, following me out.

As we step out onto the sidewalk, a city bus pulls over to unload passengers. "I needed you on Saturday morning. Not Monday afternoon, but whatever." Eyes closed, I tilt my face up to the sun that I haven't felt in hours. I open my eyes to see Kal backing away from me, the condo towers in the background looming over him.

"Should I leave?" he says, his head cocked to the side, pointing his thumb back at the bus stop down the street.

I roll my eyes and continue down the block while Kal backtracks to get his bike. He catches up to me, coasting on his bike, standing with both his feet on only one pedal. I roll my eyes again. The only reason this guy who can easily afford a car doesn't buy one is just so he can show off on a bike. He's lucky he looks good on it.

He hops off and walks the bike between us. "Something came up at the theatre."

I stop, my Daniel drama vanishing from my mind fast. "Is it about your papers?"

"No update on that yet, but any day now. How was your weekend?" He gives me a sly smile as if he knows what went down. Impossible, of course. We turn onto a wide grassy promenade between two clusters of condo buildings, walking smack into a gust of soupy heat coming off the lake. I've barely been outside five minutes, and I'm already sweating. Or it could be that guilt again.

All right. Here goes. "It's over between Daniel and me." Even as I say it, I know that sentence doesn't make sense, and it shows on Kal's creased forehead too. Devastated he definitely will not be. There isn't much love lost between Kal and Daniel. If Kal hadn't been in rehearsal that summer day two years ago when Toronto hosted the annual Ethio diaspora soccer games, I wouldn't have gone any further than just locking eyes with *hubbahubba come to mama* Daniel in his non–Toronto team jersey in the vendors' area. Usually, I'd go to the games in other cities to specifically get my freak on with my people—or *wegen*, as Mom says—because "what happens at the games stays at the games." But that year I had vowed to Kal to only look, not touch, these kinsmen of mine, since the tournament was being held on home turf. Had Kal been there to keep this front of mind, at the closing night concert, I wouldn't have sniffed Daniel out in a crowd of hundreds and waded through all that humanity just to fall into rhythm back to front, totally blowing my *don't fuck with habesha guys in Toronto* rule, steering clear of any guy who looks even remotely like he could be from back home, recently or not.

"That's it?" Kal says.

"*Really* over this time." No need to go into the rest of it.

"Remind me, when did it get un-over again between you two?" Kal says, as we continue to stroll down the grass, past dog walkers and toddler chasers, toward the waterfront.

"Ugh who cares?" I say, annoyed that both my best friends should have the same follow-up questions. I need to diversify my friend pool. Too bad all the girls I grew up with have disappeared into the marriage black hole. "That's not the point. The point is this time, it's permanent. He did something I cannot get past. Ever." I rush to add, "I don't want to talk about it."

Kal's face hardens, a look I do not like on him unless he is in character. "Are you okay?"

"Oh, I'm fine. Nothing like *that.*"

"Okay," Kal says, sounding unconvinced. "Ice cream to . . . celebrate?" He points to a convenience store.

I nod, grinning. Given the choice, he'd pick one of the three places that sell fresh gelato around here, but today he's going to slum it and buy packaged convenience store ice cream for my sake.

"Lead the way," he says, smiling.

"He just keeps contacting me," I blurt out when we're in the store, digging through the freezer. I find his Häagen-Dazs strawberries and cream bar at the same time he finds my triple chocolate Drumstick. "Wanting to come over. I'm just not into it. And I said so. But he's not getting the message." *Are you going to mention the ring, Miz?*

We move to the register. "Stop responding," Kal says, paying for the ice creams. "He'll go away eventually. He was probably more attached to you than you realized. But that doesn't matter. He's not right for you."

Exactly! I think, and then remember that he must've also thought so because he wasn't planning on proposing to *me*. We step outside. Without so much as an exchanged glance, we reflexively cross the road and head for the giant boulders that line the water's edge. Kal props his bike on the grass behind us while I climb onto a rock and get situated.

He joins me on the rocks. "I know what'll cheer you up," he says, smiling mischievously as he unpeels his ice cream.

I stop peeling my ice cream wrapping. "Oh no. Not the sad old people music."

He grips his ice cream bar in his teeth and takes out his phone. "You still owe me your opinion on 'Ende Iyerusalem,'" he reminds me, scrolling through Spotify. Asni's version is one of the tracks Kal is considering adding to his parents' anniversary party playlist of love ballads from their era, something he's been compiling since last summer. Even though I find those kinds of songs bittersweet as fuck (heavy on the bitter), and despite my understanding 10 percent of what they're even saying, he's made me his unwilling co-producer.

"Let's start with a strong candidate on the *Maybe* list: an Alemayehu," he says, before playing the track.

I close my eyes in a show of listening attentively, but I'm lost in the goodness of melted caramel. "Mmm, it's how an ice-cold Orange Crush would sound," I say over the tune.

Kal laughs. I've been texting him similar comments every time he sends me a link to a song from his *Maybe* list by Muluken, Kassa, and Bizunesh, among others.

"That's why you're putting me through this, isn't it? To get a laugh."

"I need all the laughter I can get," he says, with a tinge of sadness in his eyes, and I know he means it. Going through love songs that remind you of your parents, one of whom is dead . . . I can't even imagine. "For your info," he says, "this one is about a lover trying to tempt his beloved to elope with him because her parents are too snobby to permit their marriage."

I nod. "Ah, makes perfect sense. It's literally your parents' story." The celebration this January will also act as the wedding his parents never had since they eloped when they were young. "Move that to the *Definite Yes* list then."

He gives me a thumbs-up and plays a couple more *Maybes*. Happy to be his comic relief, I indulge him by listening and offering my kooky, totally unhelpful takes on "Ambassel" and "Yekereme Fikir"—technically about the agony of apartness and the sweetness of old love, respectively, although I say they make me feel as if I'm alone on a cloudy mountaintop and evoke my mother's Paris perfume, respectively. Anyway, those too get bumped to the *Strong Maybe* list.

"Okay that's enough, or I'm hurling that phone in the lake," I say, fake snatching at his phone. "I'm beyond cheered up, thank you. Too bad for Daniel. From now on, I'm being firm and not responding." I have to, of course. I can't keep putting the guy off forever. I have his—her—ring. Unfortunately, figuring out a natural way to get my paws on his gym bag isn't proving as simple as deleting my photo of the ring was. "I mean dudes always pop up when you think they're gone for good, but . . ."

"You can't control dudes," he says, putting his phone away. "But, maybe, you can take a break from dudes?"

I stare at him. "And do what? Apply for the other team?"

"Just be on Team Miz. Game of one."

"Yeah, no. Aimé already tried that tack." *When I lied to her Friday night and told her that I had managed to slip the ring back in Daniel's gym bag and officially ended our not-relationship.*

For a few minutes, we're both silent while we eat our ice creams, watching the water, the skyline of Toronto off in the distance. "You know what they say . . ." Kal starts slowly, as if not to interfere with the soothing rhythm of the waves lapping against the rocks. "If enough people tell you that you're drunk, then . . ."

"Yer, yer," I say, with melty ice cream mouth.

"It may seem counterintuitive, but that might be how you meet someone good, who doesn't just drop and pick you up when he feels like it, like you're a toy."

I gulp down my bite. "Excuse me, the toy-ness was mutual."

He crosses his wrists, making an X in front of his body. "TMI!"

I laugh, as I do whenever Kal gets slangy, still using terms that I introduced him to when we were kids. "Besides, neither of you losers knows what you're talking about. *You* especially don't even count as a serial monogamist because that would mean you've dated more than one person in your life." Kal had been in a kind of widowerhood himself since he and Muna ended, his first and only relationship that spanned from when he was fifteen all the way to twenty-six. "I'm not like you, friend. Stuck in the past like a bug in glass."

A flicker of a shadow passes over Kal's face, some part of him receding. He checks his watch. "I better get going," he says a bit stiffly.

I bite my tongue. "Shit, sorry." *Dammit.* A swell of tension, like the rolling water before it breaks into a wave, fills my chest. Over the years, Kal has got better with my teasing him about Muna and his tragic attempts to date here in Toronto—at my urging, of course—but sometimes he can still be so sensitive. Or I can be *in*sensitive.

"You're good," he says, smiling. "You'll be happy to know I've retired the Questionnaire."

"Say what? You mean you *won't* ask a woman what her parents' marriage is like on the first date? I'll believe it when I see evidence of an actual date where no binding promises have been extracted from the poor woman," I say dryly, taking a bite of my cone. I get the sense that Kal isn't truly interested in finding someone right now and has, instead, been using the cover of protecting his family from Addis-style gold-diggers, as if he's still a target, to scare away women with his intense questions. But I suspect his real focus, understandably, is on work, securing his papers.

"You'll see," Kal says, making his meticulous, symmetrical way down his ice cream bar.

A little bloop of alarm sounds in me, to my surprise. I have got so used to single Kal, taken for granted that he would always be around. Sort of, anyway. Please refer to this past weekend, when he was nowhere to be found.

"Right now, I have call time," he says, taking an extra giant bite of his bar.

I jut out my lower lip. "But it's only four. Your call times are at seven."

He inhales the rest of his bar with another bite, dragging the stick out through his teeth. "Oliver wants to go over some notes."

"*Oliver*, huh?" I say suggestively.

"Honest! Call him."

"Since when do you have notes during the last week of the show? On your one day off? Please. Hold on to her—er, I mean, *your secrets*—if you want. Meanwhile, here I am, spilling my guts."

Minus one shiny detail. "But really, how's it going with you?" I say, to delay him at least a little bit. "I totally hogged the convo. How's the show? What's the holdup with your papers? We're not getting any younger here."

He makes his way carefully down from the rocks, pocketing his wrapper and ice cream stick. I shift to keep him in sight. "Papers will be put in motion soon. Don't worry about that. You're coming on Sunday, right?"

"Of course. When have I ever not come?"

"Just confirming."

"Nothing will keep me from your closing nights. Even when you have, like, two lines."

"Oof!" He grabs at his chest, pretending I've wounded him. "Ten, this time."

I laugh. "Are you counting the ones that are just one word again?"

"Oh, civilians. In art, it is not about how many words you have but what you do with them."

"Those be a lot of words." I emphasize each word with a wag of my now mostly hollow cone.

He mounts his bike. "And by that, I think you mean that nothing will keep you from the afterparty."

"A girl needs something to survive all that Shakespeare." I drop my head as if I am nodding off.

"Bringing anyone?" he asks, ignoring my antics.

"Nope. I'm supposed to be a nun now, 'member?"

He rings his bell and starts pedalling. "Uh-oh, someone should warn the convents."

"Boy, bye!" I fake a lunge as if to push him off, but he slips away.

6

MIZ

The highlight of the rest of my week is taking Mom shopping for an outfit to wear to her retirement party, even though chances are she's just going to wear one of her regulation traditional dresses. But one can hope. I also wanted to pick up something to wear to Kal's afterparty. I figured that having Mom along would help me get something more modest since I was semi-considering trying out Kal's advice to *take a break from dudes*. And what better way to ensure I don't hook up with anyone than by showing up looking as if I came from Sunday service?

Daniel was still bugging me about coming over, and I was still playing dumb as if I assumed it's because he wants to make up, and responding along those lines: *I still need time* (Monday night). *Maybe it's for the best* (Tuesday afternoon). *I'm sort of talking to someone* (midnight Wednesday). What was I supposed to say? *Sure, come on over, but can you make sure to bring your gym bag with you?* That's not suspicious at all. Hey, at least I was responding. Meanwhile, my bedroom has become a guilt-ridden radioactive zone, and I am losing more of my self-respect daily. But he's backed off since Wednesday. Being the daughter of a woman who's worked in the insurance industry all her life, I wonder, hope, that he's gone quiet because he had the ring insured and decided to make a claim.

When I was shopping with Mom, I started to ask her, in a very roundabout way, how one goes about doing that. But I backed off immediately when she asked me point-blank, *You have something?* What I heard was, *You have someone?* (I.e., a boyfriend.) I seized up so fast that I almost flattened a whole mannequin display. Quickly, I redirected back to talking fashion, convincing Mom to get something she would never have picked out on her own (and ditto *moi*). But by Sunday evening, I realize that, new no-dating resolution or not, I won't be caught dead in something so blah. The calf-length button-down dress is the fashion equivalent of a eunuch, Kal's role in this play. As I shower to get ready for the show, I sound out the word as I had done last spring when I rode along on another one of Kal's outings to research his upcoming role.

We went to a hookah lounge because the eunuch fires up a water pipe for Cleopatra in one scene. I remember Kal on the cushion perpendicular to mine, elbows on the low armrest, making a slicing motion across his lap to explain the idea of a eunuch.

"Ow!" I covered my lap with my hands, gently sucking on the pipe to get it going.

"Job requirement for serving the royal ladies back then. We call it *seleba*, castration."

"Mm-hmm," I blew a thick plume of green-apple-flavour tobacco smoke in Kal's face. "So, how are you going to achieve that, ahem, *I got robbed of my junk* effect?" I'd asked, purposely not attempting the new-to-me Amharic word. I knew all too well the galaxies of difference that a misplaced or mis-stressed syllable could make in spoken Amharic.

I waved the pipe toward Kal's crotch area. "Because there are videos out there on how to tuck *that* away. I can send you some links." His hairline scurried back a full inch. "I mean, I wouldn't want you stumbling across stuff that you can't unsee."

"That you, however, have seen?" he said, arching one eyebrow. I fluttered my eyelashes innocently. "But it has to be a good video. I have a lot to put away," he said, puffing himself up.

"Puhleeze!" I passed him the pipe. "Men! Did I imply that you didn't?"

I carefully apply liquid eyeliner in perfect extra-long lines at the corners for my Cleo look. And, oops, a scandalous dress after all: li'l black sequin number that hangs by a strap laced asymmetrically across my back. "Wow, are you going to a show or trying to be the show?" I say to myself, winding my hips in the mirror when I am done. I look like a slice of Addis night sky, if I do say so myself. Am I a little overdressed for sitting on the grass in a park? Yep. But a girl has places to be afterward, hobnobbing to do.

My dollar store beach mat slung across my back, fancy clutch tucked under my arm, I slip on a pair of flats, toss my heels in a shopping bag for later, and head out. At the park, I rent a cushion to put over my mat and stand at the lip of the amphitheatre, combing the sea of people for Kal's and his roomies' friends so I can sit with them. I see the absurdly tall director, Oliver, from afar and wave hello. When I can't see anyone else I recognize, I give up and wind my way down to the very front of the spill of bodies and snuggle up on a patch of grass next to a friendly looking lady about my mom's age. She offers me a corner of her blanket and some Korean dried jujubes. We're nibbling and chit-chatting, me humble-bragging about knowing someone in the show, when the lights start to dim. I take out my phone to silence it but get sidetracked into checking socials while the pre-show overhead announcements drone on.

Until my ears suddenly catch on the words *Kalkidan Legesse*.

"What? Huh? What'd they say about Kal?" I say to my new friend, Betty, feeling panicky that something has happened to him. She shrugs. I whip my head around, searching for Oliver, but of course, it is too dark by now. I'm about to call him when *bam*, the lights come on and Kal is suddenly in front of me, close enough to touch, all up on Cleopatra in way-too-revealing ancient pyjamas but throwing a line directly at me, it seems, instead of her.

Something-something love that can be reckoned.

Eh? I understand the individual words but not what they mean in that order. *What's going on?* I actually mouth this to him as if he'll respond to me from the stage. Why is he . . . Antony? I stare open-mouthed, feeling all tingly. In no time, I become lost in Kal's performance in a way I never have been. How could I have been, with his sprinkling of one-liners?

But tonight is an avalanche of fancy words pouring out of him in such a state of constant sweaty, frothy passion, churning through all the emotions, talking talking talking, oh my god so many words. Letting himself be so obviously emotionally manipulated by Cleo. For a lady whose name is half the title, Cleo is absent from big chunks of the action, but when she's onstage, she does plenty of damage. The more I witness Cleo purring all over Kal, then shoving him away, then luring him back to her, the more I want to storm up there and smack a bitch. Kal too. Knock some sense into the idiot. Can't he see she is using him? Why are men so freaking *dumb*?!

And then, as if the practically see-through togas (yes, he had a lot to put away; shut me up) weren't enough, Kal rolls up dressed in a *breastplate*. Pecs, abs, and lats galore. I haven't seen anything of Kal's body other than his extremities since . . . must have been when we all used to go swimming in Addis back in the day, but I'm pretty sure he's not chiselled like that under the hood. *And a leather skirt? Over knee-high laced sandals?*

Kinky outfits aside, I do start to zone out when the political manoeuvrings and reports of battle drag on.

But then Kal starts to die.

I know it is all make-believe, but it hits me hard, *watching* him die, slowly, agonizingly, by his own hand, for the love of a woman whose love for him is suspect. Incapable of maintaining disbelief, I straight-up sob. Betty, looking pretty rough herself, hands me a tissue. I thank her and mumble some jumble about being so emotional these days because I just got out of a messy relationship. For the rest of the show, she grips my hand like only a mother could. And by the time the ordeal is over, I'm so wiped out that she's the one who has to help *me* up.

7

KAL

After the show, Oliver stops by my green room—one of the five-by-five pop-up blackout fabric tents in the backstage village of shipping containers, portable washrooms and handwashing stations. I am flattered but also surprised. *Notes?* I think. *Even now?* But Oliver is a perfectionist, and whatever feedback he has for me, I will take it and apply to next season's shows, which haven't been cast yet. I feel confident that after showing what I can do this past week, my days of walk-on parts and "itty-bitty" lines, as Miz says, are behind me.

I know that had it not been for Oliver seeing me as a talent worth developing and not a backdrop against which the talent of others could shine, I doubt I would have been hired at the company at all, let alone earned two work permits. Making me understudy the role of Antony—to no small amount of grumbling from the higher-ups, considering the age, experience, and colour difference between Grant and me—had been the peak of it, from which I could see the heady vista of all the possibilities ahead once I become a permanent resident.

As he closes the tent flap behind him, my director looks too serious. He gestures for me to take a seat in the folding chair by the dressing table. I sit, angling myself to face him as he perches on the ledge of the table, hands on his knee, and takes me in. I wait, trying not to fidget.

Gradually, his unreadable expression morphs into a face-splitting grin. "Sublime," he says.

I am at a loss, as if I've forgotten my cue. "Who?" I say uncertainly.

"You!"

My heart swells and I want to leap from my chair. "Thank you," I say instead, controlling my delight. My first night as Antony had been discouraging—many ticketholders requested refunds when Grant's absence was announced, leaving me to perform for a sparse audience. But three nights later, word had got out, and the house was at capacity and had been since. But more than the sold-out shows and the standing ovations, I treasure Oliver's approval. "Coming from you . . ."

"Where did you go, if you don't mind my asking?" Oliver says, sounding mystified.

What did I tap into, especially tonight, is what he's asking. Every understudy has a choice: replicate the original actor or make the part his own. Last Saturday, at the first performance, I had studiously done the former. But afterward, Silvio rallied me to show what *I* specifically could do with the role, that *I* could give the leading lady something new to work with. So I went for broke, giving myself over to the part, becoming bolder with each night. Tonight was the culmination. I poured everything I had been holding back into Antony, purging all that I had felt with, because of, and about Muna. The lines had come so alive that I hadn't dropped a single one.

"Let's just say I can relate to Antony . . ." I say, hoping that will be sufficient. Even after baring my soul for hundreds to see, I am far from comfortable talking about the period of my life after Muna and I broke up. Even with my closest friends, Miz included.

The last time I saw Muna was two years ago at the mourning for my mother, since our families are close. In the time since our relationship, Muna had become a married mother of two, confronting me with what I had thought would be our future, further complicating my grief. We did not exchange more than a few cordial words, but that had been enough to obliterate what little emotional progress I had made in Toronto talking to a few women.

Thankfully, Oliver puts up his hands. "Better you don't share, in fact," he says. "Protect your reserves."

"Always room for improvement though?" I say, still expecting notes.

Oliver shakes his head, disagreeing. I feel a quiet pride. No notes from the great Oliver, wow. But then he lets out a long, troubling breath and pulls his hand over his mouth and down the length of his grey goatee. "Which is why it pains me, deeply, Kalkidan, to bring you regrettable tidings."

He interlaces his fingers, as if I will need divine help to handle what is about to come at me. I sit back and look away at our reflections in the mirror, fearing the worst.

"I would have preferred to wait a few days, but I didn't want you finding out through gossip at the party later." He clears his throat. "Your sponsorship is not going forward."

I cave in as if I've been hit. These are the worst possible words to leave Oliver's mouth. And in response, my own falls slightly open. My mind rushes back in time to everything that has led up to *this* moment: the years in the wilderness after Muna, when the theatre had become my only refuge; discreetly applying to theatre school and for a student visa; my family's shock when I said I was leaving. Saying goodbye to them, to my staff; the first days of class as the oldest student; the highs and lows of scene study chasing that elusive state of total presence; meeting Oliver; getting hired at this company; my first days as a professional actor; the relief of every immigration status adjustment or extension. Research outings with Miz. Her drowsy face in the audience every closing night. All that struggle and triumph and joy flashes before my eyes. All that time wasted. But I am too numb to speak or cry. I only stare back at Oliver.

"The board moves in mysterious ways," Oliver says. I nod reflexively, trying to look professional even though I dissolve inside. "I am truly sorry. What it boils down to is resources. They didn't feel they were warranted in expending the resources to sponsor you," Oliver says, then adds, "at this time."

But I know that is just a bone he is tossing me, to soften the crush of failure. I have fired people too, in my previous life as a manager of multiple branches of our bakeries in Ethiopia, a life I would have to return to. These decisions are always final.

"Oliver, can I ask," I say, clearing my throat. "How long have you known about this?"

"I didn't want to ruin your week."

"I appreciate that." So they had known they were letting me go before Grant's accident. Not even my soul-baring work over this past week could have made a difference.

Oliver is still talking. He leans in. "Did you hear me, Kal?"

"Hmm?" I look up, eyes glazed.

"I said, it's not over for you. Don't give up. The politics here, as with politics everywhere, are ever in flux. I refuse to believe your journey ends here." He stands, towering over me. I get up too, though the weight of my failure makes me feel even smaller next to him. Silence looms save for the ghostly echo of tonight's applause in my mind.

Because the show is over. Really over.

Oliver shakes my hand, pulls me in for a shoulder bump, all of which I barely register. Then he leaves. I feel so hollow the gust of air in the wake of the tent flaps parting should knock me down, yet I stand motionless, frozen, as I had been just a week ago after Donna's call. But what a world of difference between how large and proud I had felt then and my present sense of being small and worthless, no more than a speck of dust.

I had spent my heart, emptied my emotional pockets, and been rejected.

In art, as in life.

8

MIZ

By the time the show ends, summer night has fallen. It's almost pitch black along the trail out of the park, the occasional streetlamp glowing weakly through the trees and bushes. Betty and I, elbows interlocked, head out with the crowd, guided by dozens of phone lights swinging about like lasers. At the fork in the trail that leads to the backstage area, I stay behind to wait for Kal. Betty wants to wait with me because it's so dark, but I tell her he'll be out in no time. "Besides," I say, "this is literally like my dad's compound in Ethiopia, minus the armed night patrols." I wink. Sure enough, this reassures her of my wilderness survival skills, and we say goodbye to each other. Once alone with the crickets, I take a selfie with the flash on to see what's goin' on with my face. "Ah!" I yelp at the shock of seeing my sultry Egyptian eyes transformed into those of a terrifying raccoon.

"Miz."

"Ah!" I shout again, whirling to see Kal suddenly materialize from the dark looking classy in black pants and maroon shirt.

"You almost gave me a heart attack!" I call out, walking up to meet him. I smack him lightly on the chest.

He staggers back as if I pushed him with all my strength. "Was I that terrible?" he says, his voice thick, heavy, just like in the show.

"Oh, please! Let's just say, I've never stayed that awake." I beam at him. "Seriously, though!" I say, hand on hip. "What happened? Explain. Weren't you supposed to be a whatsitagain?"

"Eunuch. And I was. But I was understudying for this part, remember?"

I bare my teeth into a toothy smile. "Um, yes?" Nope. I had been too distracted by the whole eunuch thing to remember what role Kal had an infinitesimal chance of playing.

"Well, I got called up for duty this past week. It happens rarely," he says to his feet.

"I know *that*," I say. *Why isn't he looking at me?* "No wonder you were double-triple making sure I came tonight," I say. "Oh! *That's* why you became Mr. Unavailable all of a sudden. Oh my god—and there I was, wah-wah-ing about Daniel." I lean closer, goofily twisting my fists over my eyes like a baby, hoping to at least make him crack a smile. But he continues to stare at the ground, looking as if he has the weight of the world on his shoulders.

"That's all right. It's my job to be there for you," he says softly, more to himself than me.

"Except you went and died on me. Wow, that is one sentence I never thought I would ever hear myself say." I laugh, downplaying my emotions. We start walking out of the park. "I couldn't do anything. I had to just sit there and watch you die! It was torture."

"I'm sorry." It's as if he is still in character—he's so quiet, almost depressed. I guess that kind of immersion would take a while to shake off. Part of his soul is still hung up on Cleo. Great. Used to be Muna, now it's Cleopatra, who's not even real. "I apologize for dying," he says, pausing to offer me a hug, though he looks as if he needs it more than me.

"Apology accepted," I say, taking it gladly. "Don't die again, okay?" I croak into his neck, squeezing him hard.

"Promise."

I lean away, seeking eye contact. "You'll always be around?"

"To the best of my ability," he says over my head.

"Why aren't you looking at me?" I finally ask, pushing away and staring at him. "What's going on, Kal?"

"I'm here," he says, meeting my eyes with such an intensity that I feel my knees soften a bit and my mind go briefly offline. I realize I've been holding my breath and remember to inhale. *Whoa, Nelly.*

"I know I'm being silly," I say, starting to walk again toward the parking lot where we will order a ride to the afterparty. "You just got me rattled, that's all." And himself, apparently.

He is quiet, hands in his pockets, eyes still pinned to the ground. This emotional bender is getting to be too much. No more method acting.

"Okay, come on, shake it off. If Muna wasn't completely history before, she's definitely been erased tonight, am I right? Delete!" I say, curling my index finger and jabbing an imaginary button. "To think about how long I've been on your case about needing to date, when what you really needed was a solid part! I feel like I get it now, like really *get* it, you know? The attraction of the stage, of acting life out, on a gut level." But he doesn't seem to have heard a word I've said. "Very belated congratulations though!" I screech, getting in his face, trying to snap him out of it. "I'm so proud of you. You were phenomenal. You're in the big leagues now."

He finally meets my eyes and shrugs. "Miz, it was just a fluke that the lead actor got in an accident."

"But they could have cancelled the rest of the run," I say. "There was just a week left. But they didn't. They *like* you. Because you're *good*."

"Me doing the part has nothing to do with them liking me," he says. "It's business."

"Oh, come on! They like you a lot. They're into you big time, my friend." What I don't say is that it's about time that he is experiencing this moment. After losing his mom and then putting years of hard work into his itty-bitty parts, he deserves to shine.

"They don't like me for anything," Kal says through gritted teeth.

His tone startles me. "Are you okay? Do you need to decompress?" I touch his arm. "We can go to Roncy Village for a quick drink before the party." But he doesn't respond. I sigh. "Help me out here. I have no experience with post-major-part Kal."

He takes a few steps back, anguish now written all over his face. I can't imagine what could be so troubling, tonight of all nights.

"They're not sponsoring me anymore," he says sadly.

I gasp, and the air stops in my chest. *Think fast think fast say something helpful say something fix it.* "Oh, but . . ." I start, feeling helpless. "They were so sure about you. Oliver said . . . he's been doing this for a long time and knew a keeper when he saw one."

"He doesn't have the final say. And the ones that do . . ." Kal shrugs, his eyes shiny.

"Oh." This truly wasn't something I saw coming. Things had been going so well since his graduation, I had relaxed, as had he. But now I have no words and can only blink at Kal's hollow expression.

"So, needless to say, Miz, I am not in the mood for a party," he says, shoving his hands into his pockets. "But you can go. You look nice."

I shake my head. "I'm here for you. Not for myself."

"Well, I'm going home."

I nod. We get onto the road that will eventually bring us out of the park. A minute later, Kal takes a breath and hesitates. *Please speak, please say something. Because I'm still blank, and I need to know you're okay.*

"Oliver just told me. Something about me not being worth their resources. Why bother developing me if they don't think I have any leading man potential?" I open my mouth to disagree, but he goes on, talking to himself more than me. "Well, I can say I tried. So many people live their entire lives without going for their dream. That's the number one deathbed regret."

He looks so sour I have to step in. "Hey, you promised no more dying," I say, wielding the only power I feel I have, humour. But even I know that I know shite about having one's life limited by a piece of paper. I've only heard about it second-hand. "Sorry," I say quickly. *Follow his lead, follow his lead.* "Look, it's okay. You tried. I've read that somewhere, about regrets. But you did it, gave it your all, so you won't have regrets."

This doesn't feel right in my mouth, and Kal's brow twitching confirms that it's the wrong thing to have said. I zip up my lips for

the rest of the way out of the park, which we walk in an awkward
silence, like a couple post-fight.

We reach Parkside Drive and wait to cross at the light. "Are
you hungry?" Kal says over the rush of traffic. "We can grab some
dinner to go."

I'm about to say *sure*, but I can't stand the thought of cutting
short what had been and promised to be an incredible night,
spending it instead with takeout in front of the TV like two losers
who have been banished by the powers that be.

"Fuck that!" I spit out, startling Kal. "Fuck them!" I take his
face in my hands and force him to look at me. "I get why you
don't want to see them right now. Believe me, I get it as best as I
can get it. But hear me out—aren't there going to be other important industry people at this party?"

"So?"

"Other important people that are in a position to sponsor
you?" I can tell by his confused look that the idea of finding another sponsor hadn't crossed his mind. "Answer me, Kal."

"Yes. But—"

"You're going," I say. "It's actually more important now that
you go to the party. Hold your head up. Make the motherfuckers
have to look at you all night. A Son-of-Legesse doesn't go down
so easy!" I beat a drum on his chest and toss my bone-straight
hair as if it is a lion's mane, boasting like a guerrilla warrior about
to deploy. "*Zeraf! Bale-gameh ayseram!*"

"*Ayferam*," he says, mildly amused, emphasizing the *f*. "The
lion-maned one doesn't *fear*. You said the lion-maned one doesn't
work."

"That's what I'm talking about!" Eff the *f*. All I care about is
the tiniest glimmer of life I see returning to his eyes. They might

as well have been blazing fire, for how victorious I feel, as if I've brought him back from the brink of a depressive hole. "No fear! Party, schmooze like there's no tomorrow! Hustle, baby, hustle! Time is a-ticking. Never say die!"

He makes a low fist, still somewhat detached and, I know, only humouring me. But it's a start.

"All right, paparazzi time. I want to be able to prove that I knew you when." I aim my phone camera at us for a selfie. Kal curls his lips in more of a grimace.

"Cute couple," a passerby says. Or it could be the voice of God, since it's so dark and I can't see where the speaker is. Not the first time we've been mistaken for a couple. We look at each other in the frame and smile. Kal's is an improvement on his grimace. Thank goodness.

"And also, PS," I say, my finger over the shutter button. "You were born a leading man." That's when Kal smiles a real, if tiny, smile. I capture the moment.

9

MIZ

During the week following Kal's closing night, I keep finding myself staring at the one wall of my treatment room where I have photos of my favourite patients: the retired flight captain in his eighties riding a bicycle again after a stroke. The construction worker with vertigo who is now a rock-climbing influencer. The MS patient who managed to walk unassisted for the qualifying distance of a clinical trial. I know it's not the same thing, but it irks me that I can rehabilitate nervous and musculoskeletal systems but can't figure out a real way to help Kal.

Other than text-spamming him with ironic affirmations and graphics, that is. Which might have amused him at first—*When life gives you lemons, throw them at someone. That awkward moment between birth and death,* etc.—but it's probably got on his nerves by now. Does that stop me from googling for more while I wait for my next appointment? Nope. I need something to distract me from the reality that Kal's chances of securing a new sponsor from schmoozing at one party are slim. Two Olivers don't come around in a lifetime. I am really feeling the advantage of my passport, and it's about as pleasant as wet wool. A text from Kal interrupts my GIF search.

> **Kal: I don't think I should go anymore. To my parents' thing in Jan. I better stay out the entirety of my visa, you know, in case—**

I don't bother to read the rest of the message. I call him immediately. "How about no?" I say, skipping the greetings. "Hell no. Do not talk like that. You are not missing that party. I did not suffer through all your old people songs for nothing. Even if it's cutting it close, if your work permit is valid, it's valid."

"You never know. A border agent might decide only one month before expiry is not enough to readmit me."

"By then, your situation will be different."

"How do you know?"

I quit pacing and start rearranging the multicolour pins on a bulletin board instead, yanking them out and jabbing them back in in no specific pattern. "I just do."

"It's better if I tell them now so they have time to accept it."

"Eske will flip like a pancake if you tell her you won't be there." I huff. I don't have to ask whether Kal has run this by her because he knows better. "What if they moved the date of the party?" Kal laughs in response. "What? It's been postponed twice."

"This party isn't getting postponed again. Everyone just wants to put it behind them as soon as possible." He pauses. "It would be great if you could make it, at least."

Eek. I sink into my office chair. "Haven't decided when I'm going back to Ethiopia yet." For a few years, we've been tossing around the idea of going back at the same time, ideally for this party, but nothing concrete. It's probably been at least ten years since we were there at the same time.

Kal's tone haunts me through the next set of patients so that, at lunchtime, I skip a group outing to Red Lobster to spend the hour scrolling the Immigration, Refugees and Citizenship website instead of shelling endless shrimp. I go so deep into the nesting documents regarding work permits and sponsorships, my head aching from the bureaucratic lingo, that I don't realize that Omar is behind me until he speaks.

"Passport renewal?" Omar says, peering over my shoulder.

I twist around, my swivel seat following. "No," I say, tapping my finger lightly on the mouse to close the window. "A friend of mine is in a situation."

"Kal?"

"I have other friends besides him, you know."

Omar shrugs. "When I see it, I'll believe it." He isn't wrong. Only Kal ever swings by my work. I don't think Aimé even knows where the clinic is.

I sigh. "Yes, it's for Kal."

"If it's for citizenship, marry him, *naturellement*," Omar says, as if it's the most obvious thing in the world.

I level him with a deadpan stare. "You know what, Omar? Never mind. I thought you would be helpful, give me actual usable ideas."

"What? I'm serious. Many people do that," he says.

"Well, good for them. Getting married for papers is one thing I guarantee with a thousand percent certainty Kal would never, *ever* do."

Omar jiggles his eyebrows. "Even when it is you?"

I snort. "Not for love or money. We cancel each other out. Come on, what other ways are there?"

"Okay, well, you insist on making it difficult . . . Let me see . . ." I listen as Omar dishes about other Bourne-level extremes to which people go to try to stay, and feel deeply thankful that Mom and I never had to go through all that. Our privilege was part of why it meant so much to Mom to help newcomers with their papers as much as she could. I wish I could ask her for advice for Kal, but then she'd assume there was something more going on between me and Kal, and she and I do *not* have the kind of relationship where we talk about the men in our lives.

My phone pings on my desk, and I grab it.

Daniel: What time do you get home today?

"Oh, fuck off," I snap.

Omar gapes at me. "Excuse me?"

"Obviously not you." I point at my phone.

Daniel has been so quiet the past week I convinced myself that he had insured the ring. I even confessed to Aimé that I still had the ring. To say that she was not pleased with me would be putting it mildly. She also wasn't impressed by my Plan B: to just sell the thing and donate the funds to charity. She's holding me to my original promise to return it to *exactly* where I found it, without much help with the how.

But I have to respond with something, so I quickly tap out a message. I'll admit that it does bother me that even after two years of knowing me, the guy still can't remember my very simple work schedule. Not that I'm about to refresh his knowledge.

**Me: Sorry, going over to Mom's to help with food
prep.**

At least this time, there's some truth in my response. I am prep-
ping something special for Mom's retirement party this weekend:
real actual doro wat. But by myself (with the help of Mama Adane
on YouTube), at my own place, from scratch, carving up the
whole organic chicken, chopping all the onions by hand, bubbling the spicy stew for hours on my balcony and everything.

"I'll miss seeing Kal's pretty face around here," Omar says
wistfully. *You and me both*, I think.

"It often doesn't turn out so well, though, does it?" I say. I
shove my phone in my desk drawer and nudge Omar off the treatment table, where he had perched himself, and pull out a fresh
sheet covering for my next patient. "When people get married
for papers? I doubt it is as simple as they expect it to be." And Kal
would never, right? Well, he did, in the play. As Antony, he married his rival's sister for the sake of peace in the empire. But look
at how *that* turned out.

Omar shrugs. "Less tough than the real thing, probably. No?"
We blink at each other, clueless. "I guess you have to decide,
what's it worth to ya?"

"You mean to Kal."

"That's what I said," Omar says, with a wink.

"Ha ha, *beaucoup* hilarious," I say, with edge in my voice so he
gets that this Kal-your-boyfriend shit is getting tired.

10

MIZ

I step into Mom's cozy two-bedroom bungalow, carrying my Tupperware of failed doro wat. The greenhouse, a.k.a. living room, is an empty no man's land between the women's voices coming from the kitchen around the corner, and the men's YouTube Ethiopian news blaring up the basement stairs.

Depositing my fusion berbere baked chicken on the dining table, I join Mom and her friends in the sauna-hot kitchen, entering just as Almaz, the combative one, currently mincing cubes of red meat into a fine mush for the kitfo, squawks, "What is she?"

Apparently, a heated discussion is in progress. A political one, judging by Almaz's question, likely about ethnicity. I pass myself around for greetings, breathing in the artery-clogging, heartburn-igniting aroma of foods I can't wait to eat.

"Who knows what *she* is!" Yeshi answers, in her signature sour tone, so potent I fear it'll contaminate the collard greens of the gomen besiga she's stirring.

"But he is Gurage," Elsi, the bringer of tea, confirms, reaching into the open oven to stir the bubbling tray of string-cut tenderloin zilzil tibs in its beefy juices.

Almaz nods sagely. "Those people are serious about their money."

Mom looks at me and gestures to a bowl of hard-boiled eggs on the kitchen table. I pull up a chair to begin peeling the shells and scoring the whites, readying them to be eased into the bubbling vat of real, multiple-chicken doro wat (why did I even bother trying?) to absorb the flavours of the stew.

"*Indee!*" Zainab, ever the peacemaker, exclaims, sawing through a fresh-baked wheel of difo dabo with a bread knife as long as her forearm. "His people are threatening to set fire to her family's home in Bole!"

"Can you blame them?" Mom counters, layering napkins between dishes. I look at her funny. *Did my mother just defend criminality?*

"How does a person spend fifty thousand dollars in three months?" Almaz challenges, drizzling the minced red meat of the kitfo with herby clarified butter.

If they're planning a wedding . . . I think sarcastically. As the hot takes fly fast and furious all around me, I make a mental note to send a photo of the spread to Kal once everything's laid out, so he can put in his takeout order.

"It was a trick. She tricked him!"

"The moment he paid her, it was her money to do with as she wished."

"But fifty thousand?"

"Let it be fifty million!"

"Was there a condition that she touch it only if the case succeeds?"

"What case?" I whisper to Zainab. Of Mom's friends, she gives me what most resembles answers to my questions. *Resembles* being the operative word. At age five, when I'd wanted to know where my father was, she told me he was a walia goat. It would take me a few years to understand that she meant he was, and would always be, in Ethiopia. Like that endangered species.

"Some marriage-for-paper arrangement in America," she says to me now. "INS threw out the case, so the man's side wants their money back from the American woman. Except . . ."

"It's all gone," I guess.

"They say she informed the INS that it was a fake case."

"That's bitchy," I say, earning a reproachful frown from Mom. I can't wait to tell Omar about another marriage of convenience gone sideways.

Out come more distasteful paper-marriage stories—a bucktoothed, weak-chinned man back home who couldn't get women to look twice at him, but the moment he won a US Diversity Visa lottery, they lined up to marry him; the guy somewhere in the US who married and brought over every single one of his sisters, divorcing one after the other, but then got his case thrown out when he wanted to bring over his actual new wife; a couple getting taken into separate rooms for their immigration interview and asked about the colour of the bedsheets, the pattern of the curtains, when they only lived together on paper. Enough to make a girl lose her appetite. Not this girl, of course. I've already snuck one egg into my mouth whole, feeling my stomach unfurl with gratitude.

"These children, if it is not papers they are after," Yeshi says bitterly, "it is 'happiness.'"

A round of derisive hmphs . . . but no follow-up opinions pro or con. Everyone's suddenly acting as if they don't smell a fart. *Ooh*, the silence that equals premium tea. Almost too hot to pour. I dart my eyes to Zainab. *Who's daring to want to be happy*? To this pioneer batch of very reluctant exiles from the '70s and '80s, happiness is low on the priority list, compared to what they've endured: trying not to get shot to death by the military junta, surviving imprisonment and desert crossings, creating community from scratch in Sudanese and Kenyan displaced persons' camps, making injera with North American self-rising flour and water, getting their children educated, keeping the girls away from the boys, temporarily deporting the rebels. The struggle was real. Happiness was an afterthought.

But Zainab avoids my searchlight gaze by carrying the platter of cut bread into the living room. *Whoa, that major, huh?* The lull drags. I flinch when I hear her peeling back the tinfoil that covers my container of fusion chicken.

Finally, Yeshi speaks up, probably figuring she might as well finish what she started. "These days, there's no *mechachal*. Just *meleyayet* at the first sign of problem."

Shite, there they go with them ten-dollar words. What does that mean?

Another lull, save for tut-tuts of agreement.

Zainab returns from the living room. "I see you made your contribution, Mizu."

I force a tight-lipped grin, and everyone jumps on this as if it's a lifebuoy. I have to explain, to great amusement all around, that I used yellow onions instead of shallots by mistake, and that I wimped out on dicing six pounds of them by hand and used a food processor. I tried to explain that ain't nobody got time, and that my eyeballs and gel nails had barely survived just peeling them, despite my goggles and latex gloves, but it was no use.

My berbere baked chicken turns out to be a surprise hit though, gone by the end of the night. When it's just Mom and me left and I am packing Kal's (and my) takeout, I seize my chance.

"So, Mommy," I say, filling Kal's half to the brim with doro wat from the pot. "What's *meh . . . mechal . . .*"

"It means to endure someone, over the long term," she says, putting incense on the stove on a piece of tinfoil.

Coming from her, the words land heavy, as if she knows more than most about true endurance. Long-distance endurance—*ha, like mother, like daughter*—since she is technically still married to Dad; a fun fact I discovered upon my deportation, when I saw the wedding ring on Dad's finger.

"Which one?"

"*Mechachal.*"

"And . . . the other one?" I know I'll bungle it up if I try to say it.

"*Meleyayet* is . . . to be apart."

"Like divorced or separated?"

"Either."

"Uh-huh. So, who were they talking about?"

"Yeshi's kid."

I splutter. Sosina's wedding was my first bridesmaid gig, almost ten years ago now. I may be marriage-allergic, but a party is a party, and weddings are always a blast. And Sosina's was *lit*. I've seen her maybe five times since, and we text only occasionally. Has she been unhappy all this time?

I feel bad for her, but I can't help also feeling vindicated a bit. "Ale Gena" rings out in my head. *There's misery yet*—how's that for a lyric update? "But . . . the wedding took so long!" As if all those parties, spread out over three cities and two years, all that effort, which was not out of the norm, should somehow guarantee that a couple stays together.

"Take more for your friends," Mom says, opening the cupboard where she keeps containers and closing the topic. I'll have to fill out my intel elsewhere, I guess. On the streetcar home, the stack of containers warming my quads, I take out my phone to text Sosina. What to say? After a bit of brain-racking, the perfect excuse comes to me.

> **Me: Was doing cleanup and guess what's still in my storage?!**

In all the wedding commotion, her bridal gown had somehow ended up at my place. All these years, no one had bothered to come pick it up. Red flag much?

> **Sosina:** 🫥 😳

> **Me: Your monster white dress! Shd I take to the dry cleaner? Never too late haha.**

An hour later, by the time I'm home tucking the leftovers into my fridge, when there's still nothing, my heart sinks. Wow, even now I can't breach that wall that goes up as soon as that "Ale

Gena" song ends, huh? But maybe she doesn't want to say too much because she's going through only the separation version of *meleyayet*. Fair enough. I can wait. I have three decades and counting of experience waiting for a couple (called Mom and Dad) to tell me what went wrong. One more marriage mystery is nothing.

11

KAL

I get a text alert from Miz as I am unlocking my bike outside of the low-rise redbrick building where I've just had another gruelling on-camera acting class. *Not another affirmation, Miz, please.* The first GIFs she sent me were a little amusing, but now I'm regretting bringing up skipping my parents' anniversary party. I open the text, hoping for a regular message.

> **Miz: Did you do the TV show audition Oliver promised?**
>
> **Me: Nope.**

I pocket my phone, toss my cross-body bag toward my back and hop on my bike. Setting a brisk pace, I barrel down the road, eager to slough off my foul mood from class. Days after the after-party, Oliver had reached out to tell me about a comedy show that he'd just joined as one of the executive producers. They would begin casting soon. He could get me seen for a part, and if I was successful, that would earn me a new work permit.

Grateful as I was for his support, I couldn't feel truly optimistic about this prospect. Drama, not comedy, is my strength, and there was a condition with the offer: that I take an on-camera acting class. We both knew this was also my weak area. I have hated screen acting ever since I was introduced to it in school. It feels so disjointed and small compared to the immediacy of stage acting.

And sure, I could extend my stay by another year, but at the end of that permit, I would be back in uncertainty. What I want is the real thing or nothing. But I had accepted Oliver's offer regardless.

Just as I am starting to feel myself relax, I am forced to slow down in Trinity Bellwoods Park to navigate through lovers, friends, and young families meandering along the tangled paths. Rather than overuse my bell like those obnoxious cyclists, I hop off to walk the rest of the way. Soaking in the greenness might even do me good, not to mention save me from taking a Frisbee to the head.

I fall behind an elderly couple walking hand in hand and smile at the sight—one I never see in Addis. Young people with interlocked hands, yes. But not the elders. Every time I see it here, it reminds me of my parents, a rare pair who did. Who am I trying to fool? No, I cannot miss their party. I must have faith like Miz that my situation will be different by January. And even if it isn't, I'll still go and accept whatever happens at the border.

As I come to this decision, the tree branches, heavy with blossoms, all dance at once, raining soft pink petals down. My father would take this as a sign of approval from Emay, and in this moment, I agree. My phone vibrates, interrupting the hallowed moment.

Miz: Have you thought of applying to grad school?

I know she is just trying to help, but it's starting to feel as if she sees me as a problem she has to fix, like one of her patients. For a millisecond, I regret ever reconnecting with her in Toronto, then I immediately regret thinking that. When we were younger, I'd show her around Addis during her summer visits, but our roles flipped when I moved to Toronto—and that has given us the best memories of our friendship.

Me: Nope.

Miz: Okaaay . . . would be easy to switch status to study permit while you're still here . . . They would enjoy charging you international student fees! :)

Instead of responding, I put my phone back in my pocket and continue my walk, but it buzzes again a few moments later, just as I'm approaching the other end of the park.

Miz: What about the US Green Card lottery? Friend of Mom's friend just got it.

I shake my head in frustration. She's relentless. With a deep breath, I jab out a response so full of errors I have to retype it several times. This irritation toward Miz—I hate it.

Me: Literally one in a million chance. And there are people who need it more than me.

Miz: A lot of random people get it.

I don't know what she means by "random people," but regardless, I opt for silence again.

Miz: Worth a try.

Miz: Feel me?

Miz: Okay, saint. I will submit the app for you. It's very basic.

But she knows she can't, not without my passport information. I watch the screen, waiting to see what else she could possibly come up with. Nothing, it seems. I send her a silent apology for having quashed her spirit and straddle my bike to ride again. *Buzz*.

Miz: Don't get mad but . . . claim asylum? You'd just be telling a story. You do that for a living.

This one I can't ignore.

Me: I would only be making it hard for people with real cases who NEED asylum.

Miz: What about what you need?

Me: I have never really NEEDED anything.

Miz: Wow. Ok. I feel like I'm pulling teeth here.

Me: Then don't.

Miz: Man, do you even want to stay??

**Me: Didn't you say it's ok if I leave? That at least I
know I tried?**

That, I know, is low, and factually inaccurate. She never said
that it would be okay if I left Toronto and headed back to Addis;
she said that because I had tried, I couldn't have any regrets. I linger
by the roadside, my legs on either side of my bike, expecting her
to call me out, remind me that I said it first and that it's true—
better to have loved and lost than not at all. But this time, Miz
goes quiet. After about five minutes, I give up. Why shouldn't she
ghost me? If Miz has decided that she doesn't want anything more
to do with me, then so be it. I deserve that. It will make it easier
for both of us to move on once I am gone.

12

MIZ

"I'm just trying to help," I insist. Aimé's sitting opposite me at an outdoor patio table at Rendez-Vous Ethiopian restaurant, scrolling through my texts with Kal yesterday about his situation. She's wearing her oversized sunglasses so it's hard to tell what she's thinking. Resting my arm on the black fence of the patio, I pick at the potted fir plant on the other side, observing the flow of traffic. What I'm really keeping an eye out for, even on a Wednesday, are any blasts from the past I'd rather not run into here. I take pity on the fir and switch to fidgeting with the notecard advertising a drink promotion. I *know* I'm dancing on the edge of being too much with Kal, but I can't help it. I also *know* that what I'm about to do, the final idea I have for him, will be equivalent to sailing right off the cliff. But if it works out, it'll all have been worth it.

Aimé returns my phone and pushes back her sunglasses, pinning me with a look. "Keep it up and you'll help yourself right out of a friendship," she says with her best Judge Lynn impression.

I flinch, as if she's actually thrown down a gavel. "I bet you K-Money's too depressed to even think about what lies ahead," she goes on. "And here you are smothering him. You know Mr. Mellow—he likes his *space*." Aimé has all kinds of affectionate nicknames for Kal. She cranes her neck and signals for a server's attention from within the restaurant.

"Um, that's some mama bear slash girlfriend slash wifey shite," I say, affronted. "I do not *smother*."

"Hookay." Aimé mouths *thank you* to the server who brings us one menu.

I watch the server return inside. "Anyway, Aimé, the reason I wanted to meet up today," I say to the top of her head as she peruses the menu, "is that I have one last possible solution for Kal." She looks up at me warily. "I promise after this, I'll stop," I say. I know I sound like a person with a problem, a compulsion, but I don't care. I do a drum roll on the tabletop. "I'm gonna . . . find someone to sign for him!"

"Sign what?" Aimé looks confused.

"Come on, don't be thick."

"I *am* thick."

Discreetly, I mime sliding a ring on my left ring finger. "Someone to *marry* him."

Aimé snaps her attention back to the menu. "I did *not* just hear that."

I tug at the laminated page she's holding. "Come on. *Everybody* gets married. We even have a song about it. Remember 'Ale Gena'?"

"Most people don't get married just to get papers."

"But everyone gets married for *something*. There's always some kind of convenience baked in with the 'love.' "

She shakes her head sadly at me, as if I have just gone beyond the beyond. "How romantic."

I roll my eyes. "The time is not for romance. The time is for bold, decisive action."

Aimé rubs the bridge of her nose and pointedly turns her eyes to look out at the pedestrians walking by. She looks as if she's giving every person's outfit a once-over, but really, she's considering my idea. I know it. I tap my nails against my teeth, waiting for her to reach the same conclusion I had after I heard about Sosina. I'd mulled it all over and realized that a person can do the unthinkable if pushed into a corner. They can always change their mind about positions they'd been so firm about. Despite all my pessimism, I have never in a million years dreamed Sosina and her man would change their minds about each other, leaving me stuck with her wedding dress in my storage closet potentially forever. So why can't Kal change his woo-woo mind about the sacred foreverness of marriage? Last time he had a crisis, he changed his mind about his entire identity! Threw deuces to his country, family, career and moved to Canada!

"And K's on board with this?" Aimé says, mouth twisted to one side.

I grin. *Someone is aboard the rescue train with me.* "That's the thing." Aimé's eyes narrow. "My idea is to first scout out women who might be good candidates to sign for him. Then, if anyone looks promising, I will casually pass the idea by him." She gawks at me, and I use the opportunity to take her menu and use it as a fan, stealing glances at the inside of the restaurant. "I thought here would be a good place to start, where there are Ethiopian women working for a low enough wage that the prospect of making a year's income for just filling out some forms would be very attractive to them."

"Oh my god, Miz," Aimé says in a whisper, as if she's terrified someone will hear us. "Did I already say the levels of wrong this is rating at?"

"I just need you to help me with the chit-chat."

"Miz! You need help."

"I need *to* help. Aims, fifty thousand dollars could change a woman's life. That's a worthy, honourable cause that benefits everyone." I put the menu down and cover her hand with mine and stare at her. "I'm just asking you to help me test the waters. How does one broach the topic? Like, should I go for the direct approach? 'Hi, are you married?' "

"Immediately no!"

"I remember words Mom used to say." That subtle, roundabout lingo she dropped when coordinating favours in the community, making call after call like a switchboard operator. "*Chigir* and *metebaber*. They might as well have been my first Amharic words."

"Well, they ain't about to become mine, honey."

"It's basically *difficulty* and *cooperation*." I chuckle. How ironic, me an Amharic interpreter. Another server sails toward our table. "Oh, oh, here she comes. Be cool," I hiss.

"Oh, I'm chillin'." Aimé smiles sweetly at the server, who is wearing snug black dress pants and a short-sleeved top with an Ethiopian patterned scarf tied in a bun at the back of her head. She has the height and fine bones of a model.

"Hi," Aimé says, barely audible. "Could you cooperate with helping me? I am having some difficulties."

I kick her under the table. She thinks she's funny.

"Hmm?" the woman says, confused, using one hand to shield her eyes from the sun.

I butt in. "So! What's good today?" I'm being over-the-top friendly.

Weak shrug. "Everything."

"Anything you *don't* have? Haha." I wink at her. "Easier if you tell me before I pick it."

She does a combination forced smile and head wobble. "No, we have everything."

God, if talking about the food is this painful . . . No, I can't be discouraged so easily. "You've been working here a long time?"

"About a year," she says, glancing back at the interior, which is not busy. But I get the message. I shoot a look at Aimé. She's nose in phone, playing *Candy Crush*. Guess I'm riding solo.

"Do you like it? Is it good pay? Sorry, I'm just asking for someone." I smile at her.

She looks at me as if I have two heads. "It's good, yeah."

"You plan to stay a long time? Are you new here? I mean to Canada."

She finally meets my eyes, and I see a hint of *I don't get paid enough for this shit* in them. "It is my work," she says to me, as if that is all the explanation needed. "Can I bring you drinks?"

"Water would be great," Aimé exclaims. "Thank you so much." I swallow, feeling like a bumbling, selfish idiot. As soon as the server leaves, she turns on me. "Hopeless."

"See! I need you!"

"*Mon dieu.*" She sighs, just like her grandmother. "Kal, you owe me your firstborn."

When the server comes back with our waters, Aimé gets to work. I make mental notes, paying attention to how she's establishing rapport before going for the big time. But the server is just as curt with Aimé's questions—whether she has any family here (some), siblings (no), long-term career plans (not sure)—as she was with me. We try to come up with all kinds of excuses to have her return so we can get further with the chit-chat: more napkins, more mitmita to add heat to our food, then a side of plain yogurt to stop our tongues burning . . . but nada.

"You think she sensed what we're up to?" I say, after she has left us with the bill. It had appeared before we even finished our meals, the fastest I've ever seen a bill arrive. It's as if she couldn't wait to get rid of us.

"I feel gross," Aimé says, pushing the bill to me. "How do men do this all the time?"

"You and me both. I'm tipping twenty-five percent," I say, filling out the bill.

"Good. That's the least we can do." Aimé scoots out of her chair. "Well, we gave it a shot."

Did we though? I think, as we leave the patio. Like the scent of the spices still on my fingertips, my plan doesn't want to let me go. A bakery across the street gives me an idea.

"Dessert?"

"I thought I'm supposed to be off sugar," Aimé says, but her eyes have lit up.

"Are you?" She smiles guiltily. "We're right in Greektown, might as well." Except where I lead us to is Mocha Cafe and Pastry, an Ethio-Eri spot.

Aimé looks skeptical. "Here?"

"We got this," I say. I know she's dreading getting stared at. But that never killed anyone, and by now, Aimé should be used to the Ethiopian national hobby of staring at each other and any-one who looks remotely like one of us. Inside the modest café

ONLY BECAUSE IT'S YOU

wallpapered with a red stonework pattern, she distances herself from me, standing at the far end of the display case of tiramisus, sponge cakes, and baklavas, reading the coffee menu as if it's the original ten commandments. The cashier, a plump woman in a denim shirt dress, comes up for my order, tossing a long thin ponytail over her shoulder. Right away, I notice she's wearing what looks like a wedding ring like a pendant on a thick gold necklace. Dammit. I do the obligatory rapport building anyway (i.e., weather), then say, "That's nice," tapping the base of my neck to mean her necklace. "You were married?"

"Oh, I am still, thanks to God," the server says. "Only, it's not comfortable to wear for work."

"I get it. I work with my hands too," I say. I order and pay for two baklavas and take them out to Aimé, who has escaped outside.

"Mission fail," I say glumly, giving her one of the pastries.

"Oh," she says, taking in my very obvious disappointment as I peel off the top layer of phyllo and crush it in my mouth. "Can I ask you something?" I nod. "Why do you need Kal to stay so much?"

The dough sticks to the roof of my mouth. "Wha—? Obviously, he deserves—"

"No, *youuu*," she says, pressing her index finger into my arm with her hand holding the pastry bag closed. "What's it to *you*?"

"It's for him. It's not about me." I frown at her. "What's with the third degree?"

She raises her free hand in surrender, backing off. We fall silent as we eat and walk toward the subway, a feeling of defeat in the air. Suddenly, she stops and points up under a sign that says Jolly Bar. "One last try?"

I smile, touched. "Thanks, boo, but oh god." I eye the door apprehensively. Though the signage on this bar is new, I know the place intimately. I haven't been here, in the daytime no less, since those wild days, before the epidemic of weddings started to take out my partners in crime one by one. "Too many ghosts."

"Okay," Aimé says, backing off again. "But bartenders are the chattiest people in hospitality . . . *and* they know a *lot* of people . . . just sayin'."

"All right, all right," I say, following her into the bar. *What I do and the places I go for you*, I say to Kal in my mind. Thankfully, it's not even happy hour yet, so most of the no-fuss seating is empty, the three different games on as many giant flatscreens over the back bar playing for just two loners hunched under their ball caps and popped collars. "My girl will have a rum and Coke," Aimé says to the bartender as we hop onto the barstools. "Same for me. Easy on the Coke."

The bartender nods knowingly and begins to prepare our drinks. I like her funky, short layered haircut and sleeveless, flowy capri-length jumpsuit showing an inch of midriff. She appears older than Kal. Slight bummer, but it should help keep things strictly business, if this is a go. And I don't see a wedding band anywhere on her person. Sweet. Unless she hides it so that it won't affect her tips? I realize I'm staring when I feel Aimé nudge me.

Our drinks arrive quickly. I stir mine and feel tipsy just from the vapours of the double shots of rum. "Holy! This is strong."

"Made by Hani," the bartender says with pride. She rests her arms on the counter and studies us. "Okay. What's the matter? Who is in trouble?"

Aimé and I look at each other in surprise. Hani laughs. "Young girls like you, in here, at this hour. In all my years, when do I see this?"

I like her already, so I decide to cut to the chase. "My friend is having serious paper problems."

Hani gives me a sympathetic tut. "I know how it is."

"And we are actually looking for someone to . . ." I almost say *cooperate* but trail off, suddenly terrified at the idea of her saying yes. Am I ready to hand Kal over to someone we don't even know?

"Sign for him," Aimé says, smooth as a single malt.

"Oh, I'm married," Hani says with a laugh. "I just don't wear a ring." Like my mama, I think, and wonder if hers too is a marriage in nothing but name, held on to by both sides for who knows what reason. If her man also still wears his ring, like Dad.

"Did your friend come from America?" Hani asks me.

"From Ethiopia direct," I say. "He's on a work permit now, but he was a student first."

Hani nods, impressed. Next thing I know, she's asking all the questions—how cooperative is Kal's family, when does his work permit expire, what would be the payment amount and payout schedule, does he have any police record or a girlfriend, is he healthy and a Christian, does he mess with drugs or alcohol? I nod and shake my head like a bobble-head doll while Aimé watches the Q&A like a table tennis game.

"Their documents will be under his address," Hani says, winding down. "But they don't have to live together. It's good for the case. But not necessary. Let me see a photo." I hesitate. This feels like another point of no return, but I don't know why I'm tripping—this was *my* idea! "I must see if I've seen him around," Hani adds. It doesn't sound as if it'll go well for Kal if she has. I move ever so slowly for my bag and root around as if I can't find my phone. Eventually, I open to a photo I took of him on his last birthday, on my balcony at home, the sunset turning one side of his face golden, and hand it over.

Hani's eyes sparkle. Dang, back up, lady. "Very handsome!" She asks me his name. I tell her. "Good name!" She gives me her phone to put my number in. After I do, I call myself so that my number is at the top of her recent calls. "I'm sending you some contacts," she says, moving away to take care of a new customer.

Aimé leans in, chewing on her straw. "Third time's a charm."

"Amen to that," I say, and down a big gulp.

"So . . ." Aimé says. "When's Daniel coming by again?"

I almost choke. "Friday," I say. She nods approvingly. Like Daniel, she doesn't need to know either that, come Friday, I'll hit him with an *I had to step out unexpectedly, but I've left your things with Everest*. None of said items will include a diamond ring, of course, thus continuing my absurd streak of finding excuses to buy myself more time until I can personally put it back in his gym bag. As much as I pray he hasn't noticed the ring is missing, he must have. Hence why he's all up on me.

We're on our way to the subway station when I receive a text from Hani, with six names and numbers. Aimé laughs when she sees the list, pointing at a name. "Is that—"

"Yup." One of the names on the list is a Muna. Just my brilliant luck that one of these contacts happens to share the same name as Kal's ex. Lovely. "Already mentally crossed her out."

Which leaves me with only a precious five.

13

MIZ

Miz: So I met one of the women on the list—Gelila (aka Gigi). We skyped.

Aimé: Oh yeah? And?

Miz: Nice, funny, works at the Yorkville Sephora.

Aimé: Ooh, connections 😉

Miz: She is saving for uni to study coding! So she'd use the $ for that.

Aimé: Sounds perfect.

Miz: Except she looks EXACTLY like Muna, even has her same voice. fml ☹

Aimé: Maybe her long-lost twin? Lol.

Miz: Too spooky.

Aimé: It will be good for K-money to get to know a
different Muna to cancel out the old one that broke
his heart.

Miz: Not the point of this mission.

Miz: But ok. I'll put her as a Weak Maybe.

After Gelila, next on my list of contacts from Hani is a woman
named Khadijah. She wants to meet outside the Rabba mini-mart
that's on the same block as my work. Of all the Rabbas in the city?
I avoid that location on account of one very judgy woman from
back home who works the prepared foods section and makes me
feel as if I'm ordering too much food. A girl who runs the equivalent of a marathon every week's gotta eat, *okay*? But time is tight,
and Khadijah's available in the middle of the day, on my lunch
break, so I agree reluctantly, hoping I won't run into the prepared
foods lady. *Again, what I do for you, Kal!*

I should have knocked on wood because, when I get there,
who do I see sitting at a table outside the store enjoying an iced
coffee and scrolling through her phone? The prepared foods lady.
Brilliant. She's wearing the store uniform of branded black polo
and pants, her chiffon scarf (green today) covering her hijab cap
thrown over her shoulder.

To create some distance, I wander off toward a grassed area
where a dog walker is wrangling leashed dogs and text Khadijah.

Me: I'm here.

Khadijah: I'm outside sitting.

I look back at the woman and see on her face the same thing I'm sure she reads on mine: complete disappointment. But I plaster a fake smile on my face and approach her. I'm pissed that I'm automatically down to three candidates now because no way in hell am I handing Kal over to *her.*

"Hi! I didn't know it was you," I say, as if it's a lovely surprise.

She puts away her drink and turns sideways in her chair, as if she's about to leave. *Be my guest, and save us both the trouble!*

"You live in this area?" she says, all accusatory.

"Oh no, only work. Too fancy for my pocket," I say, gesturing at the high-end condos.

She smiles, tight as plastic wrap. "Sit?" *Must I?* I drag out the metal chair noisily. My butt has barely touched the seat when she asks to see a picture of this man who needs a sponsor. Sensing my hesitation, she adds, "Maybe I know him."

"You don't," I say with total certainty, trying to think of a quick and painless way to end this interaction. Tell her he already found someone? But then why did I agree to meet?

"Okay." She takes a sip from her iced coffee. "Did you bring the deposit?"

"What deposit?" I ask, confused.

"To start the discussing," she says, as if this should be obvious.

Is she joking? But she holds my gaze, dead serious, unblinking. Who ever heard of upfront payment just to talk? Come to think of it, she's way too unblinking. It occurs to me she could be purposely sabotaging this meeting because she doesn't want nothing to do with me or mine neither. At last! We have something in common.

"Ohh," I say, as if I forgot to bring the money. "How much would that deposit need to be?"

"Ten percent," she says, "of the total."

"Oh, I don't have five grand on me right now," I say, perfectly straight faced.

She doesn't miss a beat. "Call me and we'll meet again when you have it?"

"Let's." I leave her to finish her refreshment. *Like hell we will.*

Aimé: So did you call her back?

Miz: What you think?

Aimé: Lol

Miz: No way, met up with Helina, Dufferin Mall.

Aimé: Mm-hmm, go on.

Miz: Born here, going to U of T for poli sci, needs $$ for studio time w producer.

Aimé: Oh, an artist! Good for K! They'll have that in common.

Miz: Was actually approached for this kind of thing before but said no b/c the guy was not Ethio.

Aimé: 😳 Slightly racist.

Miz: Points for patriotism 😜, and she's in her 20s.

Aimé: So what? Put her in the Strong Maybe.

Miz: Yeah?

Aimé: Slim pickings ok?

Miz: U right, ok. Then there was Samri. Met at the Second Cup up by Finch stn.

Aimé: Girl you been all over.

Miz: She came here 15 years ago, wants $ for house she's building back home for mom.

Aimé: 🧡 Strong Yes.

Miz: Right! So, 2 strong—Samri, Helina. 1 weak—Gelila. 1 hell no—Khadijah.

Aimé: Wat happen to #5?

Me: Melat was a flake. Giving me runaround. Just say "not interested," man! Simple!

Aimé: B/c u ppl are so good @ directness.

I set up a coffee date with Kal and schedule for Samri and Helina to meet us there, half an hour apart over the space of two hours so their comings and goings won't overlap. Hani comes through at the eleventh hour with one more contact named Nardos. I add her to the Strong Maybes only because she is available on short notice on the date I've picked for the introductions with Kal and seems cool on the phone. I give myself a pat on the back. They don't make friends like me anymore.

14

KAL

I spot Miz through the window of SanRemo Bakery, our long-established finish line. We always meet up here to reward ourselves after she finishes a long run, and I, a long ride. I feel relieved to see her. She never replied to my last text a few days ago, staying silent until she messaged me about meeting up today, and I've been bursting with shame at how rude I was toward her when she was giving me ideas for how to stay in Canada.

As soon as I pass through the sliding doors, I can feel all that butter and sugar seep into my skin, which is already porous from the heat. It's only a little bit cooler inside, but I enjoy the moderate relief nonetheless, fanning my shirt as I admire the nearly 360 degrees of decadent Italian pastries, breads and bursting sandwiches in the display cases and shelves.

As I approach Miz, I notice she's sitting at a four-top instead of our usual table for two. I look at her quizzically.

"Hey," Miz says, smiling up at me warmly. Our outfits are accidentally matching—hers a tan linen top and denim skirt, and mine a light-brown button-down and my favourite denim Bermudas.

"Hey," I say, suddenly feeling very self-conscious. It feels hard to look her in the eyes, so I direct my gaze to that wishing star above her left eye instead, a childhood scar from a feral cat, today freed from concealer. "I'm sorry," I say simply, still standing, my hands slightly behind me like a butler's.

She looks confused. "Huh?"

"I was so rude to you the other day when we were texting." I move aside so one group of people can vacate their table while another swoops down on it. "You were only trying to help." She waits me out, a smile now playing on her lips. "That's all." I sit down.

"Oh my god," she says, laughing. "Don't worry about it. You're under a lot of stress! We're apologizing for being ourselves now?" She shakes her head at me, smiling, then remembers something. "Oh, I haven't ordered yet. I was waiting for you."

"I'll go," I say, getting back up. We can't risk us both going and losing our table. "The usual?" She gives a thumbs-up, distracted by an incoming call on her phone.

It takes me a couple of trips to transport the four new pastries we'll try today, plus our double macchiatos. We toast our coffees. "Happy belated Ethiopian New Year," Miz says, putting down her cup and digging into a slice of pistachio ricotta cake. "Did you call home? And more importantly, did you tell them anything?"

"Yes," I say, taking a sip. "But no. They're all still expecting me in January."

"You'll be there," she says confidently, covering her full mouth. "Because you're going."

I break into a pistachio cannoli with my fork. "I'll miss times like these."

"Would you stop?" she says, exasperated. "You're not getting deported, you know? Trust me, things will look up for you soon." She has a mischievous grin on her face, twirling her fork at me like a magic wand.

I raise an eyebrow at her. "Oh yeah? You have a crystal ball?"

She peels the paper off a cupcake with pistachio icing. "By the way, I invited a friend to join us."

"You did?" That explains this table for four and why she has been glancing at the door every time someone comes in. "Who?" I ask, hoping curiosity will mask my disappointment that our one-on-one time is being cut short.

"A friend of a friend. I don't personally know her. But she keeps wanting to link up, and I felt awkward going by myself. What if she's weird?"

"So am I here for my opinion or for your protection?" I ask with a laugh.

"Just be yourself," she says, popping a hunk of icing into her mouth.

That's an odd thing to say. Why would I be anything else?

An Ethiopian woman walks into the seating area and looks around. Miz stands and waves her over. I stand too as they greet each other somewhat formally.

"Nardos, this is Kalkidan," Miz says. "My . . . cousin."

The word hits me like a slap. *Cousin? Since when? And why?* She always introduces me either just by name or as the only best friend she still has from childhood. Despite the thoughts rushing through my head, I manage a pleasant smile as I shake Nardos's hand. Miz asks her what she'd like to drink and goes to get it, leaving me alone with this stranger.

"Are you coming from work?" I have no idea what else to say to her. She is about our age, dressed in a black skirt suit and red shirt, her hair slicked back into a painfully tight-looking bun.

"I took the day off," she says, assessing me intensely. "You're an actor though. How interesting!"

I start, immediately feeling exposed. "Oh, Miz told you?"

Nardos confirms this by bizarrely reciting to me the main points of my own life, including that one of my sisters is very close in age to me. I'm beginning to suspect this is a setup, which is weird. But moreover, why would Miz bother with a setup when I'm so close to going back home?

Miz returns with Nardos's drink and an extra fork. "I see you guys are hitting it off," she says overenthusiastically.

"And how do you know each other?" I ask, narrowing my eyes very subtly at Miz.

"Friend of a friend," Nardos says.

Miz proceeds to give me the bullet points about Nardos, who sits there grinning at me: when she came to Canada (fifteen years ago), what she does for a living (dental assistant), where her family are (back home, big, and reliant on her), what hobbies she has (movies). When Miz pauses for a breath, I excuse myself to go to the bathroom but only so I can be out of sight when I text her.

Me: Are you trying to set me up with this woman?

Miz: ☺

Me: Why in God's name?! I'm leaving, remember?

Miz: Not if you two vibe and she agrees to sign for you. SURPRISE!

Holy creator in the sky! I fall back against the wall. Sign for me? No wonder Miz has been so quiet. I thought she was mad at me, but she's actually been trying to find me a *wife*? A wise man once told me to pay attention to what is *not* said. Miz, while cycling me through all my options for staying in Canada, had specifically *not* mentioned spousal sponsorship. Not that it's not an obvious solution. Everyone knows someone who's done it. But I'm still annoyed.

Me: When were you going to inform me of this?

Miz: Well if u hadn't run off! Hurry back. 2 more women to meet, and I don't want them overlapping.

Me: What??

Miz: Options, man, OPTIONS, don't make me have to come in there and get you.

I know it's not an idle threat—she would barge into the men's washroom to get me, breezily declaring, "Nothing I haven't seen before!"—but I need a moment to absorb this, sort through my jumbled thoughts.

Marriage is serious, something that shouldn't be abused, and this plan is exactly what that would be: an abuse of the sanctity of marriage. That's not me. I step aside to let another man enter the washroom, and scratch my chin. I *should* be *really* mad at Miz for ambushing me like this, but I actually feel touched by the amount of effort she must have put into organizing this, all so I can stay in Canada.

Me "marrying" a stranger, could it work? I know there's a strong chance that this audition Oliver has promised me won't pan out, which means I will be forced to leave everything I've built here—my life, my friends, Miz. What if signing a marriage licence with someone I don't know could be less of a holy union and more of a mutually beneficial exchange? Is that so absurd?

Yes, Kal, it is.

I sigh and head out of the washroom and return to the table.

Nardos winks at me jokingly as I sit down. "No need to worry," she says. "I have experience. This would be my second time, so I know how everything goes."

Miz's cup clatters on the saucer. "Say what now?" she says.

Uh-oh. Eyes wide, I inch my chair away from the table.

"You've done this before?" Miz says.

"Yes," Nardos says matter-of-factly.

"When?" Her tone is slightly sharp, and I swallow nervously.

Nardos looks up at the ceiling, unperturbed by the looming danger from Miz's side of the table. "2010 to 2011. That's around when you came," she says to me, and again I feel far too overexposed.

Miz scowls. "Why didn't you tell me this?"

"I don't . . ." Nardos falters. "It's a good thing."

"How's it a good thing? It's five years before you can sponsor someone new. I'm guessing you got divorced very recently?" I am impressed by how much research Miz seems to have done. "How is that going to look? You think they won't realize you're up to something when you show up with a new husband you're sponsoring?" She throws her napkin down on the table. "You've wasted our time. Fuck!"

"Excuse me!" Nardos says, now getting heated, putting one hand up. I make some useless sound that is supposed to be calming or peace inducing, but I may as well not be at the table. She continues, "I will not be shouted at. I have more people who need me, you know!"

"Excuse me?" a new voice says above us. We all turn to look. It's another Ethiopian woman, this one very short and bright skinned, with her short hair dyed maroon. "I'm Samri. I'm supposed to meet Mizan?" She looks from one woman to the other, then settles on me with a silent *What's going on?*

Miz grazes Samri's arm. "Just a sec, hon." She swivels back to Nardos, her voice murderous again. "And you think you're the only person *I* would consider?"

I get up. "I'll get you a chair," I say to Samri.

But she follows me, whispering, "I had no idea it was a group interview. I'm gonna go."

She slips away, mouthing *sorry* over her shoulder before I can attempt to convince her to stay. Just as well, I would not have done a good job of this interview. A horrible scraping sound from the direction of our table turns out to be Nardos springing out of her chair. It teeters dangerously. I move fast and catch it. Not that we could possibly attract any more attention than we already have.

She points her finger down at Miz. "I'm warning Hani about you!" Then storms off.

"Ha, it will be the other way around, honey," Miz yells in her wake.

"Marry him yourself if you're so concerned!" With that, Nardos is out of our lives, for good, I hope.

Miz rolls her eyes, then peers behind me. "Where's Samri?"

"I think this," I say, sitting back at the table, "was too much for her."

"No!" Miz moans. She drops her face into her hands, elbows on the table, defeated. "And Helina cancelled earlier while you were hiding in the bathroom. I had really liked her for you. She's also an artist, a singer."

I rub her back. "It's okay, Miz. There's still Hani?" I say that for her sake, of course, not mine.

"No." Miz sighs. "Hani was my . . . broker." She pulls the plate with a Grand Marnier Italian pistachio babà and the remnants of the other pastries toward her. Devouring everything bite after bite, she tells me about all that led up to this, starting with her mother's retirement party. Before long, I'm clutching my stomach, muscles sore from laughing at her run-in with Khadijah. I haven't laughed like this in what feels like weeks.

She lobs a crumpled muffin liner at my head. "Shut up. It's been exhausting to coordinate! How do people do it all the time?"

"You know, Miz," I begin. "This kind of thing works best when it's between people who already know each other well enough to dive into such a big commitment. Like siblings, extended family . . ." I pull back from adding *established friends*.

Miz swallows a bite. "Yeah, but I know you don't have anyone here, so . . ."

"No, no, I don't . . ." I gaze out the window at the row homes across the road.

She pushes crumbs around the plate, takes a hesitant breath.

"I mean, you *could* go down to the States and—" She knows my extended family is all in the US.

I stop her with my hand. "If I wanted to be in the States, I would have moved there in the first place. I'm here because I want to be *here*." Here where I could be just me, where my time could be mine and mine alone.

"And I'm glad for that," she says, reaching across the table to grasp my hand. "I'm glad we've had these eight years."

"Me too." We smile at each other. I feel wistful, sad. "So, 'cousin,' huh?" I say, the word like a literal lump in my throat. "You know you've never, not once in the twenty-two years we've known each other, called me that."

"I thought it would sound more reassuring than if I'd introduced you as a friend," Miz says, shrugging. She takes her hand from mine and scrapes the dry foam inside her coffee cup with a stir stick. "Don't overthink it."

"I think it bears some thinking."

"Oh boy," she says, lowering the stick.

"I think, you're not wrong. You're the closest person I have to family here."

"There you go, then."

"However, you know I have more actual cousins than I know what to do with."

"If only one of them lived in Canada." She gives me a wry look. "Okay, it'll never happen again." She puts her hands together in front of her heart and bows. "I'm your friend. Full stop."

"My *very* good friend," I say. "As today's events have shown."

"Well, I'm sure Miss Nardos," she says with disdain, "is already out there dragging my name. 'Marry him yourself.'" She scoffs. "As if!"

"As if what?" I keep my voice even, but I can feel my heart beating a little faster.

"I mean, come on," she says, eyeing me with her chin down as if I am missing the obvious.

I'm starting to wonder whether Miz is the one being avoidant. Say what she will about Miss Nardos, but the woman made a valid point. Here, no one will care for my well-being as diligently as Miz. And honestly, if I was going to take as drastic a step as getting married, there's no one else—

No no no. I stop myself and revert to reality. "She doesn't know you," I say. "She missed the memo about you not being the marrying kind."

"Exactly," Miz says, jabbing the stir stick on the tabletop. "If I were, I wouldn't be out there hustling like there's no tomorrow."

I laugh lightly but still very aware that our tomorrows are, in fact, dwindling. "And if you were, you wouldn't get fake-married. I know this, speaking as the marrying kind."

"*Exactamento.*"

We get quiet. I wait, feeling as if we are teetering on the brink of something monumental.

"But," Miz starts, pushing us closer to the edge, "in life, there are extenuating circumstances."

"There are," I say as evenly as I can.

"And obviously, it wouldn't be like me *actually* getting married to you in the forever sense. It would be me just doing you a favour. A sponsorship is a sponsorship is a sponsorship . . ." She looks at me intently, almost as if she's holding her breath.

". . . is a sponsorship." My heart is full on racing now, from thrill or terror, it can't decide.

"But . . ." she repeats, pulling us back. My heart with it. "I don't know. It's . . . you and me. Wouldn't it be . . . ? I don't know if you'd want that." She clasps her hands in front of her and almost looks nervous. "If you'd want . . . me."

"I trust you," I say simply. "What else is there to it?"

Now it gets really quiet at our table. Finally, Miz speaks, mostly to herself. "You know, it *is* a no-brainer. You and me." She flicks at the crumpled napkin. "It's just a piece of paper, but let me flip it back to you: Why won't you let me sign for you?"

"I never said that."

"But you've never brought it up. I'm sure it's crossed your mind."

It hadn't, to be honest, but I decide to dodge the question. "It's a big huge ask. How can I ask that of anyone?" I look up at the ceiling. "How can I ask that of *you*?"

"Hey," she says, reaching her hands out again and taking mine in them. The soft warmth of her skin and firm clasp immediately ground me. "What are cousins for, eh?"

It's a joke that neither of us laughs at. That's how I know we've left the realm of the hypothetical. Our gazes lock as tight as our hands. Everything falls away.

"It's many pieces of paper," I say carefully. I can feel her pulse trembling at her wrists. "And bureaucracy, time, energy. Most people don't take that on . . ."

She tugs our hands. "I'm not most people."

No. Miz is not most people. She is *my* people and has been for decades. "I trust you too," she says. "I would do it only for you."

"Same." I sound out the words like a protective mantra. "Only because it's you."

"Only because it's you," she repeats smoothly. We both take huge breaths and let them out forcefully. She smiles shyly. "Whoa, this is happening, my guy!"

"I believe so!" I'm suddenly feeling shy myself.

"So when're you sending *shimagile* to my dad?"

"What!"

"You know, your uncles and them, to do the proper asking?" she says deadpan, then cracks up, letting go of my hands. "I'm kidding! You should see your face!"

I wipe sweat from my head. "Phew! You had me."

"I wish I had a picture," she says with a laugh. Then, more seriously, "I don't think we should involve our families in this. Do you?"

I imagine Abay's reaction, how he would struggle at the idea of marriage as a tool, a means to an end. "Are you kidding?" I say, shaking my head emphatically. "No, definitely not."

"This is between us," she says. "Me, you, couple of random witnesses on the day of. That's it. And, you know, the government."

"But we will need someone to help with documents from back home though . . ." I say, knowing from her smile as I say it that the person who comes to both our minds, our only option really, is she who has never liked me being here: Eske.

"Good luck with that, future hozband." She cracks up, throwing me a wink, and lets go of my hands.

Husband.

15

MIZ

*W*hen I drop in on Mom after work on Tuesday, she is on a call in her bedroom, so I go to the kitchen to scrounge retirement party leftovers from the freezer. I'm running hot water over a container when I overhear something that makes me freeze.

Our daughter.

Forehead wrinkling, ears twitching, I shut off the faucet. Only two people in my life have any business using *our daughter* in a conversation, and that's my mother and father.

Which means . . . my parents are on the phone? With each other?

I race to Mom's bedroom and stand at the foot of her bed, staring at her curled up like a teenager talking to her boo. My parents. On the phone. With each other. My parents who, as far as I know (and I *know*), had not spoken a word to each other from when I was two until I was fourteen. Even then, as I learned later, Mom had waited until I was already in the air to give Dad a heads-up that his daughter was on the way for an extended corrective stay. That was the first conversation my parents had had in twelve years. And after that, they communicated only through me to arrange my subsequent visits.

So how come they are parleying on the phone right now, as if—

Mom holds the phone out to me. "Talk to your father," she says nonchalantly.

Those words yank me back twenty-two years to the weeks of screaming matches between Mom and me. Mom demanding that I stop seeing "that boy." Me reverse-demanding a logical reason why. Mom finally yelling at me that I'd left her no choice but to send me to my father.

Fast-forward to now. I feel caught out again. Have they found out about Kal? But nothing's happened; we just got a marriage licence and an appointment for the ceremony this morning. I swallow hard. Of course they don't know anything. I reluctantly take the phone from Mom.

My chit-chat with Dad is the usual, an almost scripted routine that can sometimes be maddening. But considering my mind is working double time, squealing that my parents were just talking to each other, I couldn't be more relieved to cover how I'm doing, how he's doing, the weather, and how I'm overdue for a visit.

"Oh!" I say, remembering something new. "I am thinking of coming around Christmas, I mean, *Gena*," I say, switching to the Amharic word before he reminds me to. "With—" I almost say *with Kal* but catch myself just in time because Mom is right there. Kal and I have agreed to coordinate our travel so that I'll go back home with him for the party. It will look good for our case. "Will that be okay?"

"Yes, of course!" Dad's excitement is contagious. "Miz, I'm so happy you're coming!"

"Me too, Dad," I say. "Listen, I'll let you know when everything is booked." I eye my mom on the bed. I'm itching to give the phone back to her—I feel newly invested in their relationship, and I so badly want to keep them talking.

Then Mom scoots off the bed. *Oh no.* I know another chance like this may never come. I put the phone on speaker. "You're on speaker now. Maybe Mom will come with me this time. She's the most overdue of anyone. Right, Mom?" I beam at her, ignoring the look she's giving me. "It's about time! It's a good time, right, Dad? Everyone is saying how the situation there has been great lately, and she really should visit now when everyone else is going back home!"

Without saying anything, Mom heads to the kitchen, and I quickly follow her. When she sees that I've already started running water over the frozen leftovers, she turns the tap on and continues. "Dad, did she tell you she's taken early retirement? Does that exist in Ethiopia?"

"That is why I called," Dad says. "To congratulate her on a long-deserved rest. Though in my personal opinion, Genet," he says, "you are too vibrant with youth to enter the seniors' category!"

Uh, is he . . . flirting? "Here, Mom, take the phone," I almost shout.

But Mom, calmly breaking apart the semi-thawed food in the container with a fork, answers before I can pass the phone back to her. "Better you help me search for where my youth is gone."

"*Lijinetachininma abren new yatefanew,*" Dad says.

Speak English, people! Literally. I hold the phone out to her. "Do you want the phone, Mom?"

"Thank you for calling, Gashaw," she says, putting the container in the microwave instead.

I guess that's a no then.

"Wishing you all the best for your next chapter," Dad says politely.

Boring. I take the phone off speaker and wander off to say bye to Dad, but he goes into a time-slowing exposition on the subject of the labour laws of Ethiopia. Maybe it's to make up for lost time or because of the certain distance between us that will never close, but anytime I show the tiniest interest in something, Dad does an instant deep dive, and tonight I've walked right into this one. But if I'm being honest, this is something about Dad I've learned to just let be, even grown to love about him.

When I was fourteen, I landed in Addis full of attitude and battle-scarred from weeks of emotional combat with Mom, ready to beat Dad to the punch by showing up mad at him. Thirteen hours in flight was plenty of time to dig up questions about his absence and his and Mom's estrangement, many of them questions I'd given up asking Mom by the time I was six. But all that pent-up ammo fell away the moment we met. I loved him instantly. Maybe because he wasn't mad about the boyfriend situation. He barely acknowledged it, almost as though I really was there just for a reunion. He only said that knowing someone for two semesters, which had been my core argument, did not mean much. That was it. Boy topic closed ever since. My parents' origin story though—he wouldn't shut up about it (not that I wanted him to). He even took me on a tour of the spots where he and Mom used to have their secret rendezvous, long before he sent elders to her family for her hand. Between the two of them, I pieced together my guiding principles on relationships: keep your dating life to yourself, and never get married because that's when things go off the rails.

After we say goodbye, I return to the kitchen and cut open the fresh packet of injera I've brought, trying to wrangle my day-dreaming thoughts. One phone call between my parents and a whole movie of them getting back together has flared up like a dormant virus. But can you blame me? These are my parents, hello. They're the poster couple for being married only on paper and for keeping their actual relationship comatose for decades. And apparently, they're both perfectly content to let that be.

But still, it would be nice to go home with Mom, for once, especially for Gena. "So, Mom, what do you say? You and me to the motherland?" I put the injera on a plate and look at her expectantly.

Mom doesn't take her eyes off the microwave timer. "We'll see," she says wearily, as if I've asked her a thousand times.

16

KAL

*M*iz has delegated me buyer of the wedding bands, saying I can pick anything. And I believe her, not least from all her complaining every time she was dragged along on a ring-shopping expedition as a bridesmaid. She once told me that they all look the same to her. In fact, the only wedding ring she has ever shown any interest in was her mother's. On her second summer stay in Addis in 2001, we were enjoying a backyard bonfire, the dome of stars that Miz calls her "Ethiopia friends" twinkling above us. We watched eagerly as the cook, Zebiba, stoked the flames under a barbecue pan filled with marinated strips of lamb.

"Check it," Miz said out of the blue, handing me her phone opened to a photo of a gold ring sitting on a bathroom countertop, worryingly close to the edge. "My mom's wedding ring. I found it rolling around in the back of her bathroom drawer. I was looking for a safety pin. It's identical to Dad's."

Following her lead, I kept my reaction casual too. "I bet it's a Teklu Desta. In their day, that's where everyone had their jewellery made." She swiped to the next photo, a zoomed-in shot of the engravings along the inside of the band. I leaned in to get a closer look. "Their initials?"

"Yep."

"I love the plus signs between the letters."

"Those are crosses, heathen."

"Or plus signs representing their union. Becoming one."

"It can't be plus signs. Do you see any equal sign? Any result?"

"The equal is implied. The love resulting. Infinity symbolized by the circularity of the ring." I smile at her.

Miz pretended to faint and then snatched her phone away. I guess I failed at casual. "Oh my god, so sentimental. Poor Muna doesn't know what she's in for," she said, jerking her head at the windows of the living room where everyone else, including Muna, was watching *Love & Basketball*.

On the contrary, I was the one who didn't know what I was in for, I think, deep into the third hour of shopping for wedding rings. The task shouldn't have taken me more than half an hour. There's a jewellery shop at the main intersection by my house in Little Portugal, one of those old European ones that hasn't updated their inventory since the seventies. I could've gone there and chosen the most inexpensive piece. But for some reason, I rode right past it and found myself downtown, at the Eaton Centre.

The rings are props, of course, but it felt wrong to not put any thought into it. I got picky, nixing every big brand store in the cavernous mall, opting instead to head west along the edgier Queen Street where unique independent businesses still held sway. I popped into every jewellery store, asking to see every ring, ignoring the salespeople's questioning looks. *Why is this man shopping for wedding rings by himself?* A prospective groom should be with his best man or the maid-of-honour. I wish I could consult Silvio or Aimé, but Miz wants to keep our plan between us.

From one of the stores on Queen, I text Miz photos of truly atrocious rings. Miz must be between clients, because she replies right away.

Miz: Looks great.

I smile. *Okay, let's play.* I send her a picture of a ring with a thick pink band and a heart-shaped mood stone sticking straight out of its centre, like a golf ball on a pin, from Ardene.

Miz: I'm not worthy.

She attaches a GIF of a swooning princess.

I laugh, but I know I'm the one who is not worthy—of Miz's generosity, that is. If I can't pay her, then I have to at least thank her adequately with some kind of gift, something I've been losing sleep trying to think of since that life-changing coffee date at SanRemo. Saying the words *thank you* is not enough. And she doesn't want to hear one word about payment either. But I need to give her something.

An engagement ring seems the obvious answer, especially given my current undertaking, but I know she wouldn't receive it well, and I guess, given our circumstances, it would be a weird choice. We're not entering into a real marriage, fine, but still, I would do well to heed the maxim "Happy wife, happy life."

Another hour later, my feet sore, my mind drained from decision fatigue, already having buyer's remorse about the plain pair of wedding bands I've purchased back at the mall, I sink into one of the corridor sofas and call Eske. She'll find out about our plan sooner or later, so there's no point in not telling her now. Besides, I'm not getting anywhere trying to find a thank-you gift for Miz on my own.

"Kiki? Are you okay?" she says. I can hear the noise of traffic in the background—cars honking, drivers yelling, traffic whistles shrieking.

"What? Yes, I'm fine," I say. "Why?"

"Because you never call me," she says. "I'm always the one who calls you."

"Oh." I'm surprised. Is that true? Do I really never call her? "Listen, I need your help with something."

"Mm-hmm," she says, then yells at some offending driver. "Don't you see me here?!"

"I'm shopping for a gift."

She taps her horn three times in quick succession. "For a woman?"

I widen my eyes. It's as if she has a radar. "No, not for a woman. Just Miz."

"Why?"

I decide to have a little fun with this. "She's getting married."

"Why are you wasting my time?" she snaps.

Right—patience was never her strength. Taking a deep breath, I tell her about my company backing out of the sponsorship. As I anticipated, she doesn't break down into tears. Her reaction is the same as when I told her about being promised the sponsorship in the first place, the same as when I told her about each of my permits getting extended over the years: unreadable silence.

After a few moments, she surprises me by breaking the pattern. "Are you . . . okay?" she asks, as gently as I've ever heard her.

"I wasn't. But I am now." I pause and say a little prayer before continuing. "Miz will be my sponsor."

I give her a moment for that to sink in, but the silence just expands. "Hello?" I check the display. The connection is still active. Then I hear the automatic window closing, the sounds of traffic from outside gradually fading, leaving us in a deep silence. When she speaks again, her voice is soft and low, reminding me of our mother's when she was serenely leading us toward our own indictment for some misdemeanour or other.

"After all you experienced, this is how you decide to get married, Kalkidan?"

"I am not *getting married*. Come on, you know how this works." I stand up and rub my face. "I need your support on this, Eske. I will need your help getting some required documentation for the application."

"Incredible! The lengths you will go to permanently abandon your country and your family," she says sarcastically.

Now I feel myself getting heated. "Listen, Eske, it's either I do this or I miss the party." I hear her sharp intake of breath, but I press on. "Leaving Canada with only a month left on my work permit is as good as locking the door behind me and throwing away the key. And I refuse to do that after how much I have invested here. This is happening, Eskedar," I say with finality. "This is not some random—"

"If it was a random woman," Eske says, "I would swim there and drag you home by your hair."

No idle threat, I know, so I decide there's no need to regale Eske with stories of the "random women" that were in the running. Maybe in the future, when this is all history.

"I don't have hair at the moment. I shaved it for the part."

It's quiet again. She sighs. "I would personally deliver the pre-nup papers." She huffs. "But I guess if Miz was after what's yours, she could have had you by now. You've been around each other long enough." She pauses. "Still, I'll have to see what Aba says."

"Not a word of this to anyone, Eske," I say firmly. "Keep it private. You are our only trusted person." I know this will appeal to Eske's need to be ahead of the curve, just as she is always scouting for the next food trend to incorporate into our menu of products. If it weren't for her, we would still be selling the original dozen varieties of bread and cookies instead of the hundred plus we have now. "Look, it's just a couple of years. This can't work without you," I say, blending flattery with truth.

"You asked her, or she offered?"

"I can't say she offered. And I can't say I asked her, either." I started the conversation, but Miz created the conditions for the conversation. "We met halfway," I say. Then, remembering my culturally touchy audience, I add a proverb of our own. "Like saints whose paths cross without their planning."

"Ha, you two, saints?" she says, with a snarky cackle.

"But," I continue, glad that at least she's being jocular, "I feel she deserves a proper thank-you gift."

Eske sucks her teeth in annoyance. "What more *thank you* does she need when you are surrendering your heart and your inheritance with both hands!"

"In the name of God, Eske, don't be dramatic."

"Hmph! You would know, I guess." I can feel her scowl through the phone. "Anyway, her fee should be enough."

"There's no fee."

"She's doing this for nothing?"

"She's doing it for me," I say.

A beat, then Eske lets out a long two-note whistle. "God help you two."

I'm not sure how to interpret the whistle, but I do know now, without doubt, that Eske is invested in this, and in us. She's not one to get casually religious.

"Thank you, from both of us," I say, immediately proud of today's accomplishments. Rings: done. Key collaborator: done. Only the one loose end remains. "So? A gift? Think about what would be good for her. But don't take forever."

"Yes, sir," Eske says, muffling a laugh.

I decide to ignore her. "Until next time then, Sister-of—"

Click. She hangs up before I can finish speaking.

The perfect idea for Miz's gift comes to me days later—Eske had proved incapable of suggesting anything that wasn't cheesily engraved, embossed, or embroidered—when I am out for a long, exhausting bike ride with Silvio. We're both slogging up Redway Road hollering our wildest post-ride recovery fantasies at each other: "A two-hour soak in a mountain hot spring *while* getting a massage!" "A fifteen-hour nap in a Himalayan salt sauna *with* an IV drip of cold beer!" . . . And it hits me. It may not be the biggest thank-you to put all thank-yous to shame, but it is no small thing either. I tell Silvio that we'll need to detour on the way back. I'll need him to act as a second opinion and product tester.

17

MIZ

Kal: I have a bit of a development.

Me: Uh oh. What?

Kal: Silvio knows.

Me: WHAT? How?

Kal: He found the rings.

Me: So??????? Couldn't you have said they're props?!

Kal: Sorry. He wants to be our witness tomorrow. He'll take photos for us too.

Me: Oh Christos.

Kal: Might as well ask Aimé to be yours . . .

Me: Fudge

He sends me a link to an Aster song.

Me: Dude, now is not the time to work on your playlist.

Kal: It's for you, an apology song.

Oh. Right. I missed the title: "Yikirta." *Sorry.*

Kal: Having people we know in the photos is a good thing. You'll ask her?

Me: Not leaving me a choice, are ya?

Kal: Of course you have a choice. But we have to think of what's good for the case. We have to do everything possible. We owe it to ourselves. And our best friends being there is natural.

Me: Okay, easing up on the WE . . .

Kal: Sowee.

Despite my panic, I burst out laughing. How am I supposed to break all of this down for Aimé now when I'm still digesting the idea myself? I would have liked, like, a month or so to get used to the idea of signing for Kal, but our time being tight, I sucked it up and accepted an early date of October 1st.

But now it's September 30th, and I still haven't told Aimé, who slept over because we are going on her first morning run. She's even taken the day off work tomorrow, expecting to be out of commission after the long run. While I get ready in the bathroom, I give myself a pep talk in the mirror. "Tomorrow, you are not getting *really* married. You're just signing a piece of paper. And saying some words. Easy peasy."

"Who're you talking to?" Aimé says groggily, surprising me by popping her head in. As she lifts a coffee mug to her lips, I spy powdered sugar on her upper lip. She snuck a stale doughnut from the box of leftovers I brought back from the clinic yesterday. A terrible idea, eating one of those before a run, but I guess we can be queasy together, just for very different reasons.

"It's a little psyching up I do before I head out in the mornings," I lie.

"Oh cool," she says, genuinely believing me. I almost feel guilty.

Outside, the dawn air is perfection for a run—cool, foggy, with a drizzle as light as a baby's breath. Is rain the day before your wedding good luck too? Nature doesn't care what's fake or what's real, right? I do my ritual of doing a squat and touching the ground as Aimé watches.

I set a brisk walking pace up University Avenue so that we will be warm by the time we get to the Queen's Park loop. The avenue is so open this early in the morning I'm almost tempted to run in the middle of the road, as if it is a race day. We speed up to a jog as we enter the loop. At Aimé's draggy half-asleep pace, one trip around, just under a kilometre, takes forever. I feel like I'm dying. If there is one morning when I need to pump it out, it's today. A little into the second and final lap for today, Aimé perks up.

"You know what?" she says. "I am gonna do a marathon."

"Said sugar and caffeine," I say with a smirk.

"No, really. What's the sense in doing something half-assed like a ten k?"

"It's not half-assed," I admonish. "Pace yourself, or you'll burn out. You're high right now."

Aimé's old muscle memory for explosive speed reactivates with each stride. "I quote, the body is capable of much more than we realize!"

Oh lord, words I used to talk her into doing a long-distance race come back to haunt me. "Not right out of the gate! I also said, *With the right gradual training*. You're going too fast."

She lifts her chin haughtily. "I don't appreciate a defeatist attitude from my coach."

She has that look on her face that means business, and then she shoots off like bullet. I, on the other hand, stop. It's kind of beautiful to witness this old Aimé, but this actually is *old* Aimé, so the consequence is going to be epic and not in a good way.

Sure enough, within moments, she starts to slow. She wilts, bends double with her hands on her knees, crouches to a squat, then sinks to the ground under a tree. Once she has completed crashing, I swallow my *I told you so* and stroll over.

"I'm so old," Aimé wails at me.

I kneel in front of her. "Easy there. Longer on the exhale."

"I should have consecrated the ground like you."

"There's no superstition to it," I say with a smile. "You just don't sprint until you see the finish line, love. And in long distance, that comes way later than in four hundred metres."

"I think my uterus is cramping. Has that ever happened to you?"

"Lie down, and put your feet up against the trunk." I guide her into the position. "Close your eyes. Breathe. This too shall pass." I copy her, with a view of the tree canopy and our feet, and wait until her ragged wounded-animal heaves even out into steady breaths.

"So," I begin, preparing to confess. I know I don't have to—I could still choose to go with a random witness. After all, it was Kal who couldn't hide an itty-bitty jewellery case properly and got himself caught. But it will be worse for me if I sign for him, *then* tell Aimé. She is bound to find out anyway.

"Hmm?" Aimé says, turning her head to look at me.

I take a deep breath. "I found a person for Kal."

She puckers her mouth and frowns, looking back up at the sky, confused. "I thought we let that go after the gong show at SanRemo." The version of that day that Aimé knew ended with Nardos storming out of the bakery and Kal and I finishing the pastries and then going our merry ways. I was perfectly happy to keep things between Kal and me as promised, but now I don't have a choice.

"The person is me," I announce. I bite my lip, waiting for her response.

She twists her head, slowly, and stares at me. I begin counting the clouds in the sky. *Don't talk me out of it don't talk me out of it don't talk me out of it.* An ambulance rushes by, sirens blaring, matching the alarm bells going off in her head, I'm sure.

"Mizan Begashaw," she says. I know she's waiting for me to look at her, tell her I'm joking. I turn to face her, the bits of wood and dried-out soil scratching my scalp.

One look at my face tells her I'm not joking. "You?!" she gasps. "*You?* Who doesn't do marriage? You're the worst person on earth to do this, and *you're* signing for him?"

"Why you gotta make me sound like I'm diseased?" I come up to my elbows to make my case. "As his best friend who has no interest in actually getting married myself, I'm, in fact, the best person to sign for him twice over. And we're not *doing* doing it. We're just signing on it."

She rolls over and sits up carefully. "Never thought I'd live to see the day Ms. I-Don't-Get-Married gets married."

I sit up fully too and begin stretching my leg. "Ears on, Miss Audio Specialist! Ain't nobody getting *married* married. No *tidar*. No *gabicha*." These are ten-dollar words that one picks up over the course of being in six weddings.

"*No hablo bien español, mamacita,*" Aimé says, bouncing up, her aches and pains suddenly forgotten.

"It means *matrimony* and . . . also *matrimony*," I say, as we walk back toward home. The traffic up and down the four-lane avenue is slightly thicker than when we left this morning, people trickling into downtown from all 'burbs in all directions. "Don't ask me why we have two different Amharic words for the same damn concept."

"One must be for when friends get married."

I grin at her. "Touché. But my point is that there is no hubby-wifey concept here. This is strictly paper."

Aimé stops walking and stares at me. "What is happening with you these days?"

"Why does anything need to be 'happening' with me?" I say, exasperated. "What has our civilization come to that people are so skeptical of altruism? People give organs to strangers, and that is permanent. I'm not offering Kal a kidney, or a heart. You give a heart, you die. Permanently." I cross my arms and raise an eyebrow at her. "Now if you're jelly that I'm getting married before you, then I can't help you."

"Didn't you just say you're not getting married?"

"I know you know what I mean." I clasp my hands and walk toward her. "Speaking of which," I begin. "Please be my witness?"

Aimé laughs loudly. "Who the hell else is gonna do it?"

"Yes! Thank you thank you thank you." I grab her and plant a big kiss on the side of her head, then flop on her heavily, making her practically carry me as we walk.

"All right, calm down. But you know what . . . ? Maybe this is a good thing for you."

I stop. "Eh?"

"Now you get a taste of what all the fuss is about, a walk-through, a dry run."

"You've been talking to Kal way too much."

Aimé stops us and looks at me, real concern in her eyes. "Are you sure you've got this?"

"Absolutely. I'm so happy I can do this for Kal. Why should he have to lose his future because of racist board bitches? He deserves to—"

"I'm talking about you," she interrupts. "Can you handle it?"

This reminds me of when she cornered me with a similar question the day we went scouting for wives for Kal. I brush her off now as I did then. "Girl, please. A little bit married for a little bit of time? *Pfft*, bring it! I am Mizan Begashaw, the child of parents who've been a little bit married their whole adult lives."

"All right," she says, sounding more like she wants to be convinced than she actually is convinced. We continue our walk in a peaceful silence.

"Oh, by the way," I say as we near home, "the ceremony is at eleven tomorrow."

She sighs. "Of course it is. You're lucky I took tomorrow off. Anything else you have to spring on me? You two planning to adopt an orphan too?"

I rub my fingers along my jawline, as if she's presented an intriguing notion. "Hmm, let's put a pin in that. No, just gotta figure out my dress. But I have something that could work."

I have an actual wedding dress, in fact—Sosina's.

18

KAL

The bells in the Old City Hall clock tower mark quarter past ten. Silvio and I await Miz and Aimé by the enormous Toronto sign in Nathan Phillips Square, which is mostly deserted this morning. I look up at the iconic curved towers. Somewhere in there is where, in about an hour, Miz's and my fates will be intertwined for the foreseeable future. For better, not worse, I hope.

A flash from Silvio's camera brings me back to my immediate surroundings. "Save your film for the real star of the day, man," I say. He has already taken many unnecessary pictures of me from every conceivable angle.

"Just checking the lighting," Silvio says.

"What lighting?" I hope the sun will come out eventually. I don't feel good about getting "married" on such a grey and damp day.

"You have the rings?" he asks. Though it's clear that I do by the little bulge in the breast pocket of my jacket. I give the box to him. Contrary to what I've told Miz, the rings are not how Silvio found out about our arrangement. He found out when I took him along to help me choose her gift, but I couldn't tell her that without ruining the surprise of the gift.

At the far end of the square, a bright spot of white catches my eye: a wedding dress. Then I realize the woman in white, the bride, moving fast as if she has a pair of sneakers on under that dress instead of formal shoes, is Miz.

I stare in shock.

Silvio follows my gaze. "Is that . . . ?"

I nod, unable to form words.

"Where's Aimé? She didn't tell her?" Silvio says, craning his neck. "Oh, I see her."

Aimé, behind Miz, is doing her best to keep up while holding the train of Miz's dress aloft. We should go meet them, but both Silvio and I are glued to our spots. Miz looks incredible in the shoulderless dress, like an angel floating toward us, veil billowing out like wings. It doesn't matter that the sun is nowhere to be seen today; Miz lights everything up.

In comparison, the rest of us—me in a plain black suit and tie, Silvio in one of his rockabilly ensembles, and Aimé in one of Miz's West African print dresses—almost look too casual.

Belatedly, as Miz is graciously accepting complimentary words from a passerby, Silvio nudges me toward them. I approach them tentatively, even though Miz is smiling encouragingly at me, as if to say *Come on, one foot in front of the other. You can do this.* When I'm close enough, I stop to take her in from head to toe. I have seen her in formal dress before, including as a bridesmaid, but this is . . . different.

"I didn't know you were bringing flowers," she says, gesturing to the forgotten bouquet of roses in my grasp. Numbly, I hand them over.

"Don't freak out. It's just a white dress," Aimé says wryly, reading my expression.

"I don't think he's ever seen one before," Silvio jokes, snapping photos that will not make it into our application package because I know I look like a slack-jawed mannequin.

Miz waves her hand in front of my face. "Hello? Anybody home?"

I blink and come to. "You look . . ." Stunning. Perfect. Like a divine goddess sent from the heavens above.

"Did I overdo it?" She turns to Aimé. "See, I should've just worn the other one."

Other one? My brain short-circuits even more.

"Can you believe she wanted me to slap on one of her old bridesmaid dresses?" Aimé says, making up for my dazedness. "Hey, Silvio, long time."

She starts the hugs all around. When I lean in to embrace Miz, touching her confirms her realness and helps me find my voice. "You look the part. You look great," I finally say, my hand lingering on her hip.

"That's the idea." She strikes a runway pose.

"You are *wearing* the hell out of that dress," Silvio says.

"Thank you." She beams. "Go big, or go home! Y'all are lucky I didn't wear the hoop slip under it, or it would've been like, *Take my haaand!*" She curves her upper body away from us, reaching out dramatically as if she's far away.

"Is it a rental?" I ask Miz.

She hesitates for a nanosecond. A look passes between her and Aimé, who nods.

"Yeah," Miz says.

I almost say that I will reimburse her but catch myself in time. As per Miz's orders, I am not allowed to bring up money. Eske's mysterious low whistle when I told her Miz was doing this for free resounds in my head. I banish it.

"All right!" Silvio says, adjusting his leather camera holster looped around his shoulders. "Before we get you two beautiful humans matrimonied, the 'before' pictures!"

Miz bares her teeth. "Here we go. Life is wild, huh?" she says, as we arrange ourselves for the first shot, Silvio backing up to get the Toronto sign and City Hall in the background. "Who knew, when we met, we'd be doing this one day?" She slips her thumb into her neckline to hitch up her cleavage, a subconscious gesture I've seen her do a thousand times, but this time it sends a tingle down my spine.

"Not this gal," Aimé says pointedly but with good humour. "I didn't wake up yesterday morning planning to be eyewitness to a fraud today."

The kernel of truth in her teasing chills my blood, reminding me how serious this could get. "Loosen up, man," Silvio yells. "You're stiff as a board. This is not good. Smile!"

Miz pinches my cheek gently. "You should see yourself. How am I more relaxed than you?"

"Not so nervous, K-Money," Aimé says through her smile.

"Me? What do I have to be nervous about?" In an attempt at normalcy, I slip one of the dangling straps of Miz's dress up onto her shoulder.

"That's supposed to be like that," she says, shimmying to get it back down.

"Oh, pardon me," I say softly, my hand brushing along her collarbone and down her arm as I slide the strap back off for her.

"Oi, get a room, you two," Aimé says.

"Are you cold?" I say, ignoring that.

"No, Grandma," Miz says, laughing and jostling me.

Miz continues to be her usual jokey self as we take more photos around Osgoode Hall Gardens and the University Avenue fountain, her arm linked with mine, getting a kick out of strangers' congratulations. This helps to relax me somewhat. Other than the fact that Aimé's been sussing me out like an assassin from the corners of her eyes, and I can't quite feel my face, this could be just another day, just another hangout.

Around 11 a.m., we're ushered into the wedding chambers after we've all signed the Marriage Licence and Record of Solemnization. I hand the rings and my phone over to Silvio, who makes his way to the front row with Aimé. Miz steps up beside me at the entrance, linking her arm with mine to await our cue.

"What?" Miz says with a sidelong glance, catching me beaming at her. I bring her hand to my heart and feel a tremble run through her. She smiles. "Only because . . ."

"It's . . ." She finishes our catchphrase by firmly pressing her index finger into my chest. I feel as if I've just been tattooed. I inhale deeply. She follows my lead and does the same. We exhale together slowly. My heart rate steadies. The music starts.

Miz lights up. "No, you didn't!"

I grin. "I did."

She and I are not a real couple, but the lyrics of Gildo's "Lageba New," as far as I'm concerned, can be for us too. We groove our way down the aisle as if we're on *Soul Train*. Silvio's camera goes into overdrive. I would have loved, and Miz as well I'm sure, to dance to the whole song, but alas, we have to stop and get serious in front of the black-robed officiant, who has remained solemn and still, like a statue.

"Welcome!" she booms. She confirms that Miz and I are both free and willing to be married, then asks us to join our right hands. My stomach is jelly, my sweat flowing like a river. Meanwhile, Miz is vibrating, her eyes shimmering not from tears of joy but from what I suspect to be the intense effort of holding back a giggling fit. I know her well enough to know that when she's nervous, she giggles.

It's all a blur as we exchange stilted, scripted vows and our rings, which Silvio fumbles and has to crawl around to retrieve. I send a quick prayer up, hoping it isn't a sign of bad things to come. Before I know it, the officiant is booming all the way to the back of the empty chairs, "I now pronounce you legally wed! You may now—"

Suddenly, Miz's lips are on mine, and just as quickly, they are gone, leaving me with a phantom sense of something I would be certain I imagined but for Miz's *yeah I did it* look and Aimé's gob-smacked stare and Silvio's camera shutter going off like a flock of doves taking to the air at once.

Miz kissed me.

And I missed it.

I roll my lips inward, as if to capture whatever trace of her lips might still be there. I've never wanted a do-over, a second chance, so badly. But history never warns you that it is about to happen. You can only hope to keep up or catch up.

Next thing I know, we are being herded over to a table to sign the Marriage Register, receive the completed Record of Solemnization from the officiant, and take "after" photos. Then, we're done. Within half an hour of our arrival, we are all back outside, Aimé tucking the Record of Solemnization into her purse, Silvio still playing paparazzo.

Miz is nimbly hopping over puddles, using her flowers as an umbrella against the drizzle, my jacket draped over her head. I don't remember riding down the elevator, or exiting the building or giving Miz my jacket. Miz, my now-legal wife. I watch her with a smile. But she's also still the same old Miz. Just as I'm the same old Kal . . . but also not. How is that possible?

"You good with that?" She's looking at me expectantly.

I step in a puddle. "Pardon?"

"Pasta for lunch."

"Wh—yes . . . pasta. For lunch," I stammer.

19

MIZ

"Miz, what're you doing?" Aimé stares at my hands on the ride to the restaurant.

I stop mid-motion while sliding my wedding ring off my finger. "What? We're done." I turn to Kal for backup. "Right?"

But he and Silvio are watching me strangely too, as if I've started undressing in front of all of them. Speaking of which, I also need to get this dress off, like, yesterday.

Silvio takes over. "We still need pictures."

"At the restaurant," Kal says gently.

Right. Aimé frowns at me. *What's going on?*

What's going on is I was fine until the ceremony. Nervous, but not overly so. But since we were pronounced husband and wife, I've been itchy, and I blame this dress. I should have known better than to wear a wedding dress to a wedding that is not an actual *wedding* wedding. Outwardly, of course, I am, or I think I am, completely fine. After all, this is easy peasy, right?

"Oh," I say. I slide the ring back down my finger and catch Kal's eye. He gives me a sheepish smile and averts his attention out the window, looking at passengers on a streetcar travelling alongside us. I shouldn't have jumped his mouth as if there was a rule that said I had to kiss the groom. Poor Kal looked dumbstruck. I didn't think he would take a peck on the lips so seriously. Actors are in each other's business all the time! And we were acting, right?

As soon as we've taken more photos at our restaurant table with our family-style servings of appetizers and entrees and bottles of wine, I haul Aimé to the bathroom to help me out of the dress so I can get into my own clothes, which we've brought along in a shopping bag.

"This is supposed to be your new husband's job," she complains in the bathroom, tugging at the lacing across the back. I brace my hands against the sink counter. I can't wait to slip into my sweater dress and start eating.

"Hurry up, I'm hungry."

"You still got room after you ate up half Kal's face earlier?" Aimé asks innocently.

"That's an exaggeration!" I say. "I had to do it for our application."

She gets to the end of the lacing, and I release like a package freed from its shrink wrap and take in a heaving breath. "So, how do you feel, overall?"

I shrug, letting the dress fall to the floor while Aimé tries to catch it. She shakes it off before starting to fold it while I slide into my sweater dress. I sigh in contentment before answering. "Completely normal. Nothing's changed. Everything's exactly the same. Well . . . okay, that's a lie. Something does feel different. But I know it's not actually different. It's only because I'm on high alert, which means what I think feels different is really just normal, y'know?"

Aimé stops folding the wedding gown, looking alarmed. "Did you take something?"

"Just a huge fucking risk, that's all. No biggie."

"You can say that again." She puts the wedding dress into the bag, which we then tie shut. "Don't worry—you're in good hands," she says, patting me on the back on our way out.

That, I've never doubted.

Over lunch, I ramp up my normal-girl act, but Kal is still playing shy guy, refusing to look at me, talking mostly to, or through, Aimé and Silvio.

"I'd like to make a toast," Aimé says, during a lull in our conversation. Immediately, Silvio starts filming.

"Or not," I say, covering Silvio's camera with my palm.

"K-Money," Aimé says, totally ignoring me. "Thanks for finally making this girl take a break from dating, which I've been trying to get her to do for ages now."

Kal laughs and snaps his fingers. "Ah! You've uncovered my master plan."

"Oh really?" I say. "Newsflash, friends, signing papers doesn't mean I can't date still."

Aimé gasps and clutches her chest, scandalized. Silvio, still filming, hams horror. "But what if they're watching?" he says. "Have investigators on you?"

That does send a little stab of worry through me. It's not a far-fetched notion. Half my mom's job was tracking down false claims. Aimé nods along sombrely. Kal hums thoughtfully, stroking his chin. He turns to me for my comeback to that, making full eye contact with me for the first time since the kiss. *Oh thank God, we're back!*

"Puh-lease," I say, waving them off. "You don't have to worry about this guy dating though." I jab my thumb sideways at Kal. "My guy, Mr. Hard-to-Get, is not about to jump into the dating pool now that he's 'married,' right?" I say, directing my air quotes at him. History assures me that I'm right, but I feel a teensy pinch of *what if he does?*

He bobs his head side to side. "Mmm, depends. Marriage is stressful, I've heard. Don't you know that Chris Rock bit?" He acts it out for us, doing a decent impression of the comedian using Mandela's divorce as proof, which cracks us all up. "Being . . . *attached* might turn out to be just the thing that drives me to date, at last," he says just as our desserts are being delivered, causing an involuntary little jump of the server's eyebrows.

"Ah, shite, now you've uncovered *my* master plan," I say. "God knows I've tried everything else to get you back in action."

We start in on our desserts, falling quiet for a few bites except for moans and murmurs of delectable bliss. "Jokes aside though," Kal says, semi-privately to me. "I would never want to stand in the way of you meeting the right person."

"The coast is clear, Kal," I say, taking a sip of wine. "Rest assured."

"The one worthy of you is out there, Miz."

"Aw, that's one of the nicest things I've heard." I can barely conceal my eye roll.

"You don't have to believe it. I believe it enough for the both of us."

I stuff my mouth with icing. "Funk ew."

"Ouch!" he says, wounded as if I've just cursed him out.

I swallow. "I said *thank you*, you goof!"

He offers me a forkful of his tiramisu. I move in to take the bite, but our angles are slightly off, and half of it smears across my cheek. We fall into a fit of giggles as Kal scrambles for his napkin.

He's dabbing at the corners of my lips when we hear a loud "Ahem." Oops—it's the other half of our wedding party, watching us with dancing eyes.

"Y'all okay?" I say.

"But of course," Silvio says.

"Everything's great," says Aimé.

On my way home, I drop the wedding dress off at the dry cleaner. I have no intention of picking it up. I consider pinging Sosina to let her know where she can get it. Maybe now, as we're both married women, she'll finally let me in on why, after shacking up, couples act as though they've taken a vow of silence alongside their vows of love. Or what happens after "Ale Gena," after the bride and groom's grand exit from the ballroom, adorned in their gilt-embroidered velvet capes and crowns. But I've already put my foot in it once, so I think better of it. Best not to push. Besides, Kal and I are not *married* married. Nothing will change because there's nothing *to* change, right?

The next morning, I wake up and realize that something *has* changed: Every day, all week, at random times, I'll experience alarms of *I am freaking married to Kal!* and flashes of that damn kiss. Each time I think about it, I cough and clear my throat, so much so that one day, Omar asks me whether I've caught a cold. *More like cold feet too freaking late!*

Kal is supposed to come over on Friday after I get home from the clinic to get started on the paperwork, and I'm filled with anxiety about being alone with him. So naturally, I start to reach for delay tactics—because I'm obviously a pro. I just have to find a way to flake.

Me: Maybe I should come over to yours later?

He replies way too fast.

Kal: No I want to work at yours.

Alrighty then. So much for that.

Kal: I don't want you to be inconvenienced or have to go out of the way in the slightest.

Oh, please do let me get out of the way. That's the whole point. *But this is Kal, you goof,* I remind myself. *Kal who needs this, whose life's direction is riding on this sponsorship. Chill.*

So, on Friday, as agreed, Kal arrives at my place just as I am putting out snacks next to the printouts of the paperwork and some brand-new stationery on the coffee table.

"Is it too cluttered?" I say, casually leaning against the kitchen island while he slips his shoes off at the door. For ambience, I put the TV on CP24 on mute. "There's more space on the coffee table, but we can switch and work here." I'm blabbering. He walks in and surveys my arrangements. His hands are bare, I notice. I wonder whether he just forgot his wedding band or whether he deliberately kept it in the ring box. Not that I care. I'm not wearing mine either.

"Uh, no, it's fine," he says, texting on his phone as he drops his bag, then himself, onto the sectional. I sit at an angle to him, waiting for him to notice that I've bought all his favourite salty nibbles, including his fancy-ass pistachios. He finally tucks his phone under him, then takes his laptop out and makes room for it among the papers.

"Shouldn't you sit next to me so we can both see? We can fill everything out online, you know?" he says, patting the seat on his other side.

"Oh, I thought we'd practice on paper first," I say, moving to sit by his side.

"I'm okay to do it all online." He shells and pops a pistachio in his mouth. My gaze zeroes in on his lips, as if they might be slightly altered from Monday, but they're the same—moisturized, full, even. He notices my staring and swipes at his face. "Do I have something on my face?"

"Beer?" I shout, springing up. I scurry to the fridge and take out two bottles. Beer feels necessary. "TGIF!" When I sit back down, he has opened the Immigration, Refugees and Citizenship Canada sponsorship webpage.

"Okay, let's get to it." I pick up a stack of ten stapled pages. "Document checklist."

He pulls up a Word document on his laptop. "No need."

On the screen are three headers: *What I Have to Do. What Miz Has to Do. What Miz and I Have to Do Together.* Underneath each header is a detailed bullet list of to-do items.

I nudge his shoulder with mine. "Aw, you're still a nerd!"

"One doesn't go through the Canadian immigration system for eight years without staying organized, Miz," he says, nudging me back.

I hum in agreement. "So, I guess since we're together, we're concentrating on *What Miz and I Have to Do Together.*"

"Yep," he says. It's only a two-item list. Item one, *Proofs of Relationship*, has subitems *History of Contact*, *Cohabitation*, *Photos*. Item two is form IMM5532.

"Number two is also known as the *Relationship Information and Sponsorship Evaluation*," Kal says, switching to a different window. "Of which Part C is all about how we met, who introduced us, who was involved and when in the evolution of our relationship, especially our wedding day, our living situation, et cetera."

He scrolls to the first question. "When was the first time you met in person?" I read aloud then look at him, and he at me. "How far back do you want to go? The *beginning* beginning or when we reconnected here in Toronto?"

"Up to you," he says.

"Me? This is your sponsorship."

"But *you're* the sponsor."

"Someone has to be the decision-maker here." I press my closed fist firmly on his forehead, as if I am stamping him. "There, from now on, you are the designated decision-maker, and I am at your service."

"Either way, we have a good long timeframe. The officer might even ask why it took us so long to get married, at the interview."

I toss back the sip I was about to take from my beer. "Inter-whatnow?"

"Miz, we're a textbook case for an interview. By the time we submit this, we will have been married just a few months, conveniently right before my status expires. We don't even live together."

I wipe away a drop of dribble. I may be imagining it, but he sounds a smidge annoyed about that, as if I am weakening our application by not offering to share my space.

"That's why we're going to bury them in so many photos, texts, emails, all that," I remind him, sounding upbeat. "But hey, listen, if you want to crash here for a few months, you know you're welcome to." I shrug. "On the couch," I rush to add. "You know I wouldn't wish my mattress on my worst enemy."

He gets a strange look on his face, and I instantly worry I shouldn't have said that. But he has slept on my couch before, so what's the big deal? Ugh, I hate how everything feels fucking loaded all of a sudden.

"Just put the *beginning* beginning," I say, trying to move on. "The truth is easier to remember."

Kal types in the year, the city, and an approximate date that looks about right to me.

1. When was the first time you met in person?

Date (YYYY-MM-DD)
1996-04-27

Where?
Addis Ababa, Ethiopia

I read the next part. *Describe the circumstances of your first meeting.* Another huge chunk of our early history that we're supposed to compress down into a text box the width of a french fry.

My first time in Ethiopia, Kal had found me sitting by myself on a stone bench in one of the parkettes in Dad's compound. He was on his way to his friend Bini's place in the compound to cram for a final exam, arms filled with burgers and fries. I, of course, was not in school on account of Mom going bonkers and deporting me back to Dad. Instead, I was in my imitation Mary J. Blige outfit, boo-hooing for my lost real love. So when this cute, lanky boy, with his high-top haircut and shiny blue track suit, waved hello and asked whether I was okay with genuine concern, I latched on. And it didn't hurt that he smelled like burgers and fries.

Kal hovers his fingers over the keyboard, waiting for me. "Just say we met at the restaurant." He types that in, adding a few more details to use all the space provided. "Perfect."

1. When was the first time you met in person?

Date (YYYY-MM-DD)
1996-04-27

Where?
Addis Ababa, Ethiopia

Describe the circumstances of your first meeting.
We met at a restaurant in Addis Ababa in the compound where she was visiting her father and I was visiting a friend.

"Doesn't really do it justice though," he says, pulling a face.

I shrug. "What can we do? If they want to know more, the interviewer will ask us."

"*Officer*, they are called officers."

"Yes, Officer. No, Officer. Nunya bidness, Officer."

Thankfully, the rest of the questions are pretty straightforward. It takes twenty minutes to hammer out the answers (with some unavoidable massaging of the facts): why we don't live together and whether either of us lives with other people; the dates of my last five visits to him in Addis; who among our close friends and family know of our relationship; whether we had a wedding ceremony and who was there and not and why not.

In that time, Kal's phone vibrates with texts no fewer than four times, all of which he jumps to check. Before we got married, I would have point-blank asked him who he was being so shifty about. But now . . . I'm scared it will bring on the Weirdness. So I heed my own words and mind my bidness.

Kal frowns at the next question on the form, scratching his chin as if it is a tricky one. "Are either of you pregnant?" He flicks his eyes questioningly at my belly.

"Ha ha." I throw pistachio shells at him. I tick the *No* box on the form. "We should get our story straight though. As in, do we "want" them?"

"You know I do," he says.

"Me too. So in theory, if we get asked, it's a *Yes*. We want two?"

"Works for me."

"Great."

His phone rings. He snatches it and stands, giving me the *just a sec* finger. He paces over to the kitchen as he talks. My ears tag along while I pretend to read my to-do list on the laptop. But I can't piece anything together from his *yeahs* and *mm-hmms* and *uh-huhs*. He hangs up and sends off a rapid-fire text.

"Excuse me. I have to step out for a second."

"Okaaay."

"Sorry, Miz. I just have to handle this outside. I won't be long."

He shuts my apartment door behind him. Then I hear the elevator. Oh wow, *outside* outside? She must be special to have survived the Questionnaire. I have a momentary unpleasant flashback to a month and a half ago when Daniel jetted that night I found the ring. I rest back on the couch, put my feet up on my unused printouts on the coffee table, and pull out my phone. *Well shoot, I got people too.* I text Aimé.

Me: So? Any ideas?

I want to know whether she's come up with any way for me to return that damn ring while retaining my dignity.

Waiting for her response, I wander over to the window and look down at the street below, but then I feel like a creep spying on Kal so I use the bathroom instead. I'm cleaning up a little around the kitchen when Aimé finally responds.

Aimé: Why don't you just go over to his place?

Me: Eh?

Aimé: Go over to his place WHERE HIS GYM BAG LIVES, as if to hang out, then FIND the gym bag, then PUT the ring inside it, where he'll find it after you leave.

Me: Omg. Bold.

Just then, there's a knock at my door.

20

KAL

*T*oday was supposed to have been smooth going. I arranged everything with Everest in advance. He let me book the moving elevator on a Friday evening, when it is not allowed, and he promised to let me know when the delivery truck arrived. Things started to fall apart when, at first, the delivery company could not find Miz's street; then the truck was too tall to enter the underground parking garage. I had to promise them a big tip to circle back to the front of Miz's building and carry the gift through the lobby, also against building regulations. I have a newfound admiration for how Abay managed to surprise Emay on every one of her birthdays.

At last, we're outside Miz's door. I compose myself and knock, putting my hand over the peephole to maintain the surprise.

"Yeah?" she says, from the other side.

"Delivery," one of the guys says.

"I didn't order anything," she says, sounding suspicious. I'm sure she can see that the peephole is covered. The guys shuffle impatiently. They don't have time for this. I knock again. *Now*, of all times, Miz heeds my constant advice about her personal safety?

"Daniel, is that you?" she says, now sounding irritated.

My heart jumps. He's still trying to get in touch with her? Or are they back on again? She *did* warn me she would continue to date; I just didn't think she'd date Daniel again.

Before I can respond, Miz throws the door open while my ringtone blares from my pocket. "Kal, what the—"

She freezes, taking in this strange tableau of three guys—one wide eyed and anxious, two drained and indifferent. Her eyes sweep up to the plastic-wrapped mattress towering over all of us.

"Surprise!" I say, trying to read her face. It's as if time has been suspended while I wait to find out whether this is the smartest or dumbest thing I've ever done.

A throat clears. "Excuse us." The guys shuffle past us into the apartment. "Which way?"

Miz is still staring at the mattress as if it's a giraffe that ambled into her apartment. I point them to her bedroom. "Miz?" I say, taking the doorknob from her and closing the door. "Do you hate it?"

She blinks, then slams into me, hugging me fiercely, as if she wants to squeeze the life out of me. Her breathing is choppy. I feel her swallow and hear her sniff. A mixture of relief and elation fills me, and I wrap my arms around her just as tightly.

"Oh, Miz, don't cry," I say. "This is supposed to make you happy!"

"I don't have the words . . ." she mumbles.

I let out a big sigh. Of course, if she had been upset, told me that this was way over the top, I was ready to have it sent back, shower her with the usual scented bath products, wine, gift cards. But this, this is much better.

One of the delivery guys pops out from the bedroom door. "Are we removing too?"

I break the hug. "They can take away your old mattress. It's part of the service, but if you're attached to it, they don't have to take it."

"Are you fucking kidding me? Please, have at it," she says. We go into her bedroom, where I help her remove the sheets.

After the delivery men leave with their tip, Miz collapses on the mattress and rolls around on it, moaning.

"Do you need a moment alone?" I say, smiling ear to ear.

"Shh!" she says, now starfished on the bed, eyes closed. She lets out a deep sigh.

"It's my small way of saying I appreciate you," I say.

She nudges me with her foot, laughing. "You Legesses don't know the meaning of small!"

"And this should make up for your never stretching too. The sales guy told me every sleep is like an eight-hour massage. It's his job to exaggerate, but I'm hoping he was mostly being honest."

"Oh yeah, I already feel looser." She opens her eyes and sits up. "So that's why you were so determined to work from here today," she says. "Sneaky." She gasps and cups her mouth. "Oh my god, how much was it?"

I have no intention of answering that. I hold out my hand to help her up. "We should get back to work."

We are allowed to submit a maximum of twenty pictures, including those of our wedding ceremony. Luckily, Miz has photo albums of all her visits to Addis, starting from '96. One of the earliest photos is at Queen Burger in Addis. "We were such babies!" she exclaims. Miz, me, Eske and our high school gang slouch around a table in our finest '90s styles. Miz has sworn that, to this day, she has yet to taste burgers better than the ones I offered her when I found her in the parkette in Addis.

That day, she had looked so broken, all alone. I remember asking her whether she was okay, first in Amharic, then in English. Instead of answering, she had stared at me for too long with her wet, red eyes, looking badass in her bandana, hoop earrings, baggy jeans, and crop top. "*Ça va?*" I'd tried again, thinking she didn't speak English either, trying to keep my eyes off her exposed belly button. German might have been next if she hadn't snapped at me in English.

"Do I look like I'm okay?"

I sat on the stone bench opposite her.

"I hate it here," she said, her pout exaggerating her bold lipliner.

The way she said it confirmed my guess she wasn't talking about the compound but about Addis itself. "Then why did you come?"

That was all it took for her to regale me with the saga of the fight that ensued from her mom learning of her boyfriend. "Are you planning to marry him?" I asked when she finished.

She looked at me as if I had just pulled a rabbit from my ear. "That's, like, the first thing my mom asked me. What's wrong with you people? I'm fourteen!"

"So? I'm fifteen," I said. "But I already know that my Muna will be my wife. That's how it is."

Years later, after Muna and I were over, Miz had told me she'd bit back her immediate thought, *Bet Muna don't know that.* I wish she hadn't. She would have saved me from so much pain. What she said instead was, "According to who?"

"That's our culture."

"Eh? Who's *our?*"

"That's why your parents panicked."

"Mom did. Dad is sane. Thank God."

"Your father was probably distressed too. He just didn't show it," I said. "They didn't do dating in their day, and so they don't really understand the concept. Personally, I don't either."

"What century are you from?"

I laughed. "I get that a lot. But when you know, you know. If you don't, then what's the point?"

"To date!"

"For what?"

"Life! Fun! Getting to know different people!"

"You can do all that without becoming romantically involved."

She glowered at me, though it did not prevent her from devouring the last of my burger and getting started on my fries. Bini would be wondering what was taking me so long, so I offered to walk her back to her building. But she said she would walk me back to my building instead. I wasn't sure whether that was because she didn't want to be home alone or she didn't know whether she could trust me. Anyway, we walked back to Bini's together. And, well, she never left, becoming a permanent fixture of my social group every summer thereafter that she came to see her father.

We set aside the photo from Queen Burger to go in our submission package, writing the date and a short description on the back as required. "It's like each visit had its own theme," I say, as we go through the albums. "You notice?"

"Mm-hmm," she said. There are the touristy ones with family the first time around in '96 and then just us young ones the next time around in '98—to Hawassa, Langano, the whole Northern

Historic tour. Then there are the party- and wedding-heavy ones in '01, '04, and '07, the last two sets only in digital on her cloud drive. "And then," she says, sighing, after we've set aside the best ones, "the individual known as Kalkidan disappears from the scene."

"You're never going to get over that, are you?"

"Nope. Because I don't know if you're gonna do it again."

When we reconnected in Toronto, three years later, I'd glossed over the reason for my disappearance as having got busy with work. If there was ever a time to tell her the full reason why I disappeared, I realize now is it. "What if I tell you something that will guarantee I won't?"

"I'll just put a chip in you. Right here," she says, touching the back of my neck. "It's my right as your lawful—"

I catch her hand in mine and gently lower it to the couch, keeping it in my grasp. Blowing out a long, shaky breath, I launch in. "Muna left me, which you know. What you don't know is . . ." I steal a glance at Miz. She looks almost scared. "Is that she came back."

Miz takes in a quiet, terrified breath. "She did?" she whispers.

"To this day, not one soul knows about this. For over a year, she would get in touch with me sporadically, and we would get together. Of course, at first, I didn't know that that was how it would be. When she called the first time . . ." I look up at the ceiling, smiling sadly at the memory of that Kal's uncontainable joy. "I thought she had come back to me for good. That we were reunited *forever*. Since grade eight, Miz. *Eleven years*, we were one. High school, university, work life." Miz mouths *I know* repeatedly, her eyes moist while mine are dry. "I was so proud of myself. I remember telling myself, 'Good for you, Kal. It was painful, but you let her go because you love her, and because she loves you, she came back to you. So what if yours will not be an unblemished story like Emay and Abay's?' All was right with the world again. But that didn't turn out to be the case. She never wanted to meet in public, always in hotel rooms or outside the city. As if I was a secret. As if I was someone who she was being unfaithful with. And this is a shame I'll carry with me as long as I live—even after I discovered that's *exactly* who I was, I still let her control me. Every time she would leave me, it was like going through that first breakup, burning down our future again. Because I couldn't help building it up again every time she called me. I was hopeless, destroyed, a shadow of myself. Someone I barely recognized. I was hooked on her, on the hope that maybe this time she would stay. Or maybe next time. For over a year." Miz drops her head into her free hand. "Then I fell apart, distanced myself, became a stranger to everyone. Somewhere in me, I found the strength to stop seeing her, but it was as if I couldn't see or share life with any-one else either. As if she was the entirety of life. Or I was punishing myself? I don't know." I laugh sardonically. "Miz, there will never be another Muna. And I say that as a *very* good thing. So I will never disappear again, from myself, from you, from anyone."

I feel light as a bird, free. Miz, however, looks thunderous, her face pinched tighter than her grip on my fingers. "Bitch!" she spits. "If I ever see her again, I'm shaving her head. And her eye-brows!" As if on cue, thunder rumbles from a distance, like a planned pathetic fallacy.

"You wouldn't know how that feels though, eh? You always show them the door first."

"You gotta. It's a jungle out there," she says, waving her free arm in the air. "I would never do a guy like that though. I'm always up front. Some take it well. Some don't." She shrugs and looks down at our connected hands, then releases mine. I remember her irritated tone earlier when she thought Daniel was at the door. And I want to ask whether he's still trying to contact her, invading her space, or she has let him back in. But I hold back. She has always handled herself fine. And it truly is none of my business.

"Kal." Miz pokes me in the triceps. "Thanks for telling me that," she says. "It means a lot."

"You deserved an explanation. It was long overdue," I say. *You deserve a lot. More than an on-again, off-again thing with Daniel, to start.* "You're my ride and die."

She busts out laughing. "Or. Ride *or* die."

"It's like a vow," I say. We reach for the same brownie. "Oh, you go ahead," I say.

She breaks it in two and gives me a half. "Hey, you know what we never did?" she says, stopping me as I go in for a bite. She extends the arm of the hand holding her chunk of brownie.

"Oh!" I do the same. We interlock elbows and pop our halves. "Hold it there." I pass her her beer bottle. I pick up mine, and we sip, our elbows still interlocked. "Now it's official!"

We unwind and take in the collection of photographs we've chosen, scattered over the table like a collage.

"They tell a good story, right?" she says.

"They do." A story of two kids who met by chance, developed a bond, had a long-distance friendship through their teens, and then were reunited by fate in Canada as adults. There must be a plot just like ours in a book, or even many books, out there somewhere.

"Are you noticing what I'm noticing though?" she says.

"I look younger every year?"

"Goof. We don't have any . . . you know, lubby-dubby, coupley ones. Even the ones of just us scream platonic. Don't you think so? I mean," she says hurriedly, "it'll be better for the case if we do a few romantic cheesy ones, right?"

"Unless we claim that we're too culturally modest for public displays of affection." Although to my eyes, we do look very affectionate in the photos of just us.

"Come on, please, our generation?" she says. "All that alcohol and hookahs. Posing like we're an R&B group?"

We agree there's only one way to remedy this: We have to take "romantic cheesy" ones around Toronto. Luckily, we're both free tomorrow, so we plan to create history on the spot, wearing different clothes at half a dozen locations we'll pick between us. "But keep them a surprise until we get there!" she says, getting excited. We shake on it. "Shall we call it a night for now?"

"Unless we start our individual sections for 5532—"

"Oh god, I can't look at another form tonight."

"Same here." I close my laptop and start stacking the untouched printouts.

"I guess I'll take off then," I say, something making me draw it out, like a child trying to put off bedtime.

"Wait, it's pitch black out there. I don't like you riding this late."

"The streets are actually quieter now, Miz."

She goes out to her balcony. "It's raining!" she yells into the darkness. A torrent of rainwater splashes against her window, followed by a worryingly close thunderclap. She comes back in and gathers the empty bowls and used napkins. "Stay. Bring your bike up."

My insides do a flip. "I'm sure it'll be okay." *Did I just brush off my bike? Who am I?*

"It'll be a slumber party!" she shouts, looking as giddy as I feel. "You haven't slept over since . . ."

Since the time I flew back from my mother's funeral. "Yeah," I say. "Feels like yesterday."

"Won't it always?" she says gently.

I nod, feeling a sting behind my eyes, but quickly redirect. "Want to watch a movie? The latest one with my body double?"

"Wow, the confidence! Get the cushions down, John David Washington. I'll go get the sheets."

"You started it!" I yell out. *But did she?* I pause, cushion in hand. Or did I start pointing out our resemblance after she developed a huge crush on him last year? I shake it off. No, she saw it first.

21

MIZ

Aimé: So didja tell hot stuff you wanna come over?

Aimé's text interrupts my overthinking about the generosity of Kal's gift while I'm cooling down from my early morning run. I snuck out without waking Kal sleeping on the couch. Last night, we fell asleep watching the movie, so I missed my first night on the new mattress. Now I can't wait for tonight. So much so that this morning, I just had to press all ten fingers into it just to keep me until then. It took all my willpower not to sink the rest of my body onto it.

I pause to text Aimé back, relishing the warmth of the rising sun at my back. I had texted Daniel last night, after Kal fell asleep, and felt weirdly guilty about it. Based on my oopsie by the door yesterday, he probably assumes Daniel and I are back to our usual on-again, off-again. I've never worried about Kal's judgment, but I really want him to know that's not happening and will *never* happen. But I also don't want to bring Daniel up at all.

Me: Says he's busy. Obv he doesn't want ME to go to him!

Aimé: Make him an offer he can't refuse ;)

Me: Ok I'm not that desperate

Yet. I know I have to offload that ring soon. I'm starting to get jumpy every time I see a house with a RE/MAX sign planted out front, as if Daniel will run out and confront me. And I can't have another false-alarm close call like last night. My heart can't take it. But today's not the day—we've got places to be, romance to fake.

Kal's house is the first stop in our day of Zipcar-ing through Toronto taking our photos, so he can drop off his bike, shower, and pick up his "costumes" for the day. My location pick is first on our photo day: Ripley's Aquarium. Specifically, the jellyfish tank—my favourite part, where supposedly we had our first date. From there we hop over next door to the CN Tower, Kal's pick, where apparently I took him when he was new to Canada, despite his terror of heights. Like me, he has not dared the glass floor, two thousand feet above Toronto. We manage to do it together, though it turns out to be almost as terrifying as getting married was. Our third spot is Snakes & Lattes, which we'll say we frequent, especially to play Taboo, a favourite of our gang in Addis back in the day, and we have the photos to prove it. A *where it started and where it's at* kind of theme.

Kal takes the wheel next, taking us east and parking a few blocks shy of his theatre. We walk to a small park, in the centre of which is a three-tier fountain, surrounded by twenty-seven (Kal counted) dog sculptures, each a different breed, all staring up at a giant golden bone at the top. Of course! This is one of Kal's favourite spots in the city. The doggie diversity struck him as such a contrast to Addis, where the majority of the stray dogs were only a handful of breeds. "Can this count as one of my locations too? Please?" I beg.

"We're not here for them. Come," he says, taking me by the hand. I feel as if I'm on an adventure. He stops under a lamppost a few feet away from the fountain. "Heads up."

I look up. Perched on a piece of jutting metal at the top of the lamppost are a pair of little sculpted yellow birds side by side. "Aw. So cute!" I pull out my phone for the photo. "What's our story to go along with it?

"This is where I proposed."

That pulls me up short. "Oh. Huh. Yeah. We forgot that part," I say, swallowing.

"I didn't," he says, his voice low, his gaze searing into mine. Holy shit, what is going on? With a sharp inhale, I swivel my head, as if taking in our surroundings.

"Or this could be where we had our first big fight over what kind of dog to adopt. Or I wanted a dog, but you wanted a cat, so we compromised on a bird!"

He nods, taking it into consideration. "Sure, if you prefer." But he sounds . . . disappointed? Dammit, fine.

"Okay, so ahem, why did you pick this spot to propose marriage, Kalkidan?" I say, colouring his name with a stereotypically nasal white guy/officer of the Canadian government voice.

He drops into character immediately and answers me formally, laying on the accent thick, landing hard on his r's. "Because, sir, the symbolism of the birds. They represent lifelong loyalty to me. They remind me of my parents. And I always used to think of Mizan as a kind of unattainable bird." He leans in close. I hold my breath, trembling a little. "There's actually an old people song about that," he whispers to me in his regular voice.

I whisper back. "Send it to me sometime."

We stay forehead to forehead a beat too long, until an actual living dog barges in on us, snapping us out of it. We take a bunch of photos with the birds and then have to hustle because Kal says his next location is best by sunset. We head back out west, burning up another hour, and end up on the Humber Bay Arch Bridge. "You are *on* your romance game today, my friend," I say. "Remember when you called me, so sad?"

"I'll never forget it," he says, leaning on the railing. "The day the love locks died."

The bridge's wires used to be packed with all kinds of love locks, something Kal just couldn't get enough of, until one day, all of a sudden, they were gone. Turned out, overnight, the city had culled them in a major cleanup operation. Now there were only a few locks left, some new, but most looked like the really sturdy kind that no steel cutter could bite through. "I guess the gesture lost meaning for people when they realized the locks wouldn't stay forever. What does though?"

Kal unzips his bag and reaches in. I back away. "Tell me you didn't."

With a smile wide as Lake Ontario and wiggling his eyebrows suggestively, he pulls out a combination padlock dangling off of his finger. "I did."

I cover my eyes. "Oh jeez, you know we could have just pretended any one of these was ours."

"That's bad luck. Do you want to do the honours?"

"You go ahead, darling. I'll take the pic."

"I can take a picture for you two—a gorgeous couple," a voice says. We turn. It's a tall retiree pausing her power walk. I'm too mortified to speak, but Kal takes her up on her offer. She snaps a thousand photos of us putting the padlock on and choosing today's date for the code. Then, at her insistence, we snuggle up, my hand on Kal's chest, the tops of our heads touching. We're separating when she says, "Oh, you've got to smooch!"

"Um," I say under my breath.

"We kind of should," Kal murmurs without moving.

I close my eyes and tilt my face up to his. I stay like that, waiting, forever. *Hello?* Just as I'm about to open my eyes, silky soft lips press on mine. Warmth swooshes down my body. I feel him sigh, his fingers grazing my chin, and the tiniest moisture as the tip of his tongue taps shyly against my lips. I begin to part them, my heart on the edge of exploding.

"Adorable!"

We leap apart.

"Here you go!" She gives me back my phone. "Best wishes!" She marches off.

"Alrighty then," I say, watching her go, the high receding. "That was . . . that was good."

"Great!" He watches her go a bit too long as well before turning back to me, smiling and nodding.

Okay, then. I'll have to do all the blabbering. "Damn, you've been depriving the Toronto ladies though!"

"That was all you."

"Was not!"

"Lips don't lie, Mizan."

"Hips, you mean?"

He shakes his head, smirking like he knows something I don't.

"Get outta here! Okay, but actually, we better head back. I have to head to my mom's to help with Thanksgiving prep." We technically still have one more stop to do—my pick this time—but after that kiss, I feel as if we've done enough for today. *Come on, Miz, friends kiss on the lips all the time, and yeah sometimes the tongues do an oopsie, but so what. Grow the fuck up!*

"Wish you could join us for our feast," Kal says, interrupting my little mental self-spanking. "Call me when you reach?" he says, opening his arms for a goodbye hug.

"I'm driving you back home, goof." I take the hug anyway. Can't ever have too many of those. Before we leave, I give in to the urge to tug on the padlock, check that it's secure, even though I know it's going to get hacked off one day anyway.

22

KAL

I'm at a UPS store, waiting for my passport photographs to print, when I get a call from my father. "Congratulations, son!"

"On what?" I step out of the below-ground store and climb the steps to the street level. Part of me is praying that Abay has belatedly found out about my playing Antony. That was back in August, almost two months ago, but he moves on his own schedule.

"I hear you have married. When did you become engaged?"

My heart drops. Eske! "I didn't!"

"I know. You jumped right into it. No engagement. My son! You remind me of myself, doing away with the protocols. Or were you engaged all this time?"

"No, Abay. Because I am not really married." Only people who are entering into a sacred union become married. Blending clans, histories, grudges, genes. Miz and I had simply repeated a few words and signed some papers. That was all, my increasingly rebellious heart notwithstanding. "Who told you I did?" I'm giving Eske a very slim benefit of the doubt. News has a way of seeping through unlikely cracks.

"The police chief called to congratulate me on my youngest son's good fortune in Canada."

I say the man's name, to confirm. "But why—" I cut myself off, piecing the rest together. Eske had to secure me a police certificate from Addis for the application. Not only would she have had to explain what it was needed for (and knowing her, she would have been very thorough in her explanation anyway), but she would have needed to pull on our higher-up connections to get it done fast.

"Abay." I duck into a winter vestibule already installed outside a business next door, this October having been unusually chilly, to escape the street noise. "We married as an arrangement—"

"I was like you with your mother!" My father goes on seamlessly, not showing a hint of annoyance that I bucked tradition— no formal ask to Miz's family for her hand. "We took off on our own, as you know. Didn't need anyone's go-ahead. When love summons, you obey!"

It has been years since I have heard Abay sound so delighted— there's no stopping him. "I am pleased. My son has come back into life. Year after year, I have had to hear from your brothers and uncles and cousins that everywhere they used to take you, the restaurants, the clubs, the bars, everywhere, you behaved like a monk. I am so pleased that time is over now. And that it is a girl we know. Please give Mizan my congratulations as well."

"Abay, you know she is just a friend, as she's always been, helping me, her long-time friend," I say. "She is only sponsoring me as a spouse so I can get permanent residence."

Although *only* is not a fair word given the amount of paperwork we've had to do, not just for the application but to join our lives on paper to prove our fictional cohabitation: her having to prove her financials, her employment, and so much more. We were lucky Everest expedited the process of having me added as a tenant on Miz's lease.

"She is not my *friend*. She is *just* my friend," I enunciate louder, loading the first with the proper emphasis their generation gives it to mean *partner*. Were Miz and I foolish to have hoped—nay, *expected*—that this sponsorship would get taken care of without our families' involvement? In this moment, I envy Miz's tiny immediate family of three. They don't get carried away at the first sign of anything romantic or matrimonial.

"Son, I am too old to go in circles with you. Miz is the one you've added to the family."

I shuffle, looking down at my feet. "It's just paperwork," I say weakly.

"Is that what she also says?"

"That's what we agreed on." Though if she brought up moving in and sleeping on her couch for the duration of our case again . . . "You can ask her yourself." *And please tell me what she says*, I think, *because a part of me is starting to wonder*. But he won't ask her, of course.

It doesn't matter. Miz doesn't do marriage. At least, not the Miz I knew.

The morning after I slept over at Miz's, I'd woken up to her gone, out on a run. I was putting away the photo albums when a piece of paper slipped out from one. A tearaway from a high school exercise book, with Miz's handwriting telling a very different story of her than the one she has gone around telling of herself for years now.

Doodles covered the page, an outline of two hands, hearts everywhere, and Miz's name written with the last name of the boy who got her sent to Ethiopia in the first place. They told of another Miz who had once dreamed of marriage, or at least cherished the idea of it. She had that desire, that flame once, but what she got for it was punishment. No wonder it was extinguished. Though she did keep that paper all these years. Was it possible that the flame was still present somewhere in the adult Miz?

I remember tracing the outline of the smaller of those hands, Miz's, as if I had her living, warm hands underneath mine. I remember seeing in my mind's eye her arms, her legs, carving through the air like when she is running. The first time I witnessed it was when I went to pick her up from running camp. Even then, I remember thinking, this is what an Ambassel melody would look like, the way her feet kiss the ground so lightly, barely stirring up dust, and her hair lifts and falls with each stride like the wings of a bird. An uncatchable bird, that *yematibela wef* of the old songs, which will scratch your heart to pieces should you try to hold her by the tail.

"Son-of-Legesse, I know you," Abay says, snapping me back to the present. "A son whom we named *vow* would not marry a woman who was not his only, no matter what uncertainty and challenge he was facing in his life. Your former life here is not that abhorrent to you, is it?"

"No," I say. I would never have gone as far as signing with a stranger, even if vetted by Miz.

"Choosing a life mate is not paperwork. Find a time to talk, truly, to her. Reveal the inner lining of your heart. In life, the best, most beautiful melody you hear will come to you when you don't expect it, as a gift. Grab this song before she fades."

"Abay, there's . . ." But I can't finish because I'm at a loss for words. You never know when the old folks are going to drop some heavy poetry on you. What argument can one make against that? Having said what he called to say, Abay ends our call shortly after a quick update on the anniversary party in January.

The image of that exercise book page flicks back into my mind. It is what made me a soft target for my father's relentless conviction that what Miz and I have on our hands is a real commitment. It is what influenced everything I said, and didn't say, that day we drove from location to location, taking our photos. I know it. It certainly was behind my daring move on the bridge, taking the initiative with that kiss, ensuring it was nothing like the missable peck at our civil ceremony. I remember her smiling dreamily at me after, as the sun set and that lady cheered.

I have been operating in a kind of daze ever since. Outwardly, we have been back to our regular selves. But it feels as if something has shifted between us.

They say you don't know what you've got until it's gone. Is there a saying that you don't know what you want until it's in front of you?

If not Miz, for this, then who?

Frustratingly, there is nothing else in the application we need to do in person, so we haven't seen each other in some time. Perhaps for the best. If my hunch (hope?) is wrong, it would make the coming months, years unbearable for both of us, if it did not completely destroy our friendship. Yes, best left alone. Unless she gives me a clear signal . . .

23

MIZ

I don't know how he did it, but Kal got it exactly right. It feels like I've been walking around in a new body for weeks now. On the second night after the mattress was delivered, I dived in, in my birthday suit. Kal wasn't kidding. Every night *is* like a deep tissue massage. My sleep becomes so deep and dreamless, my body so supple, and my joints so juicy—all kinds of bliss, thanks to Kal. It seems unfair that he doesn't get to experience the luxury for himself. This feels like *our* mattress, not just mine. I could ask him, *Do you want to try out the new mattress?* Why not? Simple question, right? Yeah, it would have been, once upon a time. Now though, I'm scared it will bring back the Weirdness. As if, in that question, he would hear my every private thought.

Stop it, girlie. This is all just pictures-day hangover. Remember the point of all this is the sponsorship application. Which we're almost done with. Everything is set except for the marriage certificate. As soon as that drops in my mailbox, we send off the application. And then back to our regular programming.

"We've never done something like this before," I say to Aimé on my AirPods. "Actually working as a team toward something serious. I'm gonna miss having a project partner. Going back to just hanging out feels like . . . backtracking or something."

"I think all that's because you forgot to jump his bones," Aimé says.

"Me tap that skinny ass? I like meat on my bones. You do recall a guy named Daniel?"

Aimé *pffts*, not buying any of it. "Speaking of, are you there yet?"

"Almost."

It's after work on Wednesday, and I'm headed to Daniel's place to execute Operation Lose the Ring. Aimé's on the phone as moral support and to verify that I actually do return the ring this time. My grand plan on this Halloween night is to use the element of surprise to my advantage by showing up unannounced (taste of his own medicine). He'll let me in because I'm too cute to be turned away in my form-fitting giraffe costume. At some point, the giraffe will need to use the bathroom, during which I'll put the ring in a findable but not obvious place in his bathroom. Bonus points if I manage to stuff it back in his gym bag. And with that, Daniel chapter closed for good. Hallelujer and amen.

"Okay, I'm here," I say, reaching the townhouse where Daniel rents a floor. I blow into my hoofs to warm them.

"You got this!" she says. I cross myself, send a kiss to Christos, and press the doorbell. *"Wait!"* she shouts suddenly.

I leap back. *"What?!"*

"What if *she's* there?"

She who? I think. Oh, Naomi, the chosen one! "Shit shit shit!" I dash commando-style down the stairs and lunge behind a parked car. I peer over the hood at the front door. "No one has come out."

"Abort mission! I don't want you getting mauled over this."

"I could just pretend to be a passerby with a bathroom emergency."

"Would you let you in?" Aimé says.

"Hell no." But I did not come all the way out here for nothing. "Hold on. Let me text him." I pull my thumbs out of my hoofs. But I go blank. Selfie then. I send him one that clearly shows that I am on his street.

Me: Guess who?

"Okay, I sent him a message. Waiting . . . waiting . . ." I say to Aimé.

Daniel: What are you doing there?

Me: Surprise!

Daniel: I'm not home.

Me: I can wait if u hurry

**Daniel: Mom had a fall, needs hip replacement.
Am back in Calgary until she's fully healed.**

Oh shit. Poor moms! "Mission fail," I say to Aimé. "He's out of town."

"Oh."

"Am I cursed to be stuck with this ring forever?"

"Is there an open window or something you can toss it in?"

"He lives on the second floor, Aims. I'm not an actual giraffe." But I still look up at his windows with pitiful hope. That's how determined I feel to offload this overpriced, probably uninsured rock.

"What about the mailbox?" Aimé says.

"You know he shares the mailbox with the other tenants. And all I have is the ring. No box, no envelope. So now what, I'm supposed to go find mailing supplies? Come on!"

"Okay, don't bite *my* head off!"

Kal: Trick or treat!

My mood improves instantly. I laugh out loud when I see the picture he's sent me of him and his roommates in costume, he in a store-bought Roman soldier one. "Sorry, girl. Gotta go," I say before quickly hanging up.

Me: Okay I see you Tony! Is that a Halloween party you didn't invite me to?

Kal: It was last minute. Consider this your invite.

Me: Do you want to see what I'm wearing?

My mind, of course, crosses into the gutter. What are the chances he'll write back something kinky?

Kal: No, surprise me.

I smirk. Hmm, I'm not sure that qualifies.

Me: omw.

Giving myself a strict talking-to about how we must remain what we have always been—strictly platonic—especially now, I skip over to his house. Yes. Strictly PG. Except my occasional unplatonic lapses. But come on, how is any human, warm-blooded, fertile, heterosexual, well-rested young female with a vibrant dream life supposed to stay indifferent to those bedroom eyes, that drawl, that rolling, hips out–shoulders back gait? *Stop it.*

Word must have got out fast because Kal's place is jumping by the time I get there. "Should I say *karibu?*" Kal says, laughing at my costume and going for the Swahili welcome. "Did you spend your workday like this?"

"Yep! What? You worked seven nights in something like that," I say, pointing out his hunky-as-heck getup. "Got anything on under there?" I ask with a wink. Wow, two minutes in and already flirting. We need supervision. Or at least I do. We are so dancing on the edge of things.

He laughs, shaking his head. "I missed you."

My heart feels like it stops for a moment. "I'm right here."

Then he puts his hand over mine. "I know."

"And we just saw each other, like, when—"

"What I'm saying is . . ." He squeezes my hand. I squeeze back. And just like that, I know. (I think.) We are on the same page. (Maybe.) I feel 76.9 percent sure of it. Or is it that I want to? Well, there is only one way to round that up to one hundred. *Come on, girlie, be brave and say it.* I look down. *Now or never, Miz. Use your words. English! You've been learning it since you were two.*

But something stops me. Damn morals. I don't want to take advantage of Kal's vulnerable position. If he wants me at all, I want him to want me as a free agent without this sponsorship hanging over our heads. Best to wait until after we finish the sponsorship process. Couple of years tops. No biggie. The thought of my making a move and then Kal feeling obligated, out of gratitude or whatever, to reciprocate is as horrifying as the idea of being rejected by him. Unless and until such time as Kal gives me a neon green light, I am not deviating from Operation Platonic.

With the party made up of almost all actors, most of the talk is about the upcoming season and who got what gig where, which I see is making Kal feel left out. He's already done the TV show audition Oliver had him prepare for. Since then, he's gone for callback after callback.

"It's like they think they want me, but they don't know what for exactly," he says, sounding frustrated.

"Mmm," I say. I can completely relate.

"Don't you want to put your bag down?" he says. I've been clutching it like it contains the nuclear launch code. Last thing I need is to lose the ring by some freak accident. Irony for days.

"I'm good. I need to head out soon."

"You just got here," he reminds me.

"It was a long day," I fib. "And tomorrow will be worse." Safer not to stay too long where the lights are dim, the alcohol is flowing, and a certain someone may or may not have anything on under his short tunic.

"Let's go somewhere we can talk," he says. I abandon all thoughts of skipping out early in a heartbeat. I feel giddy, as if we're at a high school house party and my crush has finally acknowledged my existence. We top up our drinks and go up to the rooftop terrace, grabbing one of his blankets on the way. "Not a CN Tower kind of view but . . ." he says.

"I've always liked it up here," I say, as we snuggle on the old sofa that lives out here. "Your sunrise view."

"And sunset. Always best when shared." We catch up about this and that. Work, rehearsals, the anniversary-wedding party, my mom deciding to book her flight to Ethiopia without me.

"Before Christmas too! She wanted to avoid the peak season crush. No thought to leaving me unattended," I say, with an exaggerated hurt. "My first Christmas without my mama."

"You're always welcome here," Kal says, detecting a sense of loss in my words.

"Okay." I smile, mentally chucking plans I haven't even made yet.

"We should book our flight soon too," he says. I agree. "I'm really excited we're finally flying home together," he adds with such open sincerity that I'm filled with the sudden need to smother him in a bear hug.

"Thirteen nonstop hours with you though? Oh boy," I say instead, scrunching up my face mockingly.

"Like thirteen hours of sunshine," he says, showing me all thirty-two of his pearly whites, a smile that threatens to make me abandon Operation Platonic. *Do like ABBA and take a chance, girl.*

"So you wanted to talk to me about something?" I say, arranging the blanket.

He looks hesitant, sips his drink. "It was just an excuse to get me some Miz-time."

"Since when do you need an excuse for that?" I say, shoving him playfully. As if I haven't been antsy about the same thing for weeks.

He stares into his drink. "I don't know, you've seemed . . ." He looks at me. "Busy." Except the question in his eyes has nothing to do with my timetable. If I'm reading them right. Big *if*.

"Busy hurrying home for another night of amazing sleep," I say, sticking to the safe lane. "Hey, do you want to try it out?" Never mind.

His brows shoot up. "Your mattress?"

Shite, I think he's stalling. *Retreat! Retreat!* "Yeah, whenever," I say quickly. I feel a prickle of cold on my nose and look up to see tiny flurries coming down. "Any night. Or even not necessarily at night. Just whenever you want to. I don't even have to be there!"

Shut. Up. Stop speaking.

He opens his mouth to reply, but there's a clamour on the stairs to the rooftop. We're interrupted by half the people at the party, overly excited by the first snow of the season. Humiliated, I join in the glee. When someone strikes up a conversation with Kal, I excuse myself and bolt, sending him a cowardly *see ya* by text.

24

KAL

Me: Just sent it off!

Along with my text to Miz, I attach an exterior shot of the post office in the shopping atrium, the last in a series of photos I have been sending her since I left my house earlier, the thick envelope containing the spousal sponsorship application tucked in my arm like a precious infant.

Miz: Woohoo!

I can't help feeling disappointed by her response. Two weeks after the Halloween party, our marriage certificate, the final missing piece, finally arrived. I had hoped we would send the application off together. But that's just me being sentimental. Besides, I've already asked enough of Miz. Except, that is, the one question that's been knocking around in my head since that kiss. *Am I imagining it, or have things changed between us?*

With one last glance behind me as the postal worker tosses my potentially life-altering envelope around like it's nothing, I step onto the descending escalator. One thing I do know is that I will follow Abay's advice. I will. I am not a Son-of-Legesse if I do not say what I'm thinking about her, to her, out loud and in her presence. New Year's Eve. That is my hard deadline. The work of putting together the application is behind us, for now at least. We can move on to more delicate matters.

I gaze up at the imitation snow dusting the towering Christmas tree that soars past all three levels of the atrium. When we were on the terrace, I was almost ready to tell her that my father had found out about us being "married," but I lost my nerve. I was afraid—no, I was *sure*—her follow-up question would be *What did he say?* And I would either tell her a redacted version of the truth (that he was optimistic for us and glad that it was her) or the full truth (he is convinced there are true romantic feelings involved). That would've been the perfect segue to have *the talk*. But it didn't feel right with us dressed in silly costumes in the middle of a house party.

Me: That's it then.

Miz: That's it!

Is that it? Whatever happens with the sponsorship, I can't help feeling deflated that we won't commemorate having come this far by doing something special. We have made bigger occasions out of lesser moments!

Miz: So that's a yay or a nay?

Me: To . . . ?

Miz: Scroll up.

I do, looking for a message I seem to have missed. There it is, sent right after my photo of the sealed application.

Miz: We should do something to celebrate this!

I grin. So we *are* of like mind. And I'm not surprised at all that Miz is the one who took action, instead of me. Just like I think, *I think*, she did on my rooftop. Was that . . . invitation a subtle signal? But since when did Miz do subtle?

The following night, I arrive at Miz's place, dressed up to go out for our celebratory dinner, carrying a bottle of champagne for a predinner toast. Everest buzzes me in, so I text Miz to let her know that I am on my way up.

Her door is ajar, which means the hallway is now eucalyptus-scented, just like her body wash. I close my eyes and take a deep inhale, scolding my mind for imagining her in the shower. Not wanting to assume the door has been left open for me, I knock lightly. "Housekeeping."

From the bathroom just past the entrance, I hear her. "Kal, why do you insist on being a stranger?" she calls out, her voice bubbly.

I tap the door wider with the head of the champagne bottle and slide in like a wannabe Don Juan. Miz is standing in front of the bathroom mirror, applying mascara, her lips parted, butt poking out as a counterweight to her forward-leaning torso and spilling cleavage. Again, I give myself the mental equivalent of a slap on the wrist, feeling as if I'm crossing a line by taking her in this way. Yet as I lean against her kitchen island, my eyes go where they will, taking in the precision of her hand, the curve of her lower lip, how her black dress drapes smoothly over her backside.

A glint from her open makeup bag catches my eye. I imagine it's her wedding ring, giving me a little *Do you dare?* wink. When she switches the mascara wand to her other eye, we lock eyes through the mirror. Feeling caught in my gawking, I quickly imitate her posture, hanging my mouth in a silly way, and blurt out, "Why do women always do that?"

"Explain I could, but hurting your brain I wouldn't want," she says, imitating Yoda.

Forget my brain—it's my heart I am concerned about. "You look . . ."

She smooths her dress over her hips. "Fine as red wine? I'll also accept sensational." She throws me a red carpet over-the-shoulder look. "It's not too much for a sushi restaurant, is it?"

"Not at all. You do have to live up to this, after all," I say, sliding my hand down my completely unexceptional black-on-black dress pants and blazer.

"Whateverrr." She sticks out her tongue and gives me the middle finger poorly disguised as a nose rub.

Before I misbehave any further, I go around to the cupboards, take out two champagne glasses, and carry them to the living room, where I can't see her. But through the open door of her bedroom, I *can* see that mattress . . . to which I have a standing offer. A blip of a thought flashes in my mind about who else has a standing offer. Daniel? But I swat that thought away.

"Hey, Miz!" I call out, draping my arm over the back of the sofa.

"Yeah?"

"That offer still on the table?" I try to sound as if I'm joking, but I know I'm starting something. I feel like a hormone-addled teenager these days, always insinuating something.

An excruciatingly long silence follows, although in reality, it's probably no more than ten seconds before she replies.

"Oh, that!" Another beat. "Anytime!"

No time like the present then. Before my surge of courage leaches into the sofa, I jump up. Hands in my pockets, I stroll languidly into her bedroom, a performance for an audience of zero. I stand where I know she can see me in the bathroom mirror, where she's moved on to sweeping an enormous brush over her cheekbones in upward strokes. All that is between us is the walk-in closet, and an expanse of freshly vacuumed carpet, like the plush earth of undiscovered territory. I take one step closer to the bed, bringing my shins flush against the side of the mattress. My hands still in my pockets, I bend one knee, sinking part of my weight into the softness.

Immediately, as if she was waiting for that exact moment, Miz says, "Uh uh uh! Excuse me!" I freeze. "Tell me you're not about to get up on my bed in your street clothes!"

"Oh. Sorry." Feeling like a complete buffoon, I remove my offending knee and back away.

"Take 'em off."

The air crackles. "Are you serious?"

"Just your top layer, goof."

Of course. Slowly, I start undoing my shirt buttons, waiting for her to say *Psych!* Any second now. But she continues calmly sweeping that brush over her cheekbones until she seems satisfied with whatever imperceptible effect she's created. Kind of like

what she's doing to me, with her silence, as I get all the way down
to the bottom button, then peel both my shirt and blazer off in
one piece. I fold them lengthwise and drape them on the nearest
surface without looking. I think I hear them fall, but I don't care.
I wait, visualizing what *could* happen on this mattress moments
from now. I hear a sharp intake of breath and the sound of Miz's
makeup brush clattering to the sink. I smile. That tells me what
I need to know. There has never been sweeter music, not even
among my old people songs, than the sound of that makeup
brush hitting the porcelain. She's seen me less clothed and never
batted an eye, much less lost her precious breath. Something *is*
going on.

"Go ahead. Don't let me stop you," she recovers, still address-
ing me through the mirror.

Is the brave, bold Miz too nervous to turn around and look at
the real me? No big hero myself, I fumble with my own belt.

"Do you need help?"

"No, I have done this before."

But I feel helpless, as if I have never done this before. I try to
not let the relief show on my face when she does turn, finally, and
starts walking toward me. By the time I have mastered my belt
and shed my pants, she is in the bedroom with me. We watch each
other, no longer in reflection but in reality.

"May I, now?" I ask playfully.

Wordlessly, she lowers herself to the mattress and sits before
me. Her face is directly in line with the elastic of my boxers. Is
what I think is about to happen about to happen? I feel a rush of
blood to my head—I'm surprised that there's any left for that
when it feels as if all my life force has been diverted downward.

With a coy smile, she eyes me through the fabric, and I can feel myself aching for her. She slides up and away on the mattress, and I follow as if I'm hooked on a line. Her scent, a meld of lotions and potions, intoxicates me. Desire is roaring through me, testing my control, but I must maintain it in case we are still playing the charade of testing out the mattress. Lying on her side in front of me, her body no more than a hand's breadth away from mine, she arches an eyebrow. "So? How does it feel? Never want to leave, right?"

I reach out a finger and trace the S-curve of her body, tugging at the fabric of her dress. "Not fair."

She trails the dome of my shoulder with her fingertips, her eyes on my lips. I feel her bare toes slide down my calves, flirting with the tops of my socks. "My bed. I can do whatever I want."

I grip her hip firmly, pulling her closer by a fraction. "You can do whatever you want to me."

"I want to kiss you again," she whispers, then bites her lip.

Our first kiss was a surprise. Our second, an order. But our third is all ours, by us and for us. No script, no photos, no record but the flavour we leave on each other's tongues. She relaxes into me as we close the gap between our bodies, and I welcome her with everything I have in response to everything she gives me. She slides her hand past the waistband of my boxers and wraps it around me, and I am free-falling, no parachute, no land in sight. "Where . . . where's all that supposed to go?" she says against my mouth.

My answer is to skim my hand up beneath her dress to cup her between her legs, churning her centre over the thin lacy cloth that separates us, sending a bolt of pleasure through her that makes her seize and hold me tight, as if she's falling through space with me. She gulps in all the air in the room.

"We're really doing this," she whispers, asking, telling, begging me all in the same breath.

25

MIZ

We're really doing this. Kal, who does everything so attentively, enters me with as much care as I would expect him to, as I have imagined him doing lately, as if he doesn't want to take even a second of this for granted. Holy mother of God. I never knew my body held the answers to the questions that have lived in his, that he is finally asking me, more and more earnestly, as he sinks in deeper. And I am answering him as completely, as fully as I can without splintering into nothingness. These questions and answers that have no words attached to them, and yet they make complete sense. I take him in with my body and give all of mine to him, not sure whether either of us will get out of this alive. He digs his fingers into me, firing up all my nerves.

"Have we done this before?" I manage to ask in bursts and gasps. He nestles his face into my neck, hiking my thigh higher up his side. No, of course not. I'm trying to remember every moment of this, but the more we roll into each other, the more we slip and slide with our heat, the more I feel a terrifying loss of control over my body, my voice, and my brain, giving over to a riptide of nothing but *yes yes yes to everything, whatever it is you're doing*.

"I'm making love to you," he groans in response.

Did he just say that out loud? Oh shit. Oh. My. God.

"Is that okay?"

"Yes you should you should . . ."

"Because I do, Miz. Love you. So much, *nefse*."

That's it. Hearing Kal call me his *soul*, and *knowing*—no, *feeling* at a cellular level how much he means it by how he holds me, as if he needs my permission for his every breath, for his soul, unhinges me. I shatter into a sweet black void. I don't know how many eons later, somewhere in that delicious darkness while he's still draped over me, I feel the reverberations of his voice.

"*Techawechi*," he says, teasing me.

I can feel his smile against my skin. He knows I find the expression—the way people toss it at you to invite you to talk, chitchat, shoot the shit, *be interesting*—so annoying. I smack his butt. *Talk?* I just sang a whole opera for you—wasn't that interesting enough? He lifts his head to look at me. We take each other in, staring in wonder, as if we can't believe the other has been here all along. He rolls me on top of him, closes his eyes and sighs, tucking his hands behind his head. I watch him as his breathing slows gradually, my chin propped on his chest.

"*Psst* . . ." I say, swiping my fingers along his hairline as if I'm waking a baby. He hums. I hold his nose. His heartbeat continues its steady rhythm under my chest. "Don't fall asleep on me."

"Not sleep. Only dreams."

"About?"

"Happiest day of my life."

"Actually, Kal, it's the evening," I say with a smile.

"I should have picked you up properly."

"Well, you started to, but then you had to try the mattress, and the rest is history."

"We should have left together, kissed some knees on our way out."

"Huh?"

"Our wedding day."

"Oh!" The wedding tradition, he means, the whole charade where the couple, when departing from the bride's house, first have to make as if they *must* hit the floor to kiss their parents and other close family elders' feet, before compromising for the knees only because the elders insist. "Who cares?" I bunch my fingernails over his kneecap and slide them open. He buckles but holds fast. "We can kiss our own knees just fine. Or each other's." I run my hands up the inside of his leg. "I actually have sensitive knees."

"Runners tend to."

"*Very* sensitive. They get so offended if you don't kiss them."

He licks his lips, looking down at my knees like a thirsty man at a stream. What I'm really hoping is he'll get sidetracked about 50 percent of the way there and decide to pay a visit to another very sensitive spot. "I got you," he says. He lifts my leg up gently and bends to kiss one knee; then he rolls me over so he can kiss the other. I shiver with the pleasure of it, my toes curling. He continues to kiss me up the inside of my thigh. I let my legs fall open like a well-loved notebook.

"When did you get so bendy?" Aimé asks me on Sunday, two weeks later, when she catches me folding my body in the sauna in my condo building, where we are broiling after a run. We have the whole hot box to ourselves. She is laid out on the top bench, happy to have lived to see another rest and recovery day after a gruelling ten-kilometre-total week. I am at the far end of the bottom bench, my feet stretched up against the wall, feeling the gentle burn on the tips of my toes.

Aimé had looked at me funny when she caught me stretching before we set out on our run too. Not too different from the look I've been giving myself on every reflective surface since that night, feeling almost too shy to meet my own eyes. *Who are you, lady?* The Miz Aimé knows is a walking contradiction who spends her days mobilizing and stretching people but doesn't do shit for herself. Well, things change. So much. Never in my life have I interrupted a guy before his job was done between my legs so that he would be on and in me when I tipped over. But with Kal, I had forced him to pause mid-swirl to pull him up to me. I already missed his heat, the weight of him pinning me down, the lemony sweat of him sating my tongue.

I sit up on the sauna bench and groan, belatedly putting one ankle over the opposite knee and leaning forward, as if it's the external rotation of my hip joint, and not the memory of Kal, that's got me vocalizing. "There's somebody new been stretching me out," I say.

Somebody new but also not new at all, I add to myself, grinning. Each time Kal and I get together, it gets less scary, more addictive. When he first started to go down on me though, doing a U-turn from my knees, my mind had gone into total panicked overdrive. *Oh my god, Kalkidan Legesse's mouth is about to be on my stuff (freshly showered, thank god), and there's not going to be any coming back from this, no more being only friends again!* Right, as if we hadn't decimated that point of no return earlier. But this felt like a whole other level of boundary breaking. And he took his time working his way there too, so I had plenty of opportunity to put on the brakes. Opportunity, yes. Motive, zero. I just prayed, *Please, God, let him be good at it.*

"Oooooooh," Aimé says, flipping onto her side, eagerly wiggling her fancy pedicure, another reward for her training, like her designer run outfits and overpriced shoes and specialty socks that have *L* and *R* on them. "Who? But wait, is Kal okay with it?"

"Hell yeah. Why wouldn't he be?"

"Sensitive as he is? He doesn't know, does he? Maybe it's better that he doesn't."

"Okay, slow down. He knows," I say. *Oh, he knows a lot.* For someone who's been (he claims) out of commission in the bedroom department for years. *Liar, liar, boxers on fire.* But I can't force out of him what he doesn't want to tell. And I'm not sure I want to know, either. I'm good to just send a telepathic *thanks, girl,* to whoever she is/they are out there. Even if it is Muna.

"You think he's seeing someone too?" Aimé says.

I don't know why she's so concerned about Kal when I'm the one who's bringing the tea. "He is," I say levelly, enjoying this way too much. I feel my voltage spiking again, remembering how Kal had flowed up to me once I managed to drag him away from my very happy place, eyelids hooded with renewed desire, mouth glistening, kissing me all the way up. How naked I felt holding the gaze of eyes that had really seen all of me now.

Aimé snaps her fingers in the general direction of my face. "Yoohoo, I'm waiting. Who is he? Give me the specs. And do you know anything about Kal's girl, or are you guys keeping your side action on a strictly need-to-know basis?"

Side action makes me grin ear to ear again. Which round was it? The third? The fourth? Because of course, by then, I had already told him my favourite position. My back to his front, his hands greedy on my breasts, his leg curved around my hip, his teeth grazing my neck.

Whoosah! I turn my focus back to Aimé.

"You could say that. *Who is he?* Hmm, where do I begin?" I pretend to contemplate the question. "So, he's this guy. He's good not just to me but to my people, even the ones he hasn't met. Like my mom. Without expecting a word of thanks or acknowledgement from her, he helped out so much to make her big trip back home smooth. Limo service to the airport, excess baggage allowance, on-the-spot upgraded seats—his family has so many more loyalty points accumulated between them than I will in my lifetime. He even helped me shop for all the gifts she asked me to buy, renting a car for the day. And when she left, he really showed up for me because I was miserable. He came to the airport, stayed out of the way and then spent the whole day with me. He's just so sweet. The way he loves his family, feeds all his roommates. And, get this, not only is he a quiet sleeper, he lets me have all the sheets! And he's got these cheekbones, oh my god. And he always, literally always, smells like lemony shoe polish. And looking at him, he doesn't look very sturdy, you know? But when he holds you, really holds you, he's just so fucking solid. And strong, Jesus! He's got surprising strength, let me tell ya."

I giggle, remembering the first time he tried to lift me and how that went. I sigh dreamily. "No one makes me feel as accepted as he does."

I know Aimé has put two and two together because she's teary-eyed and her hand is over her heart. "Is this individual," she says, her voice shaky, "by any chance known as Kiki to his family?"

"Aims!" That's information that no one in Canada knows except for me, and which I've sworn Aimé to total secrecy about. With the Drake song everywhere last summer, it had got really hard to keep my mouth shut about it. I was so tempted to even make it Kal's ringtone in my contacts.

I cover my face with my hands like monkey see no evil. "But . . . yeah, he is," I squeak.

Aimé's hands flutter in the air. "You two crossed over!"

I peer at her through my fingers. "Pearly gates, baby!" I squeal in excitement.

Her eyes go full-on puppy dog. "I'm so happy! This is so beautiful."

"Say what? Is it too hot in here?" I was expecting a stern *I warned you about this, what are you doing, this is your good friend, are you ready for the consequences?* All of the above. Basically, all the things I've been trying not to say to myself, not Disney levels of swooning.

"I've wanted this for you for so long."

"I don't know why. I mean, your girl has never been one to go unserviced for an extended period."

"Come on, you know what I mean. That you're finally in a serious relationship!"

"Whoa, Nelly!" I push my hands down. "Slow down."

"Look at you, *married* before me!"

"Time out, time out. We are *definitely* not 'married.' We're just—"

"But did you hear yourself just now? You gave me zero dirty details. Like, was his junk as advertised through those flimsy wraps and skirts and tights he used to march all up and through the stage in?" She hunched up her shoulders and flipped her palms. "I dunno."

I sway, twisting my body girlishly. "For the record." I lower my voice to a hush. "Yes."

"Eee!" Aimé shrieks, bopping in place. "Win *and* win!"

"I feel weird gossiping about his junk," I say, chewing my thumbnail. I can feel him in my mouth, the taste of him, for hours afterward, and the heat and thickness of him in my hand, how pantingly weak he becomes when I take my time teasing him, circling and flicking him until he quivers to be inside me again.

"Of course, you do. This is Kal, not just some dude. It's special. Maybe this is how the real thing was meant to happen for you."

"Again, hold your horses. Look into my eyeballs. We. Are. Just . . ." I had anticipated she'd interrupt, but she leaves me hanging with a daring look in her eyes. "Us. With a bit extra." I know it's not nothing. It's precisely because it could never be nothing with Kal that I've not messed with Kal in all this time. Not that we ever had a window of opportunity early on in our friendship, since he was already hardcore taken.

Aimé very obviously mouths the word *boyfriend*. "Mmm," I say, preferring *lover*. But I concede. "Boyfriend-in-progress."

"Ohkaay," she singsongs. "Are you guys on the same page about that?"

"Absolutely." Then of course, I zip through my mental storage for any tendencies Kal might have shown that he might be under the wrong impression. Red flags. Fine, he called me *nefse*, his soul, but so what? That's practically clichéd. *While inside me though?* Okay, that was a wtf. *And that daydream afterward, reimagining our wedding?* Cringe. But that was just him redirecting the scene as if it were a play. Perfectly natural thing for him to do.

Still, Aimé's words have put me on hyperalert.

26

KAL

"Is there anything I should or shouldn't do?" I pause at the entrance of Miz's clinic, one gloved hand on the door, the other balancing a party platter of sushi, our potluck offering for her work Christmas party. I want to get this, our first social engagement as a couple, right.

Miz shuffles closer to me in her moonboots, a bottle of wine cradled in her giant goalie-like mittens. *My childhood trauma is winter* is her retort whenever I tease her about how vigilant she is with staying warm. She prefaces her answer with a moist, minty kiss to my lips. "Just go easy on the eggnog. I'm gonna need you functional later," she says with a smirk, eyes dancing like the tiny Christmas lights that frame the window. I wish it was later now.

"Got it." I pull the door open and usher her in ahead of me. She sheds her mitts and reaches for my hand behind her. We interlock our fingers, and a flash of joy, hot as a straight shot of liquor, spreads through my body. We take off our coats and add them to the pile on the reception sofa.

"Well, *bon soir*," Omar says, coming up to us and laughing approvingly at our obligatory reindeer headbands and Christmas sweaters—*Merry Christmas Ya Filthy Animal* and *Black Santas Matter*. Our hands find their way to each other again. Omar takes in our silent announcement with a triumphant smile. "Well, well! I like it," he says. "I do like it. *Mashallah!*" He holds out his hand to the side just as Eve comes up behind him. "Put it here. Fifty bucks."

"You guys placed bets on us?" Miz says incredulously, as we hug all around. Between the clinic staff and their guests, about two dozen people, and the added food table, the space is almost at capacity.

"Just fifty?" I say.

"It started out much higher," Eve says. "You guys took so long we almost gave up."

"Wait, what exactly did you bet on?" Miz says as we squeeze our way through the crowd, murmuring quick hellos.

"Whether you two would hook up. What else?" they say between them.

As we find space for our sushi tray on the food table, Miz gives me a private look that says *Good, no one suspects anything.* Even though we have become intimate, it remains important to her that we maintain our privacy about being married. *You never know who has it in for you, just for spite*, she said. So I'm respecting that, reminding myself it's for my own good, even though I'd love to shout it from the rooftops. One thing at a time. Like, perhaps, hearing *I love you* back. Maybe she's thinking that I only said it that first night we slept together in the heat of the moment. The solution to that, of course, is to say plainly what's going on in my heart, as Abay had advised me to. But what am I afraid of? We're together now, we're a couple. More and more of my belongings have ended up at her place. Silvio has been joking about subletting my room. I haven't seen any signs from her that she minds, not even when my bike got permanent parking on her balcony for the winter, another broken rule Everest has overlooked. He too seems very happy to have me around more, although he doesn't ask or even insinuate anything, which I appreciate. Yes, everything looks and feels like love now, but I crave hearing those three words from her.

"So, what's your situation with the papers?" Omar asks me while we're mixing our drinks in the kitchen. Seeing my surprise, he adds, "Oh please, we talk about everything here. How do you not know that after all this time?"

I laugh. That's very true. I take a big gulp of my rum and ginger ale. "I'm all sorted out. Thanks for asking."

"You found a sponsor?" Omar asks. I nod. "Oh good!" I keep nodding and grinning, bursting to tell him more but literally biting my tongue to stop myself.

So much for that. At my overnodding, Omar's face begins to stretch with a gleeful realization. "I see," he says, pointedly looking over at Miz, who is talking to a couple of co-op students down the hall.

I force myself to focus on my plate of assorted mini quiches, silently begging God to help me stop nodding.

"A kind of . . . saviour angel came along." My traitorous eyes wander over to Miz, like a wanderer seeking the North Star.

"This is marvellous!" Omar exclaims. I shush him. He clinks glasses with me. "I know. I know." He zips his mouth and turns us both to face the bar table, our backs to the room. "So that's why she's been so tra-la-la since last summer."

"Tra-la-la?" Since last summer? My interest is piqued.

Omar waves his hand. "Like Cinderella at the ball. And those songs," he says, dropping his palm dramatically on his forehead. "I can't tell you how many breaks I had to sit through listening to her rhapsodize about the power of love like I don't have Celine, thank you very much."

I perk up. *My* songs? The "old people songs" she's been poking fun at all this time? Just to be absolutely certain, I pull up my wedding-anniversary playlist, now complete, on my phone. "You mean these?"

Omar watches as I scroll through the covers, frowning and shaking his head, my spirit sinking. Then suddenly he says, "That one! I'll never forget that face. Reminds me of Billie Holiday." It's the cover of Asni's *Éthiopiques: The Lady with the Krar* album. I smile knowingly to myself, as I piece together why Miz never responded to that link to "Ende Iyerusalem" with one of her witty takes. One of these old people songs finally got through. And from as far back as this past August. Everything comes into sharper focus.

"Wow, your wife's slick," Omar is saying. Heat spreads up my spine at hearing the word, a surge of pride that makes me stand up straighter. *I am a married man.* "When I suggested the idea of marriage to her, she swore up and down to me that you would never do that and that she would be the last person to pair up with you, even if you were to. Talk about acting, eh?! Well"—he taps my drink with his again—"I wish you both the best luck." I'm not sure whether he means for our new relationship status or our case, but I'll take either. "It's about time. And don't worry, your secret is safe with me."

"Thank you," I say. "And I appreciate your discretion."

"What are you two looking at?" Miz says, suddenly behind us. I jump a little and then hug her close, mostly as a distraction, though I'm also moved by an intense happiness at what Omar has just told me.

"Oh, talking holiday plans," Omar says, thinking fast, and raves about his planned ski vacation to Mont Tremblant. I mention that we're going to Ethiopia together. "Oh. I didn't know it's together you're going. My. So this new development between you two is serious, eh?" he says, overplaying his innocence in such a way that he reminds me of my harrowing self-tapes for on-camera acting class.

I stiffen, fearing that Miz will see through his act. "It's just a coincidence," Miz says, not batting an eye. "We have different reasons for needing to be there around the same time." This, unfortunately, is true. She expects to spend the majority of her time with her parents. As is only right, especially considering her mother has not been home in decades. But I am already dreading our impending apartness for the better part of two weeks.

"Is now a good time for you two to be travelling there though?" Omar says, and again, my body goes rigid. "With the political situation," he adds, covering a smile with a sip.

"Things have never been better, in fact," I say, relaxing and interlocking my hand with Miz's. "Right, nefse?"

She blushes, as she does every time I call her this. "Better than ever, yene keremela."

I almost hit the ceiling. I am her candy, a lifetime supply of it.

Later that night, as we're spent and intertwined in bed, whispering in the dark as has become our habit before falling asleep, I ask, as casually as I can muster, "You know what you never told me?"

"Mm?"

That you love me. "What you thought of the last song I sent you."

"Which one was that?"

Oh, Miz. "The Asni. 'Ende Iyerusalem'?"

She hedges. *Just tell me, nefse,* I beg her silently. "Honestly? The *krar* is a bit much. She plucks at those strings like they owe her money, but I loved her voice, so I did a bit of digging around online and figured out the song is about her man that she never gets to see. Or she can see him only once a *year*, like a . . . pilgrimage? It's like I sensed that that could be me someday. It just made me so . . . sad."

I can barely stop myself from groaning in frustration. Stopping so short of telling me she loves me. Why can't she say it, that she started to fall in love with me then? In retrospect, was that not what I was doing, sending her all those songs? Though I was as oblivious then as she is now. It's taking her longer to catch up, I suppose.

Wanting to give Miz all the time she needs, I allow my personal deadline of New Year's Eve to come and go without making any grand declaration. But I do pick up on additional signs that my instincts are right that night. We spend it on a double date with James and Aimé, where Miz is a good sport about their constant teasing about our marriage. It's quite a change from the old Miz, who would have immediately turned hostile.

But I decide to help things along the night before we fly to Ethiopia. Outside of the apartment, having just returned with my packed suitcase in tow, I slide my wedding ring back on. Neither of us has worn ours since the ceremony, but I can use the guise of appeasing any suspicions from border security, if she says anything. With a deep breath, I walk in and announce that I'm back.

"Long time no see!" Aimé says, waving from the couch, though it's only five days into the new year. "We almost ate without you." I get a kiss from Miz while she opens the takeout boxes. "You'd have been eating alone. My wife and I always eat together," I say. "Off the same plate, like the OGs do. Right, nefse?"

"Mm? Yeah," Miz coos. I catch her eyeing my ring, but she shows no reaction. As we eat, Aimé does most of the talking about how much she wishes she could accompany us so she could train at that altitude, like the pros do, how she's trying to walk less and run more, how she'll miss training with Miz. But she's borrowing our apartment key so that she can continue to have access to the kitted gym and sauna while we are gone. As a plus, she'll also keep an eye on our mailbox for my Open Work Permit, which will probably arrive while we are still in Ethiopia.

"First she tells me to go slow. Now she's telling me I have to haul ass." She switches gears to complaining about her coach.

Miz, picking at her noodles, takes her time responding. "Well, the distances are getting longer, so unless you want to be out for six hours on race day . . ." she says absently.

"Is something wrong, Miz?" I ask, rubbing her back gently.

"Oh, me? Nothing," she says, nibbling at her food.

"She gets like this every time right before she flies home," Aimé says. "Ethiopia PTSD. From all that drama the first time she went back."

Miz smiles faintly. "It's true. I'm better once I'm there."

"And this time, you're not alone," I say, taking her hand. She runs her thumb along my knuckles appreciatively, again not showing any reaction when she grazes over my wedding ring. Post dinner, after Aimé has left and I've checked us in to our flights online, I crack. While Miz is laying out her suitcases to begin packing, I hear myself asking, "Are you going to wear yours?" I lift my left hand.

"I don't like it," she says bluntly.

"Oh." I look at my ring. It was just a prop then and still looks like it. So plain, I admit. I remember the intricacy of her mom's ring, which she had shown me so long ago. "I guess we didn't put any real thought into it at the time, huh?"

"Nope." She tosses a pair of sandals into her suitcase.

"Maybe carry it, just in case? Especially when we come back, it might be good to wear it."

She nods curtly. "Rings are not proof of anything, but sure."

An agreement, followed by a dismissal. I don't know what to make of it, so I let it go for now. Perhaps by the time we return, we'll have chosen better ones that really symbolize our marriage. There's nothing to be done about it now, so I focus on helping Miz pack. I fold and roll clothes as instructed and step on and off a scale with her suitcase endless times so that she can calculate the weight. There are a lot of moving things between bags and reweighing, since she's also bringing the extra stuff her mom couldn't take, plus her old running shoes for donation.

During a brief respite from my mule duties, recovering on the couch, I check my email to see whether our boarding passes have turned up yet. Instead, the message at the top of my inbox makes me sit bolt upright.

"What?" Miz says, sitting cross-legged on the rug in front of me, a pile of running socks in front of her that she is stuffing into every available cranny of her full suitcase.

"There is an update on our file."

"There is?" She crawls over to me. We log on to the portal. An interview notification. "Wow, that was fast. Either they really like us, or they really don't like us," Miz says.

"I like us," I say, hoping for the best, though I fear it is the latter, considering that we got married and submitted the application so close to my work permit expiry date.

She gives me a kiss and regards me with the first real smile I've seen her crack all night. "I like *us* too." Relief floods me.

"It's just a formality," I say, trying to reassure her as much as myself. But I remember reading in my research that fewer than 10 percent of sponsorship applicants get called in for an interview. "Anyway, we have even more proof of our relationship now," I say, to appease myself further. "Every memento of our life we've been collecting since Thanksgiving." All of it is organized into a red four-inch three-ring binder. *And this time, it's all real.*

"Exactly," she says. "We're so ready. We were born ready," she boasts. I pull her to me, and soon everything gets forgotten— the socks, the rings, the notification. And above all, we have each other. How could any officer, trained to discern true love from false, doubt us?

27

MIZ

I always thought that the day Kal and I finally managed to fly to Ethiopia together would be a happy one, but I haven't been able to pop this bubble of unease that has been growing inside me ever since I clocked his wedding ring and he dropped the word *wife* last night. Talk about a double damn. I could barely get any food down after he said that. My mind was spinning, frantically shuffling through my memory for missed warning signs of Kal's change in behaviour.

It wasn't until we got that email about a new notification from immigration that I realized I'd missed two huge red flags from when we were choosing a username and password for our joint Gmail account. Kal had wanted to use the endearment *hodiyeee* as our username. Never understood what was so endearing about calling someone *my stomach*, so I hadn't thought much about it. And the password he wanted was *husband&wife1river~* based on the Ethiopian proverb "Husband and wife are drawn from the same river." To which I'd rolled my eyes and reminded him to relax; the government wouldn't be inspecting our passwords or usernames.

Aimé, having also seen the ring and knowing I was quietly freaking out, split early, taking her second helpings to go so that Kal and I could talk.

"How'd he take it?" she asks me on the phone after Kal has gone to bed. I'm still up, doing the obligatory straightening of my hair before the flight so I will get off the plane looking semi-presentable after thirteen hours in the air.

"I literally said, 'I don't like it.'"

"Ouch. And?"

"He heard something completely different." As dreamers do. "How much more obvious could I have been?" I shrug. "I really don't want to have to sit Kal down and spell out my terms and conditions," I moan softly, narrowly avoiding singeing my ear. "He's supposed to know me. The whole reason we did this signing is because it's *me*—I'm not trying to be anybody's *W*."

"Okay, *you* know you're not really married to Kal," Aimé reassures me, not realizing how she is repeating verbatim what I told myself in the mirror the morning of September 30th. "You just have to *gently* ease him back into that reality."

The question is *when*. We toss ideas back and forth. Tonight? No way. He is already conked out. Plus, the interview notification seemed to be enough of a downer for one night. Maybe during our flight? God, no. Not something to broach when we are going to be sealed in with each other and a bunch of other strangers for fourteen hours. But after our flight, we will go our separate ways, and I'll have space to organize my thoughts and collect myself. So Aimé and I agree, it will have to be sometime while we are in Addis. But before his parents' party. That way, he will have something to look forward to if he takes it badly. By the time we fly back, he'll have got over it.

Plan formed, I feel much better. Just a little misunderstanding that will get cleared up in a few days' time. As I sneak into bed, I say a little prayer that, in the meantime, there won't be any more of Kal using the word *wife* in a sentence around me.

He starts up again at the crack of dawn.

"My wife and I are going back home together for the first time," Kal says to the Uber driver. *Goddammit.* We haven't even finished buckling in. And why must Kal look so happy on top of that? And why must it make me happy to see him so happy?

Sticking to my resolution to save the talk for Addis, I put my game face on for the rest of the morning as Kal drops our newly-wed status every chance he gets—at check-in, security, even Starbucks. On the plus side, we get lots of special treatment. We get to jump the line and check in at the first-class counter. And though we don't get upgraded to first class because it's two days before Gena and the whole flight is full, we do get a pass to the Plaza Premium Lounge. From that, it is a hard comedown to economy seats, but Kal's brimming excitement almost makes up for it.

"You sure you've been on a plane before?" I ask him, slipping an eye mask on my forehead after the first meal service.

He arranges the green airline blanket evenly over me. "Everything is different with you. Everything is brand new."

My heart melts a little, but I deflect. "You're telling me! Look at all this swag," I say, going through the first-class amenity kits a flight attendant brought us after Kal looped her in on our relationship status. By now, I am basically numb to the madness, not to mention a total ho for all the blessings and abundance that flow our way, on the down-low, for the rest of the flight: extra desserts, extra blankets, the whole entire can of whatever we feel like drinking, extra everything.

Our sunrise approach and landing into Addis Ababa bathes the landscape below in a romantic sepia glow. At first, it is a patchwork quilt of dark and light greens, with bursts of light where the tin roofs of the small towns surrounding the capital reflect the sun's rays. Slowly, that gives way to thicker and thicker stretches of medium- and high-rises and warehouses separated by major roadways, the low-lying mountains all around. Then as we touch ground, it all disappears, leaving just the blue-gold sky, the dark and, far off, the low ring of mountains, the sight of which always makes me teary.

"I'm fine. Happens every time," I tell Kal, dabbing my eyes and sniffling. "The mountains."

He nods and puts his arm around me. We stay like that even after the seat belt sign has been turned on, the tinny Ethio jazz has resumed over the speakers, and everyone has sprung up as if there aren't still hours of ordeals to get through. Like the chaotic lineup at passport control, another part of these journeys that I used to dread as much as the interminable flight. But today, it is sweetened by Kal acting as my personal support pole. Talk about someone having your back. Kal is all smiles as I lean heavily on him while talking on the phone with Dad, nudging my carry-on with my Crocs every time the queue moves.

"He's working late, so Abera's getting me," I tell Kal after hanging up. Just as well. Last thing I need is Kal blabbing about me being his wife in front of my dad too. Dad has always liked Kal—it's hard to keep any secret in that compound, so he'd found out about my new friend soon enough that first summer—and since my first trip, he's kind of entrusted Kal with my care in the city, like a bodyguard. But Dad might feel different if he were to learn of more recent developments. Different how, I'm not in the mood to find out.

"I'll miss you," Kal says, wrapping me in his arms.

I reflexively lean in and rest my cheek on his shoulder. "Me too." I inhale deeply, taking in that stale, spice-and-detergent-inflected aroma of the arrivals terminal. Once we are on the other side, it will be goodbye until his parents' party. And as much as I am looking forward to being away from "my wife" this and "my beloved" that, I will miss him.

"You're still coming on Saturday, right?" he murmurs into my hair.

"Duh, of course." I pull back and smile as he puffs up happily. I look around at the masses of Canadians who funnelled through Toronto for the only nonstop flight to Addis Ababa from Canada, on the Eve of Ethiopian Christmas no less. "I can't believe Mom just passed through here. After all these years, all my nagging her to return, I never thought we'd arrive separately. Instead, here I am, with you."

"And how am I doing so far?"

I burrow deeper into him, wanting to kiss him, but too self-conscious for PDA here. "You're good. Could use more padding. But I'm going to sleep on you like a baby on the flight back. Everybody will be feeding the prodigal son. You'll be nice and plump for me."

One of the airport staff unexpectedly opens up another lane, causing our line to speed forward. "Nooo," I whine. "I'm not ready to part yet!"

"Why don't you come over for a little bit?" Kal says.

"Hah, there's no such thing as 'a little bit' with you Legesses. I'll be there until morning. Besides, I'm way too stale, unlike you. Who you trying to impress?" I say. I'd never known a person to spend so much time freshening up in the bathroom before landing. But it shows. Kal looks his usual polished self, cologne and everything.

He suddenly looks serious. "By the way, Abay knows."

"Knows what."

"The same thing Eske knows."

"That we're—what?! How?" I pull away to look at him. When he explains, I can't say I'm too surprised. "But he doesn't know that we're . . ."

"What?"

"You know, seeing each other . . . naked?" I feel my face heat, even though what I've said is accurate.

Kal gives me a funny look and shakes his head. "No, of course not. Only that you signed for me."

"Okay," I say, nodding slowly. "I mean, it's not like anyone acts like they do the humpty-hump around here anyway," I say, trying to put myself at ease. "Thanks for the heads-up." Best case scenario, the info hasn't spread past his sister and father. Most likely scenario, however . . . Ah, I don't want to think about it.

At arrivals, there's a crowd waiting for Kal's homecoming, as if he is a political exile, or long-lost family member or, come to think of it, a newlywed. Their balloons and flowers are impossible to miss even in the pandemonium that is the arrivals hall at this peak travel time. "Holy!" I say, shuffling back. "Did you know they would all turn up?"

"Not at all," he says, grinning from ear to ear, his eyes watering. His dad is there, of course, and Eske, plus his three brothers and their spouses. A bunch of aunts, uncles and cousins. Even Bini, his next-door neighbour best friend since childhood, who's never let me forget I ate a burger and fries that was meant for him a hundred years ago.

I'm thankful that I am enough of a familiar face that my presence isn't that unusual. But as we wade through the hugs, kisses, waterworks and photo moments, I'm on alert for signs that I am being welcomed differently. You know, like . . . Kal's wife. But there are no flowers specifically for me or random showers of blessings and applause. Just regular old hugs and cheek kisses.

We herd ourselves outside the terminal, into the mercifully crisp early morning air with just that hint of woodsmoke, and make our way down the winding ramp to the parking lot where private cars, taxis and airport shuttles jostle for space right along with arriving and awaiting passengers, a snarl of all trying to leave at once. I try to sneak off to find Abera. But Eske intercepts me. "Mizu? Where you're going?" she calls out, her overloaded key chain chiming as she waves it at me. As usual, she's impeccably dressed in slacks, heels and a silky blouse with a tie neck in a dramatic, colourful bow.

I continue shuffling away as if I haven't just been found out. "To find Abera. He's parked—"

"The driver?!" she screeches, as if I'm about to go by horse and buggy. "Nobody is here for you?!" She stands with a hand on her hip, the other cupping her cheek in dismay.

"Abera is," I repeat firmly, annoyance tensing my words. I know that, to a family like theirs, my situation must seem like borderline emotional abandonment. But Abera has been with my dad for so long. Eske knows that and knows him. I cringe at how many nights the poor man slept in the car waiting for us on many a night when we were selfish club-hopping teenagers.

"What is this fuss? You are family now," Eske says, cutting through my resolution. "A feast is waiting. Let's go."

Helpless, I look at Kal, who just nods emphatically, backing her up. Of course he would.

"No, no, I can't," I say. "My dad is waiting for me . . ." I lie weakly. But the idea of a full Legesse meal courtesy of Zebiba is too enticing. "Okay, let me just find Abera and give him my luggage."

Finding Abera in the gridlocked parking lot is nearly impossible, even with Kal and especially with my suitcase along for the ride. When we finally spot him, it's a true reunion, even between Abera and Kal, who haven't seen each other in years.

"Do you mind just taking these to the apartment?" I ask Abera. "I'm sorry. If I had known I was going to Kal's house, I would have told my dad not to send you."

"No problem at all!" Abera says, with a giant smile. "Why be alone if you don't have to?"

I stare at Abera, my mouth falling slightly open with the unexpectedly astonishing realization that he's absolutely right. *Why* be alone? What am I trying so hard to prove, or prevent? I loosen my grip on the handle of my suitcase. I look at Kal, smiling as if he's read my mind, and I can't help but smile back. He wiggles his eyebrows. I feel Abera pulling my suitcase away.

"Give it here."

We bid Abera goodbye and begin walking back to the group, when a car horn blares right next to me. "Ah!" I yelp. "What's your problem?" I snap in the general vicinity of the noise. I sidle up to Kal. "You better get me out of here before I hurt somebody."

Baggage-free, Kal and I trot happily through the path that he parts for us through the melee, my heart stirring with almost as much anticipation as my stomach.

28

KAL

"We're here, *wudé*!" Abay announces, taking off his golf cap when we enter the living room, which takes up almost the entirety of the first floor of our three-storey Mediterranean-style villa. For a breath, I think Emay will come sweeping down the steps, adjusting her shawl, her arms open in welcome. I even look up to the top of the grand, winding staircase, expecting to see her stockinged feet in her slippers.

Miz, straggling by herself at the engraved double wooden doors, looks jarred and a little bit frightened. "Who is he calling *beloved*?" she says to me, real low.

"It's okay, still Emay," I whisper to her. I've warned her about my father talking to, and about, my mother as if she is still present in body. But this is Miz's first time around Abay since my mother's death, so it will take her time to acclimatize. Even I have moments where I feel like a stranger to my father's mental space.

"Just say hi," I say softly, lowering my lips to Miz's ear and guiding her in.

She widens her eyes at me like *Seriously?* I shrug apologetically. "To . . . ?" she hisses.

I point out the large, framed studio portrait of my parents. Miz puts on a brave smile as she comes along. "Hi!" she says to the picture cheerfully but not before giving me a painfully sweet pinch on my arm. But Abay looks pleased, and that's what matters most.

From then on, it's normal goings. Over the next half hour, everyone from the airport slowly trickles into our living room, and we feast, buffet style, on the spread of fasting foods that Zebiba, our long-time cook, has put together. Though Muslim herself, she refuses to prepare anything with dairy or meats during the Christian fasting season, so the table is filled with standard veggie platter fare, all the greens, beans, beets and seeds—gomen, misir, shiro, kik, keysir and duba wot, shimbira asa and her famous souf—plus the obligatory cheeseless minipizzas. Afternoon creeps on through rounds of coffee, desserts, drinks, videos, photos and stories of family occasions, holidays and vacations that I've missed.

By then, it's an open secret that Miz has signed for me, so I pass around my phone to show off the photos of our ceremony. They find our mismatched wedding party and casual lunch at an Italian restaurant highly entertaining for how tiny our party is. Only my father looks pensive as he swipes slowly through the album, and I study him, wondering whether he's more disappointed than he has led me to believe at my sudden wedding without anyone there to represent my family. I keep a subtle eye on him as the conversation turns to the wedding-anniversary party on Saturday. He has a faraway look on his face, so I know he's off in his mind somewhere. Talking to Emay, remembering their own days of elopement, perhaps?

"*Wudé* and I have discussed it," he begins suddenly, his tone serious. Everyone quiets and turns to him. "In our time, because of circumstance, we were not blessed to have a wedding celebration with our family, relatives and friends. On Saturday, we will, at long last, have that. But my Kalkidan and his bride, Mizan, also because of circumstance, were not blessed to have a proper wedding. Should the elders have all the celebration and enjoyment? No."

He turns to Miz and me. "*Wudé* and I have agreed on it. On Saturday, we will share our celebration and enjoyment day with our son and his bride. You two will make us happy by standing alongside us on that day." He beams at us.

The silence is absolute, so much so that I can hear the ticking of the grandfather clock at the end of the long hallway. My heart swells. *Yes.* I glance at Miz, but her expression, directed at Abay, gives nothing away. She slowly swallows the bite of a cookie she had been eating, and I nervously twist my wedding band around my finger, waiting for her to say *something*. After a few moments, she clears her throat, taps her chest lightly, and takes a sip of her soft drink. Then she glances back at me. Her eyes bright, too bright, almost manic.

I haven't spoken to Abay about Miz and me since that phone call, so I know he is acting purely on the strength of his conviction that there's more between us than just paperwork, purely on faith that we are together now. And if we're not, this is him nudging—shoving, rather—us along. He's not suggesting this as a good occasion to fortify our case, but our marriage.

I hold my breath, waiting for Miz to decline, to accept. And whichever it is, I will follow. But it's as if she's on pause now, alongside the rest of the room, just staring at me. I search her eyes, trying to read into her expression, but all I sense is that I must take the lead, it seems. We are in my home, and this is my father. "Thank you, Abay—"

He claps once, with finality. "Good! That makes us very happy. It is a double grace."

Cheers and laughter sound from all around us at this unexpected turn of events. "But," Miz says in a small, tentative voice once the excitement has subsided some. "I wouldn't have anyone present from my side. It's too late to invite people. Wouldn't that look strange?" I'm not sure whether this is her polite way of declining or a true concern of hers.

"Our family is your family too now," Abay says. "Only a few generations ago, on her wedding day, a bride was whisked away by her groom to his home or town for the nuptials. She would not see any of her family again until they hosted the reciprocal dinner one week later!"

"What few generations?" my uncle adds. "The *mels* is still held the same way in the rural areas."

"So you see, you will be very traditional, in fact!" one of my brothers says to me.

"A new trend!" Eske joins in. "Combined weddings, from the two ends of married life."

A chicken-and-egg-like debate enssues about trend and tradition as my family discusses the old marriage customs. On a normal day, Miz would have a word or two to say about them—eighty-day marriage contracts, battlefield concubines, bride-napping (especially that!)—but she only nibbles and sips, her face wooden except for the occasional smile she offers.

"Are you okay?" I ask her under my breath.

"Hmm?" She pops another cookie into her mouth and smiles at me sweetly.

"You know, in the old country, a wife feeds the husband more than herself," Bini says.

She cuts him a withering look. "Bite me, Bini."

"I like you!" Bini exclaims, tipsy enough to overlook that he's known her for years. "I like her!"

Eske intervenes before Miz responds. "Miz! I'm going to steal you away for a few moments. Come." She stands and beckons Miz to follow her. "We're talking wedding-related matters," she informs me.

I laugh lightly, my eyes on Miz, who doesn't put up a fuss. "Don't be gone too long," I say, watching as they disappear up the spiralling stairs. I try to fall into the other conversations around me, but as the minutes tick by, Miz's empty seat next to me feels more and more hollow, and my mood sinks. Knowing Miz will soon be leaving me for even longer, to be with her dad, I feel restless, desperate for more time, as I used to as a kid when, after a whole day of playing with my cousins, I would beg Emay to let them sleep over. Miz and I haven't spent more than a day apart in weeks, and I'm dreading the upcoming days of endless social calls and wedding-related errands without her by my side.

At last, they return, and without sitting down, Miz quietly asks me whether I can drop her off. She would rather not bother Abera on Christmas Eve, when he is likely at overnight mass. Thankful for this chance for one last chunk of alone time, I don't even wait for her to finish asking.

"Finally, right?" I say, braking to wave thanks to Dereje, who closes the gate after us. Miz is quiet in the passenger seat. I ease us off the uneven neighbourhood road and onto Bole Road. It has rained since we arrived, so the asphalt glistens like freshly mopped linoleum, and the greens, yellows and burgundies of flowers planted on the grass of the traffic islands and in raised planters really pop. The sun is still hanging on but not for long. Once I am settled into second gear, Miz grabs my forearm and squeezes it very hard, which despite my jet-lag exhaustion, gives me a rush of excitement. As I drive, commenting on what's new and not new in our side of the city—the reflective glass of the shiny new hotels and retail complexes teeming with neon signage dwarfing the aging, architecturally more unique decades-old shops and apartment buildings—relishing this first time of us taking it in together after such a long time, she doesn't say much in return. But she maintains her iron grip on me, staring at my profile with an intense, expectant look in her eyes. "What's the matter, Miz? You look like you're about to step on a glass floor," I say. She has that same tight-lipped grin plastered on her face as she did in our CN Tower photo.

She nods, then releases me abruptly and looks straight ahead. "I feel . . . weird."

"I'm not surprised. That was a lot, I know. But everything will work out, you'll see." I remember how I felt on our wedding day, flustered and overwhelmed. I can imagine that the sudden prospect of having a big wedding has put her on edge.

She hums, a faraway look in her eyes, tracking the squat palm trees as they whiz by. Even the giant billboards advertising everything from contraceptives to mobile banking garner no comment from her.

"Maybe your parents can both come on Saturday?"

She tilts her head back on the headrest, closes her eyes and lets out a long sigh. "I don't know, Kal."

"One of these days, you'll have to talk to them about us," I say gently.

I wait for there to be more, but she leaves me hanging, and soon, dozes off, leaving me with nothing but my thoughts for the rest of the ride. After thirty minutes, I roll up to the curb outside her father's apartment within a gated compound of low-rises and bungalows separated by green spaces, playgrounds and parking lots. Miz wakes up and leans out of the car to peer up at the unit's windows, visible just above a bed of hibiscus shrubs and satellite dishes.

"All clear?" I ask, though her dad's empty parking spot shows that to be the case.

"Mm-hmm," she says, stretching. I reach for her; she curls into me, and we kiss—soft, gentle, but also filled with desire. The moment is simplicity itself. Everything is all right.

"Uh-uh," she says, breaking away and laughing at the hunger in my eyes as I do a quick check in the rear-view and side mirrors, confirming we have no witnesses nearby other than the stray dogs. "Don't even think about it," she says.

I groan. "Should I come up?" I ask hopefully. "Make sure you get in safe?"

"I'll wave to you from the balcony, Romeo," she says. Seeing my face, she rubs my arm. "Honestly, I'm about to collapse."

I try to hide my crushing disappointment and make one last-ditch effort. "So am I, but we could collapse together for a bit," I say, knowing how ridiculous that idea is, when her dad could come home any moment. Him finding us together in her bedroom is not how I want to disclose my new role in his daughter's life. Miz shakes her head with a laugh, and I let mine drop to her chest.

"This is goodbye then?" She curls her hand around my head and kisses it. I want to fall asleep right here.

My phone pings. "It sounds like you're needed," she says, pulling away. "Folks blowing up your phone."

No denying that. From the moment I got on Ethiotel this morning, my phone has been dinging and shimmying and shaking. People are eager to see me, probably expecting a night out. But the only person I want to spend the night with is, at this very moment, unbuckling her seat belt.

"Will I see you again before Saturday?" I ask hopefully, straightening in my seat.

"Of course, goof," she says. She gives me one last too-short kiss; she opens the door and steps out. "Sleep tight . . . Kiki."

I can't help feeling uneasy as she winks and vanishes. I wait for what feels like forever for her to appear at the balcony. It isn't until I honk that she comes out and waves me off. Probably jet lag, I tell myself, and drive away.

29

MIZ

Backpack slung over my shoulder like a teenager, I trudge up the exterior staircase and let myself into Dad's apartment with the spare key he sent with Abera. I step into the darkened, spacious living room, which flows into the dining room, where on the table, Dad has left me a small stack of musky-smelling *birr*—pocket money until I exchange my dollars—and my local SIM card. My luggage awaits outside the guest bedroom door, which is across the hall from Dad's bedroom, our respective bathrooms between. I sit at the dining table, switching out my SIM card, my mind playing over the afternoon and the big, noisy dinner at the Legesse compound. It's not until I hear a honk outside the balcony doors that open onto the dining room that I remember Kal's waiting to see I got in safe.

"Oh shit," I say, and hurriedly go out onto the balcony and weakly wave at him. I stand there for a while, watching the last of Kal's headlights as he leaves the compound, feeling like my heart is being towed after it. I'm surprised and realize that I *miss* him, even after being apart for only a few minutes. I already regret not spending more time alone in the car or up here while we had the chance. But this afternoon's bombshell was a lot.

I call Kal's local number but then hang up quickly, remembering he's driving. I quickly tap out a text to him.

Me: 'Night!

When Kal's dad started making his speech and I realized where he was going with it, I wished so hard that my name was not Mizan and he was talking about someone else. But *nope*, all eyeballs were on me. On principle, I did think the idea was brilliant and insanely romantic—but for a *real* couple, not Kal and me! For us, it felt plain delusional. But the best my flailing brain could come up with was that sad excuse about my "people." The way everyone justified the absence of my friends and family, it was as if they were just desperate to bring some normalcy to the event; you know, an *actual* bride in attendance, not just a spiritual one that one family member regularly talks to. They were ready to grab at any rationalization to make that happen. After that, there was no way I was going to decline and watch my words break the heart of every Legesse in front of me, so instead, I sat smiling and nodding, having my little internal freakout while they got all hypothetical about traditions or whatever. And there was Kal, eating up every word. Ugh, why did I have to be such a chickenshit and put off clarifying our relationship, even as the flags got redder and redder? Serves me right to now be stuck with one mother of a special treatment.

I realize that night has finally fallen, and I look up at the sky to greet the dome of stars, my million brilliant friends that always wait right where I've left them. I take in the perpetually semi-constructed villas on the other side of the compound wall, the birds flitting around the lemon and avocado trees behind the bougainvillea-bordered fences of the bungalows across from our low-rise. I check my phone to see whether Kal has texted back, but nothing yet. Frowning, I open up our texts again and realize that he probably doesn't know it's me.

Me: This is me, btw . . . Me, Mizan.

Seconds later:

Kal: Who? Only know a Mizu.

I grin and my stomach flips. It's as if I'm texting with my crush. I pluck at the clotheslines jutting out from the edge of the balcony like a guitar, thinking of what to type next.

Me: Home yet?

Kal: Popping bottles at da club.

I laugh out loud. This is the us I like. No labels, just bubbles. We should have arrived a week early, not told anyone and stayed at a hotel gobbling each other up enough to last us two weeks of separation.

Me: Already? Not wasting time, huh?

Kal: Miss you already.

My fingers are moving faster than my rational mind.

Me: Me more.

Is he really going to the club though? I know all too well what goes down when the groom and his groomsmen are let loose on Addis in that week before the wedding, but I try to push that out of my mind.

Me: Have fun. We'll talk tomorrow!

I wander back inside, cross through the living room and into the kitchen and try Mom's number as I get a chilled bottle of water from the fridge. I'm not expecting to get through on the first try since she's in the "regions." But she picks up after a few rings.

"Mommy!"

"Mizu, are you here? Why you didn't call me before going to sleep?"

"Sorry," I say, to keep it simple. "Where are you now?" She's been moving around so much that I had given up trying to keep track of her from Toronto.

"At Bole Medhane Alem for service!"

"Huh?!" That's a church in the city. Both my parents in Ethiopia, fine. But both my parents in Addis Ababa, breathing the same air? What?! This city is not big enough for both of them. The thought of them possibly running into each other threatens to make my head explode. Oh Christos, is this the year when everything in my life is set to go up in flames?

"You're still at the Elilly Hotel? Why?"

"Yes. So many people to visit. I'm staying longer."

I feel bad that I could have gone to her hotel and seen her already. "I'll come tomorrow, after lunchtime?" I say. In the morning, Dad will be taking me around to visit with his people.

"Sure," she says. "Goodbye now." *Click.*

Okay, abrupt much? *I'm fine, thank you, home all alone here,* I think childishly. I go back inside, closing the balcony doors after me, and start unpacking my toiletries. Belatedly I think, *Hey, why didn't Mom call* me *around when I landed?* But before I can think much on it, Kal texts me.

Kal: Home safe.

Me: Yay!

Kal: Eske says she forgot to send you off with some food.

Me: Tell her I ate enough for a week!

As I shower, I replay my conversation with Eske in my head. I was so relieved when she rescued me, sweeping me upstairs under the guise of wanting to discuss "wedding matters." Obviously, unlike her clueless brother, Eske could tell that I was shitting my pants over what Kal had just signed us up for. Thank God. She could be the one to discreetly let their dear, kind dad know that this "bride" was not down with this spontaneous spectacle. She would save me from having to be the one to disappoint everyone—especially their dad. The one to remind him that I was not Kal's actual wife.

As soon we had reached the stairs landing, out of sight and earshot of the living room, Eske had hugged me tight. "Thank you, Mizu," she said. "You don't know how special you've made this occasion for me and for all Kiki's brothers. What it means for us that our brother has moved on and healed at last and with the best person possible—our own Miz, who we have known so long. You have always been like family, and now you really are!" She held my hands to her face and stared into my eyes.

I swallowed and smiled nervously. *So much for getting me off the hook*, I thought, the family in question smiling out at me from the framed photos lining the walls behind her. Fantastic. Did she leap into this fantasy on her own, like her father, or did Kal share with her that we were living in this delicate married-but-not-*married*-married bubble? I opened my mouth to set the record straight, at least with her, but then I surprised myself by getting all emotional right along with her. For just a moment, I let myself give in to the sense of really gaining a family, a big family like the one I'd always imagined being a part of, in a parallel universe where my parents had cut each other loose long ago, found new partners, and had more babies. Next thing I knew, Eske and I were hugging and sniffling and laughing at ourselves.

"Come," Eske said, pulling me into a room. "I want you to try something on." She opened the closet door and presented a gorgeous white dress on a hanger.

"A wedding dress," I said, unable to hide my surprise.

"It's the dress Emay bought in London years ago and was planning to have altered for the anniversary party." She held it out to me. "I want you to try it on."

Another hand-me-down wedding dress. Story of my life. "Oh, it's beautiful. Um, okay, sure." What could I say or do? My only hope was that it wouldn't fit and I could get out of wearing it. I took the hanger from her, scooping the dress at the waist to lift it off the ground.

Eske turned to head out to give me privacy. But then she stopped. "I wanted to ask you something."

"Shoot," I said, a part of me hoping her question would be something along the lines of, *Do you actually want to do this?*

"Your mother and father . . ." Eske said. Missed the mark. "They can come, right?" Eske knew their situation, that they were, for lack of a better word, separated, and that my mom was currently in Ethiopia. What she didn't know was that they had no clue I'd signed for Kal.

I sucked in air as if I were trying to stand straighter and shook my head. "Oh, that's way too delicate. They haven't been in the same room since I was two years old, and I really don't want to have to start choosing between them now, you know? I wouldn't even know how." I kept talking, knowing that the best shot at winning any convo with Eske was just to out-talk her. "And without them there, how can I have other people there? It wouldn't look right. Someone else will have to stand in as my mother and father on Saturday. But one day, we'll definitely have the *kilikilosh*."

Eske's laugh forced me to pause my verbal diarrhea. "*Kilikil*," she said, the term for when, in the olden days, the bride and groom's families had their first mixer. My blunder, tagging on the ending of some other wedding-related word (I think) to this one, was enough of a distraction that she let the question drop, to my great relief, and left me alone.

I laid the princess dress down on the bed respectfully. "Okay," I said, hands on my waist. It felt wrong to put something so beautiful on my grimy, unwashed skin, but hey, I didn't ask for this. I got out of my hoodie and sweats and stepped my sock feet through the bodice. *Please don't fit please don't fit.* But the waist part slid up over my hips like *Pfft, you call these hips?* The bodice slotted over my torso easily too. *Shite!* I slipped my arms through the long lace sleeves and raised them up high, but my shoulders didn't stick. *Dammit!* I folded forward, but my breath stayed even. *Fml!* Finally, I did a little twirl because, who am I kidding, that thing was divine. The beadwork running down the A-line skirt caught the light and shimmered as it lifted and settled. *Oh, kill me.* I gave up and let myself look in the mirror. With the boatneck-style neckline, it was a perfect mature-sexy. *Juuust great.*

"Okay!" I yelled to the door. Eske came in and stopped dramatically to gasp. "Oh, stop!" I said, ogling myself in the mirror. *Yep, could totally rock this for eternity if I were a ghost.*

"We should take it in a bit, up here," she said, tugging at the slightly loose bodice.

"No!" I said, surprised by how protective I felt of it. "Don't touch anything."

Eske clapped once happily. "I'm so relieved you love it!"

Yes, but for its own sake. For what it represented, not for myself. "This bride intends to *eat*, okay?!" I said, still trying, in some small way, to distance myself from the occasion.

Between the emotional deep end I've been plonked into with my family and Kal's, and the combo of airplane food and home cooking working its way through my system, my insides are a tangled mess. I pull on my sweats and hoodie and go out for an early evening run around the compound, 1.8 kilometres. The air is perfect for it, a happy medium between the last of the day's heat and the first of the evening's cool.

I walk the last block back to the apartment, taking in the bizarreness of the complex bustling with energy for the 3 a.m. post-mass breaking of the forty-day fast, housemaids hurrying to and from the mini-mart swinging small plastic bags of forgotten ingredients, aromas of multiple stews coming from every other household, as if to taunt me about my failed experiment back in September.

Tucked under Dad's balcony and feeling sentimental, I text Kal a picture of that little secluded parkette where we first met.

Me: Remember this?

I'm staring at my phone, waiting for him to respond, when I hear a voice from above. I look up to see Dad, backlit by his living room lights, the red tip of his cigarette hovering in front of him like a firefly.

I wave up. "Hi, Dad," I say casually, as if it hasn't been two years since we've seen each other. Almost twenty-three years ago, I had greeted him in the exact same way. Our first meeting had been so hasty and unforeseen, we had both acted as if it was no big deal at the time, and that pattern has stuck.

"Hi, Miz," Dad says, equally casual. "Who dropped you off?" He taps the ash off to the side.

"Kal."

"Kalkidan was here?" Dad asks, with an uncharacteristic gruffness in his tone. I feel my knees lock up. Dad has always been liberal and trusting of Kal. Why is he acting weird now?

"Yes, he was." I consider adding that we actually flew home together, but I decide not to.

Dad looks at the apartment behind him. "And he left?"

"He left."

"He left you at the gate?"

"Oh, no, he brought me right to here."

"Hmm." Oh, the parental *hmm*. Volumes could be written about the parental *hmm*. This sounds like a positive *hmm*. For a man whom I've heard say he believes fathers are not as important as mothers, Dad being super paternal all of a sudden lands oddly—he's supposed to be my cool parent.

"Can I come up now, Counsellor?" I say, and step into the stairwell without waiting for his go-ahead. I send off a last text to Kal on my way up. At the door, Dad is waiting to envelop me in one of his nicotine-infused fluffy hugs—the no-fuss welcome, same since I was fourteen, which I much prefer to the overdramatic, extended kiss-a-thons I get from my other relatives here, mostly out of pity, I suspect.

"How is Kal?" Dad says, locking the door for the night. "He is here because his father is still having that strange party? A friend asked me to come along, but I declined."

I freeze up, as if I am under cross-examination. But I can tell Dad has no clue about the depth of my collaboration in the "strange party" department. "Oh yes. I've been invited. I think I'll go," I say, as nonchalantly as I can.

He settles into his armchair and reaches for the TV remote. "It will be something for you to do."

I curl up on the couch under a thick *gabi* made of blue-dyed cotton, smiling at how that's been his standard response to whatever ways I've found to entertain myself here, the first of which was running. The country had been in running fever during my first visit, rooting for and then, later, celebrating Roba's gold at the '96 Olympics, and then hoping for Haile G to bring home gold from the '97 World Championships. But I took to running because it was the only thing that settled the turmoil of my life at the time. All those shitty firsts, just because I dared to date: the epic fight with Mom, the solo transatlantic flight and the sob fest en route to Dad's. And then finding out that my parents have been married all my life, on top of everything else. Thank the Lord for endorphins, or I don't know how I would have coped, then and now.

30

MIZ

MONDAY, JANUARY 7, 2019
11:00 A.M.

Kal: Melkam Gena! 🤍

Me: Merry Xmas to you too!

Kal: What's your plan?

Me: With Dad until after lunch. Then to Mom's for overnight. U?

Kal: Whole clan here all day. Except you 😔

8:00 P.M.

Kal: How was your day?

Me: 😴😵 just passed out at Mom's hotel.

Kal: Lol what happened?

Me: Let's just say I am glad these two people live on different continents. How do divorce kids do it?! I am emotionally and physically exhausted with all this 🏓 🏓

Kal: ??

Me: Ping-Pong, you know, one parent to another same day. Too intense for me. I'm all knots.

Kal: Oh! Need a massage? 😬

Me: Nah, just lots of 😴🛏️

A massage sounds amazing, but I'm not about to admit that. Going to spas for "cheap" mind-blowing massages is the number one diaspora activity we used to partake in plenty, but I know that maintaining distance from Kal (and Eske, by extension) is for the best. We weren't expecting to see much of each other anyway. Not that it will make any difference to Saturday, which is still happening. But it does make me feel as if I'm reining Kal in. Controlling the situation without really controlling a damn thing about the actual situation. Less time together is for the best. I still plan to break things down for him—yes to togetherness, no to husband-wifey shit—but later.

TUESDAY, JANUARY 8, 2019
9:00 A.M.

Kal: Got time for ☕?

Me: Aw, already dosed up on my Starbucks instants. Spending day w Mom.

Mom being in town actually works out nicely for my little keeping-distance strategy. Since Dad is back to work for the rest of the week, my plan is to get up early enough to chill with Mom during the days until she leaves for up north, then be with Dad in the evenings.

But day one of "chilling" with Mom turns out to mean *not* café-hopping and spa treatments and shopping to take in what's changed around the city. Instead, it is tagging along to house after house, making very belated condolence calls for people who have died in the time she's been away. People who I don't know from Adam and I've never heard Mom mention. Worse, at each visit, she hears news of more passings that she must pay respects to, so our itinerary keeps growing. The thought of more of the same cracks my resolve. Who am I kidding? I need my boyfriend.

4:00 P.M.

Me: Save me. I'm literally dying in leqso bet.

Kal: Mourning? Who died?!

Me: Who didn't?! F if I know. I'm on fourth house.

Kal: Come to dinner with us tonight?

Yes yes yes I want to say. But no. I've got to stay strong. Think of the long term. The big picture. Sure, I'd love to plaster myself to him, but I have to let us breathe a bit. So with regret, I leave him hanging, waiting to text him back until after Mom and I return to her hotel, where she insta-passes out on her bed, resting before some evening plan that, thank God, I'm not invited to.

6:30 P.M.

Me: Going back to Dad's.

I feel like a total loser cooped up in here, getting ready to go home to get cooped up some more, when I should be out. But even if I miss Kal, it's more important that I clear my head as much as possible, so I embrace it.

Kal: Want a pickup/drop-off?

Me: No, I'm good. Dad's getting me.

Not. Once again, Dad is working late, so I am actually taking a RIDE home. Mom had been really suspicious of the ride-hailing app until I showed her it is literally the same thing as Uber.

Kal: We're going out after . . . check on you then?

A flash of heat rips through me as I imagine all the homegirls in the club swarming Kal like migrating butterflies. I know the deal. I wish I didn't, but I do. I groan in frustration to myself. Why do I care so much? Besides, Kal is the opposite of the cheating type. Man stayed loyal to an ex long after she moved on, and then some!

Me: I should hang with Dad.

Meaning, the bygone version of him in his photo albums. Like Dad and I did on my first night here back in '96, I go through an old album of my parents' wedding and their marriage certificate tucked into the last page. I have since taken screenshots of all of it on my phone in a hidden album, but when I come here, I still like to flip through the originals. Just a little jet-lag ritual of mine, which I do usually in that first week when I am up half of every night anyway.

Between how often I've gone over these fifty-three photos, only nine of which are in colour, and all the anecdotes Dad has (repeatedly) told me about their wedding, I know more about this day than about the day I was born. I pore over Mom's floor-length wedding dress, with its long sleeves, high neckline, and empire waist, which Dad had emphasized was "imported straight from Italy." Forgetting I'm not looking at my phone screen, I try to zoom in on the exquisite beadwork on the bodice and laugh when I catch myself. I don't need to zoom in though; I've memorized every detail. I study Mom's face. The way she gazes up at Dad. Man oh man, if it weren't for the facts of science, I could easily believe that that was the moment I was conceived.

I put the album away. *How does a marriage start out looking so right only to go so wrong?*

WEDNESDAY, JANUARY 9, 2019
10:00 A.M.

Me: How was the clubs, stranger?

1:00 P.M.

Kal: Sorry, I was out. Can you talk?

I dial his number right away. The three hours of silence from Kal, taken up by more depressing belated bereavement visits with Mom, were like a dose of my own medicine—very unpleasant. In that time, my mind has jumped to multiple scenarios, which all involve Kal leaving me for some beauty he connected with at the club. I excuse myself and step outside to the front yard, wandering all the way across the paved car park and a neat lawn bordered by leafy greens and pink roses until there's nowhere to go unless I scale either the cinder-block wall or the water tower ninja-style.

"What's up?" I say, when he answers.

"Sorry, I was out," he repeats. "We went to the mausoleum."

It takes a second before I remember that one of his must-do things when he returned for the anniversary was to see the new marble cover of his mother's crypt. "Oh. How was that?"

He sighs heavily. "Hard. How can the place where I feel it hardest to believe she is gone also be the place where I feel her the most?"

I swallow, tracing my hand along the groove of the dried cement gluing the cinder blocks together. "I don't know." And here I was whining about too much time spent with my mother, too many dead people we had to mourn. *Fudge.*

Kal continues. "I wish you had seen Abay though. The rest of us were all crying, but he was so relaxed because he is with her in his mind. His face was peaceful, joyful even."

"That's so . . . beautiful," I say, feeling my eyes sting a little bit, remembering, for some reason, the night I watched Kal "die" as Antony onstage and how that got me so worked up. What if something happens to him here while I am so busy avoiding him for reasons that make sense only to me? I'll never forgive myself, forever wishing that I should've been there. Like a good girlfriend.

"They were asking about you. I wanted to tell you something."

"Yeah?" *Please say that we don't measure up to them, that we have no business being all up in their big day. Please say you're content just being my boyfriend.*

"Standing before Emay's crypt, observing Abay, I realized that my parents' marriage, the kind of bond that extends into the hereafter, that is the kind of love a person could only humbly aspire to, not arrogantly assume will pass on to him as a birthright, like their features and mannerisms, you know? That had been my attitude when I was young, when I was with . . . why I took it for granted that us being together since grade eight equalled lifelong marriage." I startle, realizing he's talking about him and Muna. "Now I know all anyone can do is accept that we have no control over whether we are destined to be among the lucky few who find that kind of timeless, spaceless bond. We can only try. I want you to know I plan to try as hard as I can."

I sink down to the grass, floored by this. I don't know what to do with it. What else could a person ask for, really? I shake my head. I mean a person who is actually *married* married.

"Am I being too heavy?" he says, when I don't respond.

"You?" I say, finding my voice. "Never!" But I don't know what else to say.

"I did ask Emay to send a sign that you and I have a good shot, if it's not too much trouble."

"And?" I genuinely want to know if we do. Does anyone do well skipping over an entire phase of a relationship?

"Well, they move on heaven time up there, so we have to wait and see."

"I hope it's quicker than Black people time." I mentally curse my stupid humour as an emotional crutch, and a nearby rose stalk takes the punishment as I choke and swing it roughly.

"But I think Saturday will be a kind of good luck charm." Aaaand we're back to Saturday. "When am I seeing you? I'm losing sleep."

"It's called jet lag," I say. Eye roll. He waits. "Well, tomorrow Dad is taking me to Sululta," I say. "He has to go for work, but I'm tagging along since we haven't seen much of each other. So I guess Friday? Brunch?"

"Make it lunch, then you can stay on for the evening thing!"

"Huh? Stay on for . . . ?" I don't remember committing to a Friday thing, though if it is just us two, I'm very open to it, of course.

"The eve get-together. Eske didn't mention it?"

"All I know is she is supposed to come get me early Saturday morning for hair and makeup."

"At our place. I assume you're not having a *tilosh* at your place," he says. A bridal wedding-eve party? "It's just a small fete."

"Legesse-small," I say. "Anyway, I'm not supposed to be there, Friday night of all nights. Might I remind you there isn't supposed to be any mingling of the bride's and groom's camps the night before a wedding? Especially of the bride and groom themselves!" Why am I talking like this, enabling the madness? Although lord knows I do miss . . . mingling with Kal. We've been apart three days, going on four. I'm feeling all stiff, and I really do miss him. "The bride at the groom's house on the eve. *Tsk tsk.* Scandal," I say, hoping I sound firmer than I feel.

"Didn't you take anything away from the talk over lunch last Saturday? Tradition is under renovation," he says.

"But I'll need my beauty sleep."

"Oh, I promise you a beautiful sleep."

"Goodbye, Barry White!" I say, feeling mixed up again, and end the call.

31

MIZ

riday evening finds me lounging solo on Dad's balcony, my feet braced up on the stone, with nothing for company other than the background chatter of neighbours and passersby below, and the melodic calls and chants sailing through the air from mosques and churches. At least the Wi-Fi network is on point. And of course it would be, because on a Friday night, everyone is out having a life. I'm the one at home, fiddling with my phone because I'm too principled to go where I am wanted. That is, the "small" wedding-eve party at Kal's. We talked again last night before bed and quickly this morning, but he's been quiet since. Meanwhile, in my first day of being home alone in I don't know how long, here and in Toronto, I've gone for a too-hot late run, taken a too-long nap, and watched too many hours of dubbed Turkish and Korean soaps. And I may have to repeat the whole cycle just to keep from fretting over why Kal is being so quiet. Has he never heard of *magderder*? Has he forgotten that in our culture you're supposed to make an offer multiple times? *Sheesh.*

It's also been hours since Aimé emailed us both with a scan of Kal's Open Work Permit, which had arrived in the mail at last. If Kal had seen it, he would have said something. Which must mean he hasn't seen it. Which circles me back to the antsy-pantsy mystery of what's got him so preoccupied? I cave.

> **Me: Guess what? Did you check email? Your wp arrived!**

I send him a bunch of festive emojis and then groan. Who is this Miz, obsessing over a boyfriend? I don't like her. And missing a party? What?! Miz doesn't do marriage. Fine, we know that. But since when does she pass up any wedding-related party, much less one thrown by the Legesse fam? When technically, it's not even a proper *tilosh*, since both weddings (the real and the fake) have come and gone, one of them forty-eight years ago, the other one three months ago. Which makes what I'm missing just your garden-variety party. Never thought I'd see the day. But still, I can't help imagining how, if I was really Kal's fiancée, tonight would be my night. This place would be jumping with music and dancing, packed with everyone from my side.

Another hour later, I'm so agitated I've turned into my own hostage negotiator. "You know what, why not get the full experience?" I say to my reflection in the bathroom mirror. "Well, full*ish*." I look as if I'm cleaning house: hair sticking out of my wrap, dressed in a T-shirt and pyjama shorts. "Okay, so, hear me out," I say to me. "Not that you signed for Kal because you were curious about marriage, but *if* you had, say you had, then why not go all-in, huh? You're about to experience the actual big day, so why not the lead-up to it too?"

Besides, it makes more sense for me to sleep over there anyway, as long as we're throwing tradition or protocol or whatever out the window.

I grab my phone before this latest tide of *yes yes yes* changes to *but but but* again.

Me: Come get me.

Without even waiting for Kal to respond, I jump in the shower for the second time that day to start getting ready. One thing I have no shortage of here is party dresses. I've left behind clothes after every wedding so I would have room in my luggage for Mom's goods. But I end up wearing the dress I brought to wear to Kal's parents' wedding anniversary tomorrow, a silky green wraparound dress (very easy to get out of) and tie-on black strappy heels. As for my hair, there's no time to do anything but slick it back. The final thing I put on, also a few hours earlier than I'd planned to and to complete the charade, is my wedding ring.

When there's a knock at the door a little while later, I throw it open and am immediately thunderstruck. The Kal who's come to whisk me away makes my breath catch. He's leaning against the portico column, swinging a single red rose upside down by the stem, ankles crossed and one hand in his pocket. I behold him in the only way that does him justice, in a slow, sensual pan up. His long, sleek frame is sheathed in a fitted midnight-black designer suit, creases crisp as if he's been professionally gift-wrapped for me, and his patent leather shoes are so shiny I can see my reflection in them. His skin, darker from one week in Addis, glows in the night. And that fade? When our eyes meet, I know the drunk desire I see in his is mirrored in my own.

He holds out the rose. I take it. He sees my ring. He pulls my hand in and kisses the back. I flip his hand over and reciprocate. "Come in," I say. He does, turning me with him as he goes. And that swagger? "Ahem, were you always this fine in Ethiopia?" I say, letting him lead me back inside. I run my other hand up his back. I know that diaspora up their fashion game when they are here—not about to catch anyone going out in leggings and a baseball cap, hell no—but I can't believe I deprived myself of him all week. "How're you gonna top this tomorrow?"

He tugs the edge of his blazer lightly and slides his hand down his milk-white shirt—a gesture that nearly finishes me off. "Tomorrow is a mystery," he says with a slow blink.

Whoosah. I'm not a gambling gal, but I feel as if I've hit the jackpot. This special edition Kal, my smooth stick-shift operator East African Bond is going to be mine all night and all day tomorrow? *Mine.* And not just today and tomorrow but . . . for life? *Because he's . . . my husband,* I think, testing out the phrase in the soundproofed privacy of my mind.

"Only the present is known." He closes the distance between us and plants a kiss . . . on my cheek. *Boo.* I pull my cheeks down in a pout. But still scrumptious. My response is to blatantly sniff the skin of his neck, from shoulder to ear and along his jaw and up his chin, coming around to his mouth—the only reason I haven't put my lipstick on yet. "I missed you," Kal says, pulling back.

"Where are my gifts?" I demand, my arms akimbo. The head of the rose taps my lower back softly. I swing it around and wag it at him. "You are supposed to be showering me in all kinds of gifts tonight, as your bride."

"Is that so? Well, since I have neither gold, nor silver, nor perfumes, nor a week's worth of party outfits for you, and since you already have a wedding dress," Kal says, listing all the typical goodies I'm not going to get, "how about I . . ." Eyes hooded, he scans me hem to hairline, echoing my actions on the doorstep.

"*Indee!* Hey, stop it," I exclaim, feeling all kinds of ravished. "We better go before we end up not going at all." I pick up the overnight bag I've put by the door. "I thought I would sleep over. Instead of Eske having to get up earlier to come pick me up to-morrow? We can all go from yours together, right?" I bite my lip, fearing I have overdone it. "Is that too much? Will she mind?"

He takes the bag from me. "If she does, she'll have to deal with me."

I bite the stem of the rose, shortening it, and stick it in my ponytail. Kal's hand captive in mine, we head out. For the ride back to his place along roads now lit up like a Christmas tree that a child decorated—electric palm trees and all—he puts on a play-list of wedding songs. I don't comment on it. I'm just so happy to be together again that I even acknowledge and wave back at the flirty young men and boys overseeing roadside fruit carts. One of the songs is "Ale Gena," the outro of almost every wedding party, which, based on the crickets that follow, I had always thought of as marking the end of fun and the beginning of disap-pointment. Maybe it's the happiness of being with Kal again, or my own self-talk earlier, but I find myself reconsidering the lyrics now as we groove along to it. How it says there will be more wed-dings yet, because everyone marries eventually. This wedding party is winding down, but this time next year, and the next and the next, all the single bridesmaids, groomsmen, their sisters and brothers and cousins and nieces and nephews and neighbours will, one by one, get hitched.

Am I everyone?

"What'd I say?" I turn to Kal as we walk into his yard, having had to park out on the street because of the overflow. "Ain't nothing small about all y'all's small parties." There are easily fifty people, and that's just out in the garden. The air is a heady mix of cigarette smoke, incense, coffee and liquor. Out back, there's a full-on catered buffet and nonstop barbecue, even a big bonfire like it's Meskel time.

"Hey, your songs!" I say, hearing Kal's playlist in the background.

"Our songs." He places our intertwined hands on his chest. "You helped me a lot with them."

"Categorically untrue," I say, looking around and taking it in, waving to the faces I know (few and far between). It would be overwhelming if this were all for me and Kal, but I remind myself it was originally intended for his parents. We're just last-minute add-ons. *It basically has nothing to do with me, right?* I ask my twinkling stars in the pitch-black clear night sky.

Much later in the evening, when the atmosphere has mellowed out, people nursing their glasses of preferred digestifs around the bonfire, someone requests that Tsige, one of the guests, grace us with her music. Of course a professional singer would be among the guests at this Legesse version of a small fete. Just one of those legends that the family oh so casually has in their social circle like it ain't no thang.

Tsige, regal and heavy-set as an opera singer in a loose blue robe, doesn't need much goading. Cigarette drooping in one hand in a way that reminds me so much of Asni, swirling her tumbler of cognac, she slides from preamble conversation into "Ende Iyerusalem" within the same breath, no prep needed.

I gasp. Asni's signature song! The crowd claps and snaps their fingers softly in appreciation. I immediately fall into the rhythm of her smoky voice, softly lip-synching to words I think are roughly about someone who is so near yet so far. Like Kal, sitting what feels like miles away on a lawn chair next to me. He is smiling at me knowingly. I want to climb on his lap, feel his arms around my hips, his chest against mine, his fingers digging into my hip in that way that makes my legs give out from under me.

Hoots and whistles erupt from the audience when Tsige phrases lyrics whose sounds are unfamiliar to me. "She's improvising," Kal murmurs, seeing my confusion.

"It's like she's channelling Asni," I whisper back, noticing how every time she weaves another impromptu line, she lifts her downcast, mournful eyes and delivers it personally to one of the guests. *Good thing she doesn't know anything about me*, I think, with relief.

"Well, she was her contemporary. Was actually a witness at her wedding."

"Say what now? Asni was married?" How did I miss that in all the stuff I turned up during my googling to find an English translation of the lyrics to the song?

"Sure." Picking up on my interest, Kal gives me a quick lowdown. The Queen of *Krar*, she who loved to love but looked down her nose at marriage, as far as I had gathered, was herself madly in love and married, once. "But it didn't last long." That tracks. "More later. Better yet, watch the doc," he says, and puts his finger to his lips. *A documentary?!* What rock have I been under?

Tsige does a few more songs for us, then to much appreciative applause from her listeners, retires back to her guest status. "Ale Gena" floats into my head again. Everyone does marriage. Every girl, one day, holds the biggest bouquet, wears the whitest dress, stands smack dab in the middle of every photo, sits in one of the two thrones on the dais, has the happiest day of her life. So why not me tomorrow?

"Am I getting *married* married tomorrow?" I ask myself later, in yet another bathroom mirror, this time in one of the guest bedrooms, while brushing my teeth. "I mean, I am married," I respond to me, frothy-mouthed. "Technically, but . . ." I rinse my mouth and, leaning in with my hands on the counter, face myself again, closer this time. *So this is how six-time champion bridesmaid Mizan Begashaw, who does not do marriage (but has a misplaced engagement ring still in her possession, and a hidden album of her parents' wedding on her phone and keeps finding herself in other women's wedding gowns), lands herself married, eh?* I can only guess what all those six pictureperfect brides whom I waited on hand and foot really felt inside. But if it is anything like this *bring it on, why the hell not?* fearlessness, then fuck it, why the hell not me too? I switch the lights off and go to my rightful bedroom.

32

KAL

I love this girl. Instead of waiting for me to tiptoe my way to her room once the household is slumbering, she brings herself and her overnight bag to my room express while everyone is still dispersing for the night and I'm in the middle of undressing. "Whatchu lookin' at?" she says, letting herself in. "Peoples know I'm already your wife, right?"

I laugh and finish undoing my belt, then untuck my shirt. "If anyone missed it, the memo will be distributed shortly," I say.

She tosses her bag aside and flings her body on the bed. I abandon undressing and join her. Our lips meet. In our kiss, I taste the sweet vanilla of our wedding cake. *Small fete, huh?* Miz had said—her refrain throughout the night at every "extra" development, from the moment we walked into the garden to when Zebiba wheeled out a two-tier gold-and-rose creation. I had to remind Miz she did marry into a family of bakers. My father had insisted that Miz and I cut the cake. I had a feeling that my father would keep doing this tomorrow—staying on the periphery of things while pushing Miz and me into the centre of everything.

Even if Emay were physically with us, I bet it would have been the same.

"At least there's no bedazzled stepladder," I said, as guests huddled around the cake table chanting *Kiss! Kiss! Kiss!* I had been ready to do the customary blink-and-you'll-miss-it peck on the lips, as couples do here at their weddings, as if they've never kissed before. But just as on our wedding day, Miz had other plans, as if to remind me this was not our first time and that, since November, we have almost succeeded in permanently rearranging one another's anatomy. Our kiss became a full-on make-out, live, in high definition. I knew we had gone on too long, even for this loosened-up crowd, when I felt a tugging on my sleeve and heard Bini's voice yelling, *People waiting on cake, yo!*

I want to pick up from that moment, but we're both so worn out from the night that our lovemaking is the quietest and slowest it's ever been, to the point where we have to laugh at ourselves.

"It's like we're already in old age," I say, after.

"Change of pace is good sometimes," she says, curled into me. "Literally." She chuckles.

"You had a good time tonight?"

She puts her chin on my chest to see me better. "Are you kidding? The slow dance especially," she says.

I nod. Me too. After dinner, at Eske's urging, we had relented to doing one solo slow dance in the living room, starting with a special entrance emceed by the one and only Bini. But the second he launched into his lengthy *Ladies and gentlemen!* and I heard the opening bars of "Yehiwote Hiwot," I tried to signal to him to change the song, remembering Miz's dislike for Tilahun. All that time I was sending her links to songs, I had made sure to not send her any of his tracks.

"It's okay," Miz said, her eyes moist, blinking rapidly at the chandelier to reverse her tears as we walked in. "We have to dance to this song. It's practically the law." We took our positions and started sweeping gently across the floor. She leaned into my ear. "It's just that a couple's first dance always gets me emotional, and now I'm doing it. So double trouble."

"What is it about Tilahun anyway?"

She sighed so heavily I was about to tell her it didn't matter, to not ruin the night. But she went on. "So basically," she started, talking to my shoulder as we danced slowly, "when I came here the first time, and I found out my parents were actually married?" I nodded. How could I forget? "There was more."

"What, Tilahun played at their wedding?" I said, chuckling.

She did a double take. "What are you, psychic? A Tilahun music video was playing on Dad's TV when Dad showed me, get this, *their wedding album.*" I widened my eyes, amazed. "I kid you not. Legit plastic-protected pages, gold-ringed spine, padded floral cover, fifty-three black-and-whites. Total coincidence Tilahun was on at the time, but I have not been able to stand his voice ever since." She shuddered. "I associate him with that period of my life. It was on my first day back too!" This made me stop dancing for a moment. She pointed at my face. "That, how shocked you look? Multiply that by a thousand, then add the soundtrack of a guy who half the time sounds like he's crying more than he's singing. I mean, it could have been anyone, but it had to be Tilahun? Who would ever want to listen to anything of his again?"

She'd kept her game face on since we were still slow dancing in the spotlight, but I could feel the light tremor in her chest—she was working hard to keep the full impact of that memory at bay. I wished we'd been alone.

She hesitated, then quietly added, "But sometimes, I still look at the photos."

I shook my head, speechless with fury at her parents, but keeping my smile on. Perhaps too convincingly, because she narrowed her eyes at me as if I'd said the wrong thing.

"I know you want to defend them," she says. "Say they had their reasons *blah blah*—"

I cut her off firmly. "No. They did you wrong. A terrible wrong. Messing up your first taste of love like that?"

She *tsk*ed, shrugged. "Can you blame me for turning nonbeliever?"

There was a note of regret in her voice, as if lamenting something lost. The belief that her first would be her forever. The one she doodled about in her high school notebook, the outline of her hands with his, their names conjoined under a halo of hearts.

"And now, what do you believe?"

"I think they had no idea what the hell they were doing. Love is worth everything."

Her words hit me with a force that made me pull her closer. I'd promised myself I would wait for her to say it back to me before I said it again, but I couldn't help it. Tomorrow was not guaranteed. This could be the last time I got to say it. "I love you."

"I love you too. *Afekrihalehu*."

In Amharic too! I almost shouted with joy. I brought her closer yet, and we danced the rest of the four-and-a-half-minute song without speaking, not with our words anyway. I began to pull away as the song wound down, for her sake.

"Hold on. Few more seconds," she whispered while Tilahun held the final note. "I want to."

So we stayed, until the very last whisper of his breath. For fifteen seconds, we were still, soul recognizing soul, feeling as if everyone was also holding still with us.

In the shaft of moonlight slipping through the bedroom curtains, our wedding rings gleam as Miz interlocks her left hand with mine. "From now on, you will pick what we dance to on our anniversaries," I say.

"Ooh, you might live to regret that."

"Nah." I caress her plain ring, the complement to mine, bought at random after a long day of solitary wandering. "We should order real ones with engravings from Teklu Desta. What do you think?"

She twists our wrists this way and that. "I would love that."

"Those, we will never take off. No matter what."

"Unless we have to have surgery."

I burst out laughing.

"I'm just being practical!" she says. "Or an MRI."

I adjust the pillow, propping myself up, and she shifts up with me. "You know, when I was small, I used to think if wedding rings came off, then the couple was not married anymore, because I never saw any married grownups without their rings on."

"Oops," she says. "I took this thing off the same night, back in October."

"It's okay. The hex doesn't apply to us because these aren't our final rings," I say authoritatively.

"Phew," she says, then grows pensive. "Never to come off, like my dad's."

I nod. Exactly. I'm so happy she thought of him, despite his part in mishandling her lovestruck-teen phase. His commitment to his absent wife is so much like Abay's. Such an inspiration. I doze off to the soothing feel of Miz tracing her toes along my shin. What feels like minutes later, I am partly pulled out of sleep by the sounds of the women leaving for their beauty appointment. It is dawn already? I open my eyes and look around. Miz is gone. I move to where she had been and fall asleep to the lingering warmth and scent of her, grasping her pillow to me like a man who has been left, an image I can afford to indulge in only because that is not my story. In fact, my story is the opposite. I have been found for life.

33

MIZ

*O**h, please, God, let me still be asleep, let this be a bad dream*, I plead with the man above when our car pulls up into the Elilly Hotel driveway. Whenever I am in Ethiopia, I am so used to handing over all decision-making to locals that it didn't cross my mind to ask which hotel the ladies—Eske, and her sisters-in-law and cousins, my semi-bridesmaids—and me had been booked in to get ready for the wedding. Turns out, the hotel where the salon is, where we have a suite for primping and dressing . . . is Mom's hotel.

As we file into the atrium-style hotel lobby that all the balconies look down onto, I keep my head down as if I am hiding from paparazzi. Thankfully, at this hour, it is deserted. Now all I have to do is make sure I don't run into Mom. That's all. Not while I am going from the salon to the suite or leaving the hotel later, glammed up by the city's most sought-after stylist, with the whole procession and fanfare of the groom's party, being serenaded by a live instrumentalist and vocalist, I'm sure. But no problem. Nothing like hiding in plain sight.

As the bride, I get priority for hair, so I finish at the salon before the other women. Weyneshet, the wedding manager, a fast-talking, big-haired, self-made businesswoman who favours purple in all the shades in existence and has managed every Legesse clan wedding, gives me clearance to go on up to the suite. I hurry across the lobby, eager to hide out, thankful that it is early enough that—

Saywhatnow?

I come to a screeching halt.

Dad is in the lobby. As in, *this* lobby.

He has just stepped out of the elevators and is jauntily crossing to the café. What the *what*? I dash behind a potted palm and peer out. Did the hood dryer at the hair salon fry my brain along with my hair? Dad, who was supposed to have been in Adama overnight for work, looks rumpled as if he just woke up. He is in yesterday mode: yesterday's hair (uncombed), pants (beltless), shirt (untucked), face (unshaven).

Well, well, well. Working late, huh? When I had imagined my parents running into each other, I did not picture it in the context of Dad having a rendezvous with some lady at the very same hotel where Mom is staying. Of all the hotels in the city, Dad, really? This is a freaking epic potential disaster in the making.

While Dad waits for service at the café, I feel I have to do *something*. What? Confront him? By saying what? Or warn Mom? Also, by saying what? Unsee what I've seen? Impossible. The elevator dings open all by itself, like a sign from God. Upstairs it is. Quiet as a mouse, I slip in.

Upstairs, I let myself into Mom's room with my key card. "Were they open, *maré*?" she calls out from the bathroom.

Honey? Who does *she* have up in here?! "Nope!" I answer loudly. Oh, what I would give to see the look on Mom's face in that moment. I walk further into the room, looking for giveaway details . . . and slap my hand over my mouth like a scandalized auntie when I see *Dad*'s tie, watch, wallet, keys and fedora on the bedside table.

Oh no they didn't. Oh, but they did. Because it's all laid out like an evidence exhibit. The sheets are mussed and piled haphazardly like an unmissable art installation. *Oh my god. My eyes! My eyes!* I turn away, squeezing them shut. Growing up, whenever friends told stories about walking in on their parents "doing it," I used to pretend to be grossed out too, while secretly wishing I had a similar story. *Similar* being the operative word. Not exact!

When did my parents go from ships passing in the transatlantic night to *honey*?

So, Mr. Your-Mom-Knows-Where-to-Find-Me found his way to her. Once in the past week, I oh-so-delicately broached to Dad that maybe he could join Mom and me for a coffee or something. But he'd shut me down, saying he was still at the same address he'd always been at, and if my mother wanted to see him, she knew where to find him.

While I'm still reeling, Mom comes out from the bathroom wrapped in her bathrobe, sees me seeing the room for what it is but remains totally chill as if this is just another morning of me coming by for a day of visiting the long bereaved.

She picks up the nearest object, an ice bucket, and holds it out to me.

"Can you get me ice?"

"Huh?"

"I need ice."

"But . . . it's . . . not filtered." She's been nitpicky about everything, determined to avoid getting sick. Also, do I look like a six-year-old that she can distract that easily?

In addition to her undercover agent level of cool, I notice that Mom is also wearing a wedding ring. *Her* wedding ring. The one that's been rolling around her bathroom drawer for ages.

Jigsaw pieces click into place with deafening clangs. No wonder Mom came to Ethiopia early and got "delayed" so long in Addis instead of continuing north. No wonder she never got around to making all those house calls. *Many people to see*, my butt. One person, more like. Slick! These old people's game is myofascial-tissue *deep*.

Mom puts the ice bucket in my hands and ushers me out the door. As I stand in the hallway, helplessly holding the bucket and trying to figure out what's going on, Dad comes around the corner with a bottle of mineral water in one hand and a bottle of Johnnie Walker in the other. His eyes widen a fraction when he sees me but then flick to Mom's. Without missing a beat, he says, "Oh good, you're going to get ice."

What the *huh*?! My phone rings. Eske. I decline the call and put the phone on silent. Sis-in-law will call right back. She believes that relentlessly calling makes a person magically available. Which maybe works in Addis business life, but not this Addis business right here.

"You look lovely," Mom says suddenly.

I have to double-check who she's talking to. *Moi*. Right, I forgot about my hairdo.

"So early in the morning too," Dad says.

"Thanks? I, ah, I decided to come right when the salon opened so I don't have to wait for the flat-iron guy." For some reason, the flat-iron guy in every Addis hair salon is some cocksure dude who struts around like he's a brain surgeon. "I have a . . . thing later today," I explain, very much unasked. "I just thought I would say hi before going."

"Enjoy your day," Dad says, nabbing the out I just presented them on a silver platter. He bypasses me politely, as if we were strangers, goes into the room, and shuts the door. A moment later, the Do Not Disturb sign is shoved through the bottom of the door and bounces against my shoe.

Oh hell no *they didn't.* In a daze, I pick up the sign, hang it on the doorknob, fetch ice, leave it by the door and buzz off so my parents can . . .

Nope, not finishing that sentence.

In my suite, I sink into a bucket armchair. Weyneshet has transformed the room into a princess's chambers, all white silk, chiffon and glittering rose arrangements. My wedding gown, tiara, veil, shoes, bouquet and perfume are all laid out on the king-sized bed. I twist my (temporary) wedding ring round and round on my finger, as if it is the crank that will get my brain going so that I can process what just happened. Hey, they didn't even notice my ring!

A knock at the door, then someone lets themselves in. It is *the* famous Kokeb, in the flesh. Sometimes names really are destiny. This *star* is so overbooked that none of the brides in all the weddings I've been in could get her to do their makeup. And now . . . oh, the irony!

We say hello, and as she starts to set up, I excuse myself to the hallway to make a call. It is past midnight in Toronto, but then again, it is still Friday night there.

Aimé picks up, sounding groggy. "Am I not the one who's supposed to be calling you? There's no more notifications from your portal. I'm checking the email twice a day like my life de-pends on it." One of her other jobs while we're away is monitor-ing our inbox, just in case of an internet blackout here.

"I caught Mom with Dad!"

She is instantly awake. "What? No!"

"Yes!"

"Where? How? When?"

"Hotel room. *Her* hotel room. Let's just say he didn't get here this morning. Follow?"

"Oh snap!"

"After all this time, and that's what they get down to?" Silence. "Hello?"

"Okay, don't read too much into it. Start from the beginning." I tell her the happenings. "There you go," Aimé says. "They're not ready for questions. Eventually, they'll bring you into the loop."

"When? On my deathbed? Haven't I waited long enough?"

"Don't you have anything better to do over there? Wait—isn't Kal's party tomorrow?"

"It's already today here." If I tell her that I'm about to have another wedding with Kal in a matter of hours, very publicly at a resort, alongside his parents' marriage celebration, there's a real chance her head will pop off from happiness, which will not help with keeping her focused on the current, more urgent situation.

I hear her fumbling around, followed by the sound of peeing. "So just have fun."

"I intend to. But . . . but what about my parents? I just leave them here?"

Aimé laughs so hard there are breaks in the sound of her pee-ing. "That is exactly what they want. You're too old for any of this to be your business, anyway. Leave them alone. You don't own them and their story any more than they own you and your story. What's theirs is theirs, what's yours is yours."

"Except what's theirs has pretty much determined the course of my entire life. I am owed an explanation."

"You need it right now?"

"Yes!"

"Why?"

Kokeb pops out of the room and signals to me we should get started. I know that if I sit in that vanity chair, it's game over. I will be stuck for the rest of the day. The other women will come back while I am getting my face put on, then the in-room breakfast, then getting dressed, etc. This is my only window of opportunity.

On any other day, I would have died to have Kokeb work on me, but I give her the *just a minute* finger, and she goes back into the bedroom, shrugging like *it's your money*. I beeline down the hall to the elevator, press it and wait, all while making listening sounds as Aimé chatters on about her race training. As soon as one comes, I hop in, not even telling Aimé sayonara, and press the button for Mom's (my parents'?) floor. She'll assume it's a bad connection.

The Do Not Disturb sign is still hanging on their doorknob, proving that all that earlier really did happen. Too bad. I knock, almost saying *Housekeeping!* in English, forgetting that staff would say something else here. But in a way I *am* there for housekeeping. Of musty family mysteries that need airing out!

It's a minute before the door is opened. Both my parents are in bathrobes—oh god—but Mom is sitting in one of the loveseats on either side of a small table. Are they really sitting there sipping alcohol as if it's tea? I have to blink to adjust to this sight of them in the same space. Music comes at a low volume from one of their phones, one of those familiar '70s soul melodies.

I march in and sit on the edge of the bed, the very edge, and cross my arms. They look at each other with amusement, but neither takes the lead. *Okay then.* "What's going on here?"

Crickets. Mom busies herself by wiping imaginary dust off the tabletop. Dad takes the other loveseat opposite her.

"What's going on?" I repeat, my voice climbing higher. "All those years . . ." *Thirty-four, to be exact.* "And then this? What happened?"

"Nothing," Mom says, waving her hands in a gesture I hate because it only comes out when I edge up on the big questions. I feel a rush of hot rage toward her—her nerve trying to pull that cagey shit on me, even now! And Dad being his usual passive self, placid smile on his face, like a man who's just spent all night . . . *Nope, still, not ever, finishing that sentence!*

Suddenly, I feel so overwhelmed, I burst into tears. Mom is by my side in a heartbeat, clutching my hands. "Oh, Mizu. Please! I can't see you cry." Her eyes start flowing too. "You know I cry when you cry."

I snort wetly, taking away one of my hands to wipe my nose. She gestures for Dad to give her a napkin and tries to wipe my face like I'm a kid.

"No, tell me what happened!" I demand, wriggling away.

"Misunderstandings, miscommunications, disappointments, fights . . ." Dad rambles, looking like a man who's never dealt with a toddler on the verge of an earth-shattering meltdown.

"What?!" I glare at him. "That doesn't explain anything."

"Over everyday matters," Mom says, picking up his sentence, "that seemed so important at the time but that were so small and silly."

I press my fingers really hard into my eyeballs, hoping that stops the tears and makes this all make sense. "I. Don't. Understand."

Mom pulls my hands away and forces me to look at her. "We got married too soon without knowing each other well, because we didn't have anything like dating back then, so when we started to have normal couple problems, we fell apart." She looks over at my dad. "Right, *maré?*"

Dad nods, leaning back in his chair. "Did not know how to meet our first storms." He is so out of his element, his confidence too shot for a full sentence, that I feel a little sorry for him.

"So why didn't you just . . ." I pull my hands apart. The word feels icky, as if I hadn't spent more than half my life wishing for it as much as for their reunion. Anything but the limbo. "Divorce?"

"At the time, that was very difficult. Not at all like these days," Dad says.

"So when I had to leave for Canada with you for your surgery, and he couldn't come . . ."

"At the time, it was rare for couples to both get exit visas," Dad adds in his lawyerly voice.

"We . . . just let each other go," Mom says, patting my cheek, which just unleashes a new wave of tears from me.

Dad takes the opportunity to step out to the balcony for a smoke. I fall the rest of the way onto the bed and curl up into a fetal position. Mom shuffles onto the bed and reclines so she can see me.

No big dramatic story. Just too-new love that didn't stand a chance against real life.

We stay like that for a few minutes: Mom watching me, me watching Dad on the balcony, Dad watching us. The chorus of old school soul slowly fading out, falsetto voice repeating something about not giving up. *What the hell was that song?*

Eventually, Dad comes back in and pours himself mineral water. "Marriage is serious," he says. "Knowing someone for a few years is nothing."

He'd said something similar to me about my teenage boyfriend. But Kal . . . we've known each other for donkey's years, but as friends. Been intimate for just months. Never properly dated. What does that mean for us?

Dad caps the water bottle and puts it down. "We are so proud of you for not getting married."

That hits me like a gut punch. I sit up. "What?" My entire life, they don't say one word to me about getting married, and now *this*?

"You have grown up to be so independent, so much wiser than us and your friends, taking your time to decide about marriage."

Dad takes a long swallow from his glass and sighs with satisfaction. "If at all."

"If at all," Mom echoes.

Is that what I was doing? Deciding? News to me.

Mom takes the rest of his glass, finishes it, and gives the glass back to him. "We are so proud of you for not following the crowd even when you celebrated wedding after wedding. Unafraid to be your own person. Only once, I worried for you," she says. "You were only fourteen, a baby, but arguing with me about being in love! I did not want my mistake for you."

"Mom, even if we wanted to get married in grade eight, that wouldn't have been legally possible."

"I did not want you falling into a serious situation that would be impossible to get out of."

The question is on the tip of my tongue. *Was I an accident?* But the answer seems self-evident. "So you deported me," I say instead. Mom huffs, annoyed. She hates it when I use that word to refer to what happened. I turn to Dad, expecting a commiserating smile, but he gives me a stern look. *Wow, already defensive about wifey.* "I mean, 'decided the time had come for me to meet Dad,'" I say sarcastically, switching to her official version of what happened.

"And it worked."

She actually looks proud of herself, as if scaring me off from falling in love—a privilege she got to enjoy—was her intent. "Better than you realize," I say sadly.

"I haven't worried for you since," she says, completely missing my point.

I feel woozy. I do *not* feel that I have been wise, deserve to be proud of myself or have made smarter choices than they. I've messed up big time. Wasted time. And now I'm trying to make up for it with some charade at a resort.

"We assume you have . . . friends, of course." Dad struggles to find the right word, since I don't think there's a literal equivalent for *date* in Amharic. Other than *go out*, maybe.

"Of course," Mom echoes. Kill me now. Where was this levelheadedness when I was fourteen? "But if one has to marry, take it from us, wait. Wait as long as possible."

"Like, thirty years?" I assume they're not headed for divorce, even if it's modern times now and they could easily get one.

Dad laughs. "Yes! *Now* is when we should have a wedding.

When we know who we are. When we have earned a celebration, like your friend's father and his wife, God rest her soul."

"Oh yes! Up!" Mom says, knowing only half the story, like Dad. "Go enjoy the party."

But I don't move.

34

KAL

The second thing to wake me up on the morning of my wedding is the rumble of my own stomach in response to the aroma of clarified butter and spices wafting through the house. I take what might be the happiest shower of my life, as if the silky warm flow of the water is Miz's touch coursing over every inch of my body. Both Abay and I will be wearing traditional dress today, so after showering and shaving, I put on my all-white *eje tebab* tunic and pants combo, and tie on my white sandals, the strains of my "Indegena" playing on Bluetooth intermixing with "Yeshi Haregitu" on the sound system on the porch. By then, the clatter and chatter from downstairs have amplified. Buttoning up my tunic at my window, I marvel at how the compound is already full of cars, with more parked on the street outside. Extended family, close friends and neighbours are here for brunch and photos before we drive to the hotel to pick up my bride and her entourage. The bulk of our guests are already at the Bishoftu resort, making a long weekend of the occasion.

I am in front of my mirror, coaxing the patterned hem of my shawl into draping over my shoulder perfectly, when my door barges open, revealing a frazzled Eske, wide eyed and glowing with sweat. "Oh," she says, fanning the T-shirt she has over her jeans. She loosens her grip on the door handle. "She's not here?"

"Who? Miz?" Eske's hair is styled, so they must have been at the salon. "Didn't she leave with you this morning?"

She wipes her neck with the collar of her shirt. "She did."

"So why would she be here?"

"Nothing."

"What's going on?" Did they fight? That and other unlikely scenarios flying through my head, I look at my phone and see that I have missed multiple calls from Eske, having had my phone on silent. From Miz, I have only the text she sent me last night. *Come get me.* I hadn't even texted her back. I just hurried to her apartment as fast as I could before she changed her mind.

I call Miz's number. She doesn't answer. Now I begin to feel dread.

Miz: We need to talk.

I call her again. She declines it.

Miz: In person.

Me: Miz, what's going on?

Miz: Can you come?

Me: To the hotel?

Miz: The café next to it.

"What's she saying? Where is she?" Eske says, rising on her toes to try to read my texts.

"Everything is okay," I tell Eske, keeping my voice calm. Maybe Miz is up to something good, something fun, something sexy and out of left field. Holding on to that hope, I tell Eske, "There's no problem. She's on her way back now. She just went for a walk."

"A walk?!" my sister almost screams.

I have to tell Eske many more soothing lies to get her to leave so I can hurry to Miz. I even have to lie my way out of my own house. Mocha Coffee is on a quiet side street around the corner from the hotel entrance. Rushing down the wide stone-tiled pavement separating the café patio from the cars parked along the curb, dressed as if I am celebrating Gena a week late, I attract plenty of glances. I spot Miz sitting at a table for two on the patio, partially hidden by the row of large planters holding small trees and the green sun shade hanging low over the metal railing. Thanks to a scorching morning, there are fewer customers here than inside.

Miz's hair has also been transformed by an elaborate style, tied into a soft bun at the nape of her neck, a line of sparkling gems tracing a diagonal part from the front. But the rest of her, in a velvety track suit, is looking decidedly not wedding-ready.

Still, the sight of an empty coffee cup in front of her appeases me. Things can't be that bad if she had a macchiato, right? A thought suddenly comes to me: What if she just found out she's pregnant? Joy blooms inside me. I scoot the other chair close to her and sit, ignoring the intent stares. We must make an odd sight. A hawker passes by, carrying a tall stack of locally pub-lished books in Amharic and pirated Western bestsellers—I spot *Becoming* by Michelle Obama wrapped in plastic. I tell him we're not interested, and he moves on. I hold out my hand, but she doesn't accept it. "Are you okay?"

She takes in a deep breath, and her eyes fill with tears. "No, I'm not."

My chest tightens. My mind is a riot. Something happened to one of her parents? She saw something horrific? A stranger said something awful to her? Groped her? "Talk to me, nefse." I give her the napkin from under her coffee glass, feeling myself shake with anger at an unidentified foe.

She dabs her eyes and takes a few more breaths. "I can't do it."

Her voice is so low I almost have to read her lips. But she be-comes more clear-voiced as she continues to speak. "I can't do today. I am not your wife. I've barely been your girlfriend for a minute. It was my mistake to not stop you when you started to call me your 'wife' and call yourself 'husband.'" The air quotes she puts in her voice at those words feel like lashes, so visceral I feel my skin sting. "I should have said something a long time ago. I'm so sorry. I didn't think it would get this far." She smiles ironi-cally. "Me and you? Standing next to *your parents* as if we're any-thing like them? I can't. I just can't."

I don't know what to untangle first. She hasn't looked at me once. She spoke to the table, the coffee glass, the commuters rush-ing minibus taxis on the street, the mobile credit hawkers. She darts her eyes at me for a second and withdraws them back to the tabletop. "Do you hate me?" she says, trying to crush a single grain of sugar under her nail. The air hangs between us, thick and hot. On the outer staircase of the retail complex across from us, I watch as a waitress dressed in a white coverall takes her time climbing up carrying a covered tray of food for delivery.

"No," I say at last, but I know that my long pause before and my face say different. The truth is I do hate Miz a little right now, for asking me that in this moment. And I hate myself more for realizing that I am capable of hating her even that much. Blood is pounding in my ears. A server approaches our table but backs off at one blazing glare from me.

Miz stands up, lifting and pushing her chair in soundlessly. "Please tell everyone I'm sorry."

"Sit down," I say through clenched teeth, in a voice I haven't used since I was a manager at the bakery. She stays standing. "What could have changed between last night and now?"

She pats the back of the chair as if it's a skittish animal. "I've felt this way before."

"Yesterday, all the months before, was that all you pretending?"

"No. Not really. No. I just didn't know. I didn't realize it."

I stand too and run my hands over my head, ignoring the people staring at us.

"I was being . . . I don't know what I thought I was being. Someone I thought I could be?"

I let out a long, long breath. "Let's just get through today and—"

She backs away from me the same distance I try to close between us. "Are you listening, Kal? I said I can't do it."

"As a guest, Miz! And then we can—"

"No." She shakes her head. "That would be just as bad."

I can't help raising my voice in accusation. "Do you know what this will do to my father? To my family?"

She recoils. "Don't do that to me," she says, her voice and face hard. "Don't manipulate me."

"But *you* can do this to *us*?"

"*For* us. I'm doing this *for us!*"

We start talking over each other, neither of us caring that we've become public entertainment. "Your parents deserve the party. We don't. It's *because* I respect them that I cannot share their day, in any way. I like *us*! A lot. But that's all."

"We're not saying we are equal to them, we're—I don't understand you. Then why not celebrate us?!"

"Kal!" She presses her fingers deep into her eyelids. "You're. Not. Listening." She stuffs her napkin in her pocket. "Take time and think about it. You'll know I'm right. Please give everyone my deepest apologies." Her phone rings in her pocket. She checks it, then declines the call. "Abera's here for me."

I am floored to realize she'd already arranged her ride home before I came. I've been summoned here to receive her decision, not to have a discussion or have my point of view, my feelings in this, heard.

"Today will be fine," she says, calmly now, trying to catch my gaze, which I adamantly refuse to give her. "It was going to be amazing before we got involved in it, and it still will be. Go. Celebrate them."

With that, she leaves me alone in the spotlight, in a story unknown.

35

~⁓

MIZ

*N*ow that the secret's out about their . . . affair (what else am I supposed to call it?), my parents drop the act of Dad "working late" every day and Mom having mystery plans every evening. Dad just stays on at Mom's hotel, leaving me the whole apartment to myself now that I have no one to share it with. Still, I keep hoping that each day will bring Kal to my door. I don't dare reach out to him. The kindest thing I can do now is shut up and wait for him to accept that I'm right so that we can start figuring out how to be a normal girlfriend-boyfriend couple, who just so happen to be married to each other. On paper.

All that weekend, I creep photos and stories of the anniversary-wedding party on socials. The event went off beautifully without me. I'm impressed by how fast Weyneshet and her crew swerved back to the original protocol. No one would ever have guessed there was supposed to be a whole other couple there. Or that Kal was anything but a proud and happy son. I feel horrible, thinking of the kinds of questions he must have got because of my absence from those who'd known about us. Or worse, not questions but

looks and whispers instead, for being dateless at what was supposed to have been his wedding celebration too.

During the week, I ignore multiple calls from Eske, Bini and
numbers I don't recognize. Kal is the one person I want to hear
from. A call, a text, a visit, *anything* to say he understands. I wait
for him to respond again to my last text to him: *Come get me.* But
he continues his cold silent treatment. I double my runs, going
out in the morning and evening, to destress. But no matter how
hard or long I go, I can't stop replaying our conversation in the
coffee shop.

Now and then, a sinkhole of sadness gapes open inside me,
and I have to have a good cry at the thought of what that day
could have turned out like had I never crossed paths with my
parents that morning. Had I gone on blissfully believing in the
fantasy that that day was mine and Kal's too, that we had miraculously leaped into happy-marriage land. Had I worn the makeup,
put on the dress, held the bouquet, posed for photos—gone
through all the motions, in full faith that I could be like everyone
else. But then the sinkhole fills back up, and my insides level out
again, and I calm down. No. It was fated that I would cross paths
with my parents so that I wouldn't fall any deeper into being a
fraud, a total imposter. To not cross paths with my parents would
mean that everything leading up to that point would need to not
have happened, going as far back as meeting Kal at all. And I refuse to imagine that. Kal and I were fated to meet in that parkette
and to have stumbled into this version of *us*, so many years later.

Other than running and stuffing myself afterward with burgers and fries from the compound restaurant—miraculously un-
changed after all these years—and passing out to my dubbed
soaps, I go out only twice: on the obligatory souvenir spree with

Mom, and to donate all my old running shoes that I hauled here. Each time, even though we always take hired taxis, I come back home grimy, exhausted and practically exhaling diesel dust. I am haunted by the sharp contrasts more than ever—the merchant women squatting by the roadside, protecting their tiny piles of tomatoes and peppers on plastic sheets from the shuffling feet of the long lines of government workers waiting to get sardined into aging city buses, while high above, on the rooftop bar of the mall above everyone, expats, diasporas and what Dad calls "private sector types" mingle over happy hour and tapas.

By the end of my time here, I am not sorry to leave any of it. In another mind-blowing first, both Mom and Dad see me off at the airport the next Saturday. I bawl like a child leaving home for the first time. Inside the terminal, I brace myself to see Kal at last, expecting that here we will have no choice but to interact. The flight will force us to talk this shit out. What's the alternative, taking a sixteen-hour nonstop flight without speaking?

Throughout pre-check-in security, check-in, passport control and the three additional security checks and two document checks before reaching the exclusive US and Canada departure gate zone, I keep an eye out for Kal, but he's nowhere to be seen. By the time my group is boarding, I assume he's running late, because the only other possible explanations are that he's upgraded to business class or changed his travel date. All that to avoid me? The thought feels like an actual body blow, so I dismiss it while I let everyone board ahead of me.

Then I see him. He's at the last document check, a simple table and chair setup just a few metres beyond the first row of gate seats, but that might as well be the Pentagon. The agent flips through Kal's passport too fast to be noticing anything and ignores the additional documents he's offering her. I hate seeing Kal's bent, deferential posture. *What the hell is there to question him about?* Kal's work permit, like his temporary resident visa, still has a month on it. But he's warned me that, at the end of the day, any visa holder is at the border agent's mercy, no matter the validity of their paperwork. But Kal has the documentation of our sponsorship process on him. We both do. And I assume he printed out the scan of the Open Work Permit that Aimé emailed us. *What else does the fucker want, Kal's firstborn?!*

My breathing has become fast, choppy; my body pulses with fear. Immediately, I want to call my dad. When things get hairy here, it's either him or Kal I turn to. But no, I'm a big girl. *Handle it!* On shaky legs, I start walking to the desk, but a commanding voice stops me.

"Is there a problem?" A man, off to the side. He looks official, but who the fuck knows? I keep walking. The tension between Kal and the agent at the table is really coming off in waves now. The man snaps his finger and claps at me. "Hey!"

Fuming, I stop to glower at him as much as I dare to. He points at the gate, his steely eyes fierce with real threat. "Boarding that way!"

I'm terrified. It's as if all the stories I've absorbed about horrible altercations with figures of authority are surfacing at once, making me sweat so bad I actually start to stink sharply. Do people still get disappeared nowadays? Fuck if I know! I want to call out to Kal so he knows I tried, but it's as if my throat is packed with sand. And I don't want to add to his trouble. Feeling like a total useless shit waste of space, I slink away and board the plane. *He'll be in shortly*, I tell myself. *We'll have all the time in the world to talk.*

But he doesn't board. This scares me so much that the only dialogue I end up having for the rest of the flight is with a whole lot of itty-bitty red wine bottles, and with the flight attendants. After I do a full circuit of economy to make sure Kal isn't in a different seat, I annoy the shit out of them by asking, different ones at different times, whether I could do a walk-through of business class, real quick, *just once*. I'm lucky they still left me my breakfast tray while I was knocked out and drooling. By the time the plane lands, my lips look tattooed, and I have a splitting hangover. Which is why, when I catch a glimpse of Kal walking far ahead of me down the tunnel at Pearson Airport that leads to the customs hall, I think I am hallucinating. My first response, after confirming he's not a mirage because of his interactions with people around him, is relief. But then it turns into *What the fuck? He was on the flight? What the hell?* He *did* upgrade. Jerk!

I hurry to catch up, losing sight of him now and then, barely restraining myself from breaking into a run for fear of drawing attention to myself in an airport. In the customs hall, he blends into a five-lane-deep passport control lineup, and I get stuck too far behind so that we can't even end up side by side as the line folds back in on itself. I see him step up to a border agent's cubicle. Within seconds of their exchange, he stiffens, starts making hard gestures with his hands. Their conversation drags on. *This is not happening again.* Well, at least here I speak the language, literally and otherwise. I *excuse me* and *pardon me* through the winding queue, tucking my stuck-out hairs back behind my ears to make myself presentable, agitation already shortening my breath and sending sweat trickling down the middle of my back. I step into the open area in front of the border agents' booths.

"Ma'am, back of the line!" a security officer barks at me.

I point at Kal. "I'm with him." The officer waves me on.

"I'm with him," I say again to Kal's agent, handing over my passport. "We're together." Oh god, I reek of day-old sweat, but Kal is wearing that perfumy sweetness of business class. I smile at him even though I want to kill him. *Upgrade? Really, Negro?* Mr. Business Class doesn't deign to meet my eyes. But to the agent, he grants a smile, even if it's one tighter than Addis rush-hour traffic. Slowly, he lifts his left hand to show the officer his wedding ring. Since I am, of course, not wearing mine, that might as well be a middle finger to me. I pull his hand down beneath the counter, trying to make it seem like a loving gesture. The agent opens his mouth. Between Kal's coldness, his hand limp and lifeless in mine as if I am a stranger, and the fear of all the potentially entrapping questions the agent is about the ask, I feel a buildup of tears. I bite the inside of my cheek, tightening my death-grip on Kal's hand. The tears escape anyway, and I purposely don't wipe them away.

"Ma'am. Calm down," the agent says with the slightest kindness in his voice. He taps the work permit in Kal's passport. "This expires next month."

I let more tears freestyle down my fattened cheeks. "He has—"

"Ma'am," the agent warns.

Without a word, Kal lets go of my hand and pulls out a printout of the scan Aimé had sent, just as I'd hoped, and dryly explains his situation. Oh god, if he's this robotic at our interview, we're fucked. Miraculously, the agent lets us through. Kal walks ahead of me and steps on the escalator to go down to baggage claim.

"Phew, huh?" I say on the step above him, tapping him on his shoulder, wiping my face with my sleeve.

He doesn't turn around completely. Just offers me his quarter profile. "That's your strategy, isn't it? Crying. To get your way. Well, I was handling the situation fine on my own."

I see red. It's all I can do to not push him down the steps. "You know what, you're right. I shouldn't have stepped up to sign for your sulky, *spoiled brat ass*. Excuse me," I say, shouldering him aside and barrelling down the rest of the stairs. I do not need this. What I need is a shower, a bucket of Shanghai noodles from Swatow and my bed. No, my couch. Burn the damn bed. That's what started all of this shit. Who buys a fucking mattress for a friend?

At the luggage carousel, far away from Kal, I switch my phone on. The screen spits up a whole bunch of texts, a lot of them spam, and a lot of them from Daniel. Same with the missed calls. *Fuuudge*. Ever since I hooked up with Kal, I have been straight up ignoring Daniel's messages, not even pretending to try to arrange a time for him to come by anymore. In December, Daniel had gone quiet. Since the real estate market is dead in winter, I figured he'd gone out West for the holidays. Or Naomi dropped him, so he had no more need for an engagement ring.

Daniel: Hey.

Daniel: Miz, are you around?

Daniel: I'm passing through your area later.

Daniel: Babe, pls ping me I'm back.

Babe? I've pushed the poor man to the brink. I plop down on my cart, too tired of myself to stay upright.

36

MIZ

*H*ours after I get in from the airport, Kal still hasn't come home. I look him up on Find My Friends and see that he is at his house. I tell myself he must have decided to stop off there to catch up with everyone first. Maybe he needed a man-to-man with Silvio. Even as I crawl into bed early, teeth chattering from the shock of winter—this is why I go to Ethiopia only in summer!—I still expect Kal to come home and, despite everything, warm me up. When I wake up the next morning and see that his side of the bed is flat and cold, I begin to feel the devastation. He really is gone.

For now. I just have to wait him out. He'll come around. I control myself from stalking his location or reaching out. He knows where to find me. I resume our daily routine. I buy groceries and cook for two. I don't do the laundry because that's his department. I don't catch up on the shows we watch together. I wipe the snow off his bike so it will be ready to ride. After work, I wait for him a little bit before going out on my second daily run, in case he wants to cruise alongside me, showing off his no hands steering while checking out my backside and tempting me with carbs.

On the weekend, Aimé comes over for a long run and to pick up her souvenirs. "Where's Kal?" she says, doing a full circuit of the apartment. She's all energy now. A real runner who gets up early in the mornings on her own and ticks off another of them boxes on the schedule, baby! Her endurance is increasing, her form improving. She doesn't pump her arms, keeps her chin up, eyes ahead, trusts the beautiful symbiosis between pain, discomfort and endurance. And she has decided to do a half-marathon instead of the full marathon she threatened back in September, on the eve of my wedding. Like a good coach, I've laid the praise on thick.

"He's out," I say, pulling on a second pair of socks.

"Already?"

"Wanted to let us catch up. Says hi." I know that's not much of an explanation, but thankfully, she's more interested in our upcoming run than Kal's odd absence from his home at eight in the morning. She undoes her shoelaces and reties them, tugging very precisely to get that perfect-to-the-millimetre hold that's snug without being restrictive.

"I'm so jealous you got to train in Ethiopia for two whole weeks!"

Among other things, I think, knowing that for the first of those two weeks, the most cardio I got was when I was darting to cross the street without dying.

"Did you read my new post?" Aimé has even started a training blog, subscribed everyone she knows and branded her social. Monetizing is next.

"Bet." I've barely glanced at the blog because something about her hook, the challenge of making the switch from short to long distance, hit too close to home. "Ready?" I do a few high jumps, ignoring the tingling in my knees. "Fifteen kilometres aren't going to run themselves!"

Outside, we start the warm-up around Nathan Phillips Square a bit faster than we used to. Right away, I feel myself struggling, but Aimé doesn't even slow down to pluck her water bottle from her belt pack and glug when her latest-model Garmin tells her it is time for hydration. As I exert harder to avoid ending up being her next blog post topic, I sense Aimé forcing herself to slow down for my benefit, before inevitably speeding up, then pulling back again. This isn't the Aimé who didn't know how to pace herself. This is conditioned Aimé, who simply is faster than I am. The next time Aimé picks up speed despite her efforts not to, I try to match her. She stops.

"The safest thing," she says carefully. I know what's coming. She's going to give me the same line I've given people who tried to run with me. They never come back for a second time. "Is if we both go at our own pace and just meet me back at your place."

Her implication, that she's going to finish before me, which of course is accurate, stings. "Oh, excuse me, am I cramping your style?"

"I'm aiming for two fifteen. That doesn't mean you have to."

"Okay, madam expert. Run alone. Oh, I mean, along!"

"Miz, I want you to be able to do this race safely."

"I never wanted to. I don't do races. I got into it for your sake, 'member that?"

"And I'm saying—"

"I heard ya. Bye!" I blast off like a wild horse, fuelled more by pure will than by energy. Within minutes, I start to flag. *Flag! Yes!* Remembering my motivational reel, I try to pull it up in my mind now. That three-minute clip from YouTube of Derartu winning, the people screaming. But it's unavailable. What begins to scream, instead of my imaginary fans waving the Ethiopian flag at the finish line, are my quads. Then come the cramps in my lower abs, like the ones Aimé used to complain about in her early days. *Meh. Something is always supposed to hurt anyway.* Then I start to feel nauseous. A bit of bile comes up. I swallow it. Not like it's blood. For a nanosecond, my vision goes black. But the route is a straight shot, so I don't really need to see. *It was probably just a long blink.*

The message from my body, of course, is clear. *Stop.*

On I run. Ten kilometres won't run themselves either. Next, my left toes join the strike and begin to go numb and, shortly thereafter, my right toes too. Then, on top of my gradual system shutdown, I get camel toe. *Great, how much crappier can this run get?* All of a sudden, I am flying. But this isn't the runner's high. I am actually airborne. Black ice? In my peripheral vision, right before I go full body patty-cake with the ground, I see a cyclist zip past, the rider screaming bloody murder at me. I lie sprawled on the frozen asphalt for a good while, trying to focus on the birds surfing the breeze instead of the pain thrumming in my right ankle. I feel the vibrations of Aimé's elegant, even stride through the asphalt. *That used to be me,* I say to the pale moon still visible in the sky.

Aimé comes into view, looms over me, hands on her waist. I raise my hands, like a child wanting to be carried. Wisely, Aimé crouches down to me instead. Without a word, she puts my arm over her shoulders, eases me off the path and props me up against a tree.

"Stay there. I'll call a ride. Okay?"

I nod, sipping at the pain, blinking back tears.

After a trip to the walk-in clinic, where I react badly to finding out I have a hairline fracture in my ankle, and worse to Aimé's advice that I drop out of the race, we pick up breakfast and head back to my place. Aimé only eats the orange slice and melon cubes, since she plans to finish today's run. She sits with me while I eat, springing up the second I take the last bite.

"I'll check on you later, okay?" she says, tossing my used napkins and condiment packets into the empty container.

"You're leaving me?"

She ties the takeout bag and gets up. "I don't want to miss a day. Consistency is crucial."

The tense truce we've been in since the walk-in clinic splinters. "Is that going to be another one of your blog posts?"

Aimé smiles. "I forgot you are a mean high."

I am on mild painkillers. But Kal is the painkiller I want. One dose would fix everything. Hell, I wish he had been that cyclist!

"No," she says. "My next one is on how stress is bad for training. I'll check on you later, okay?"

"Then we'll go to the sauna?" I say, feeling pathetic that I so transparently don't want to be alone.

"I don't have any of my stuff here."

"I wish Mom was here."

"Mom is busy with her man." I give her an *ew* face. She leans in, serious. "Miz, tell me where Kal really is at this hour on a Saturday morning. Something happen?"

I shrug. "Kal moved out."

"Wha—?"

"I have no idea where he is. We're not speaking. Sorry to tell you, we are through."

Aimé looks around the place. "But he had moved in."

"Not officially." We were just joined at the hip there for a while. "My apartment is husband-free. We failed. Just like you warned me we would."

"I did not."

"Maybe you didn't. Maybe you did. Anyway."

"What happened?"

"Nothing." I can feel all that Aimé is brimming to say, to ask. But she holds her tongue and waits. Which for some reason makes me dissolve into tears. "I should have known better. Marriage ruins everything. Haven't I always said so? I'm not cut out for it. I know I said *that*. Who did I think I was that I could "try out" marriage? I should have left well enough alone. Accepted Kal had reached the end of his time in Canada."

Aimé looks at me like I'm something too broken to take for repair. She lets me just cry it out against her, someone who has been married in all but name for longer than all my hookups combined. Maybe that is why she is being quiet, just patting my head until I subside to intermittent babyish hiccups.

"Tell me what happened."

"No. You go run." Nothing has been resolved, but I actually feel a little bit lighter. And I know Aimé doesn't really want to get too deep into it right now either. She needs me to be okay, for my fight with Kal to be a minor spat, for life to be drama-free between now and the day of the race. I get it. She was like this in college too. Back then it was all about whatever had to get shelved so she could go pro. Now, it's about possibly relaunching her athletic career so she won't be stuck peering into hairy wax-clogged ears for the rest of her life.

"Whatever it is, it will blow over," she says.

"Yeah," I say, believing. "Yeah?" I say again, doubting.

"Absolutely. It's one thing to know your friend is human but a whole other thing to know that about your spouse."

I groan. Aside from the fact that I don't understand how she can be so convincing, having never been a spouse herself, I do *not* have the energy to go over all that again, what labels I am willing to take on and not, and why. Once she abandons me, I put Asni on repeat, down two shots of NyQuil, and melt into the bedcovers to hibernate until Mommy comes back.

But Monday comes first. By then, I can hop and lean my way around my place. After a trip to the bathroom, I'm lingering in my walk-in closet to sniff the special laundry detergent Kal had convinced me to buy for my run clothes, when I hear a knock at my door. I gasp, instinctively knowing it's Kal. *Yay!* "You're such a nerd. Why're you knocking?" I yell, turning to the door, completely forgetting my ankle. I feel the punishment the second my full weight lands on it. I crash, howling in pain, but giddily happy at the same time because Kal's arms will wrap around me and he'll carry me back to bed and everything will be okay.

So why am I hearing Everest's voice in my apartment?

Because the face that appears over me is not that of my Kal. It is Daniel's.

37

KAL

*M*iz has made a liar out of me. It takes all my will-power to return to the house from the café by her mom's hotel. I can only take so many detours from home, to the point I found myself mindlessly circling over and over the Atse Menelik monument in the Piassa roundabout, as if the old king mounted on his rearing horse would lend me some of his forti-tude. Once I return home, I fabricate lie after lie, beginning with telling my family that Miz's dad had appendicitis and she will not be able to join us. I cannot bring myself to utter the truth: that she does not want to be with me anymore. Not even to Eske, who proves hardest to convince. If I don't say what actually happened, then it has no reality, no power. And to me, Miz and I *had* become a kind of family, of two, with a view to adding to our number in the future, so there is, in fact, a private family crisis at hand.

Only Bini senses something is off. "You all right?" he says to me, already on his third drink of the morning, as we ride on the expressway to Bishoftu in the back of the '70s model Benz sourced specifically for this day, to evoke my parents' era. The original intended passengers were Abay and my mother's spirit; then Miz and I got added, and now here I am with my so-called best man because Abay chose the more cheerful vehicle packed with his grandkids.

"Yeah, yeah." I inject my voice with energy matching Bini's. "Just worried about Miz's mother."

"I thought it was her father with the bad appendix?"

"Oh, yes."

Bini narrows his eyes. I don't blink. I'm thinking about her parents because of what Miz told me last night, trying to connect that to what she told me this morning. Because that's the only way I can begin to make sense of how she flipped so quickly.

Bini pokes me with a finger of his drink-holding hand. "You better not have fucked it up. Did you fuck it up? I told you, man. Don't fuck this up."

"I didn't fuck it up." *She did.*

"Good!" He gulps his drink. " 'Cause this is Miz, *nahmean?* Yeah! Whoo!" He winds down his window, pops out the side of the vehicle, and shouts, "*My boy is married!*"

As if the residents of the boxy, ochre-and-yellow housing developments we are whizzing by would give half a damn. They're probably sick of the sight of flower- and ribbon-bedecked luxury wedding caravans travelling to and from resorts on the city's outskirts. I want to pull Bini in and demand to know what the hell he means by *this is Miz. What makes her so special?* I think, letting all my bitterness surface freely on my face, taking what might be my last chance to drop my mask of cheer for the rest of the day.

I am in pure agony from the moment we disembark from our cars and are welcomed by the guests gathered on the resort's wide terrace designed to create an infinity effect with the grey-green water of the lake. The densely wooded shoreline curves out on either side of it to meet itself on the far shore, half a kilometre away. I feel as lonely as a man stuck on one of those steep hills. The centres of attention—Abay with his wife absent in body but not spirit, me with my wife absent in both—navigate from group to group, taking photos, accepting congratulations and concerns, playing hosts. I check my phone for a missed call or message from Miz a thousand times a minute, wishing every time I see *Come get me* that it was sent seconds ago, not hours ago.

I drink and drink, finding alcohol the only way to slow this spin cycle of my mind, creating so many gaps in my experience of the evening that I find myself standing alone on the stage with a microphone in my hand. I blink. Everyone is still at their dining tables, faces turned to me expectantly. It takes me a few seconds to piece together that Abay must have made his speech and now it is my turn.

"When Abay decided that he and Emay would go ahead with this day . . ." I start. The boom of my voice on the sound system almost knocks me off balance. I pull on the edge of my top as if that will help me stay upright, hoping my swaying is more internal than external. "Despite . . . despite . . ."

Eyes on my toes, I falter. Until this morning, I had planned to say that I had understood him completely, because I believe that true love never ends. But my lips refuse to open and utter the lie, as if pressure-sealed by all the alcohol that I've poured past them tonight to numb myself and speed up time. I shut my eyes tight, praying for some higher power to slip me different words. But all I hear, through the pounding in my head, is someone clearing their throat. Even in the dark, I can feel the energy of an audience when a performance has fallen short. With a sharp sobering in-hale, I snap my eyes open.

I raise my glass. "Congratulations to the happy couple."

No one corrects me.

The rest of the week, on the pretext of being there for Miz and her family, I manage to have all the alone time that I lacked on the weekend, with still no word from Miz. I spend days avoid-ing places where I might run into people I know. Hard to do in a city where I have lived and worked most of my life. I steer clear of Miz's area. I spend a lot of time brooding alone at the topmost edge of the coliseum-like Meskel Square, contemplating the nearly nonstop cat's cradle flow of traffic steering humanity to and fro, on the eight-deep lanes going in each direction, the lane markers merely a suggestion. If anyone had told me, a couple of weeks earlier, that I would be this idle, counting down the days until I leave Addis, I would have laughed and said, *In a hurry to leave my home city, where I am visiting for the first time with my love? You must be out of your mind!* Maybe for a honeymoon to Lamu Island, or Zanzibar, or the Seychelles or Dubai—all places I had thought to surprise Miz with, except I didn't want to deprive her of time with her parents.

Without giving anything away, I try to find out whether Emay and Abay ever had problems, something I have never thought to ask. Even a single day when they were sour with each other or exchanged hard words? Anything. I am not sure what I am fishing for. Permission to have a flawed, messy marriage? Assurance that I will not be the first in our family to stumble in marriage? Surely, between all us siblings and their spouses, some-body witnessed a moment, heard a rumour, has a slightly different recollection of one day? But I get no such assurance. Either my probing is too subtle, or my parents really were as they appeared. Whatever magic those two had, unfortunately it has not passed down to me.

I dread and anticipate the flight back to Toronto in equal measure. I am late checking in because so many people come to my house to see me off and tag along to the airport.

I don't realize it's possible to hurt more than I was already hurting until I see that empty boarding zone as I rush to the final document check. I never, *ever* dreamed that Miz, knowing my situation and the ridiculous number of document and security checks every passenger to North America must pass through, would board the flight without me. When I am finally allowed to board, I don't want to see her face, so I turn left, upgrading to business on the spot in a petty, wasteful act of one-sided revenge that shames me even as I carry it out.

Sixteen hours later, I am still nursing my grudge, waiting until we are home to confront her about boarding without me. But the repeat ordeal with border agents on the Canadian side throws me for a loop, exacerbating my acidic mood. The border agent, purposely to disorient me, is asking irrelevant questions about a ten-year US visa on my records, which hasn't expired but is in my old passport. I am trying to maintain composure, used to automatically relinquishing my personality whenever I deal with any government representative, to complete the interaction fast and without incident. When Miz intervenes, I don't know how to manage my automatic response to her presence—her face, her voice, her touch, the vibrating heat of her body, even her stale wine breath and sharp odour, all of which are like cool water to my parched insides—with the tension of the situation, so I default to being an asshole. I deserve how she tells me off. And then how am I supposed to follow her home after that?

My lies continue in Toronto, where I tell Silvio that Miz is staying on in Addis a bit longer, hence why I'm back at the house. I busy myself with meetings with several agents who had told me to get in touch once my papers were sorted out. I quickly sign with one, who promptly starts sending me out for a string of commercial and silent-on-camera auditions that I try not to feel too demoralized by.

On my second Monday back, I am out on a ride on a rented bike, taking advantage of a mild winter day, when I get an email from my agent regarding an offer from the TV show Oliver had me retrain on-camera to audition for . . . for the role of Security Guard/Custodian.

This can't be Oliver's doing, is my first thought. I suspect I was marked for the part from the first time I walked into the casting studio. Silvio is optimistic and practical about it, pointing out that the role is a series regular that pays union scale. What more do I want? He's more amused by the irony of me claiming that I didn't come all the way out here to be a janitor, and reminds me that at least it's not a gangbanger. That's when I walk away, needing to talk to someone who would get where I'm coming from. Miz. Oliver. I ache to call Miz. I call Oliver.

"If I take this on, there's really no coming back from it, is there?" I ask him, pacing on the rooftop terrace, my fingers numb, trying to be careful about how I turn this down. He has done so much for me, and our relationship matters to me. "I have to be strategic how I let myself be perceived, don't I?" Oliver had hoped I would take a chance on the part, but he completely gets it, especially when I share with him that I have an

Open Work Permit now. "Are you . . . disappointed?" I ask, my throat catching as if I'm disappointing Abay.

"Absolutely not!" Oliver says. "And were I so inclined, you would be more than justified to be disappointed *in me* for pushing you toward a role that we both know is not right for you. For what?!"

"Thank you," I say, lowering onto the frigid old sofa with relief.

"Give it time," Oliver says. "The role you are right for is out there."

That's when it hits me, like a sudden gust of skull-cracking windchill. I've done the same thing to Miz. She only wanted to be a good friend to me, to help, but I took it and ran. I shoved and shoved her into a role for which she never auditioned, let alone signed up for. Then, when she had the courage to walk off the set, I punished her. After I end the call with Oliver, I pull up the photos I haven't been able to bring myself to look at since I showed them off to my family the day Miz and I arrived in Addis. Our simple, visually chaotic civil ceremony. I see so clearly now how unaware we were of how far in over our heads we were about to dive. I revisit the night I put on my wedding ring, and she didn't; the day we arrived in Addis and I delighted, but she froze, at Abay's suggestion.

What can we do but go back to where we started and begin again? I know the onus is on me to ask for this do-over. I just hope she agrees. She must.

I believe in the power of the simple words *I'm sorry*, but because there's no harm in a small gift, I detour to the supermarket on the way to her place to pick up just the thing. She deserves something grander, of course, but limes will be special in their own way, I know, because they'll take her back to her delight when I told her, a long time ago, about how limes are to our rural folk what roses are to us city people—symbols of love. "Specifically, during Timket," I'd said, "when you toss them at the one you have a crush on."

"But why limes?" she'd said.

"Because love is tangy, refreshing, rare, aromatic, full of essential vitamins and minerals."

"In other words, you have no clue whatsoever."

I'm in the produce aisle, smiling at the memory, when Aimé calls. *Oho, the obligatory best friend intervention.* Not needed, but why not have a little fun? "Yes?" I say gruffly.

"Hello to you too. Nice of you to say hi when you got back."

"What's up, Aims? I'm in the middle of something." Trying to decide between organic limes from Mexico or Argentina and whether I should include lemons, for chromatic variety.

"Are you planning to do something about whatever's going on with your woman?"

"Why do I have to be the relationship mechanic?"

I hear Aimé smack something, probably her face. "Because that is marriage! How am I, the not-married person, the only one talking sense? I don't have time for this runaround. Handle it. Y'all are *married*."

"No. We are not. Simply taking on the label doesn't make it so." I am clear on that now. We have to both choose that status. Then, if we do, we have to earn it anew every moment.

"Listen, she's laid up with an injury, busted up her ankle trying to be the fourth Dibaba sister."

All my pretense crumbles to ash. "What?!" A vivid memory flashes through my mind—of my hands clasped around Miz's ankles pressing against my neck, her pleading yes when I hit that spot, when I ask her whether I can let go.

"She fell, while running. On Saturday. She's the worst patient. You signed on the dotted line, so drop whatever you're doing, and go take care of your business."

"Going!" I say, hanging up and tearing off a produce bag from a roll. This is Miz. Dotted line or not, she is my business, mine to take care of.

38

MIZ

"What in the absolute fuck?" Flat on my back on the carpet of my walk-in closet, I scowl at Daniel's upside-down face looming above me. Time and the hairs at the back of my neck stand on end, my heart throbbing like a tiny sedated drum. I roll over onto all fours—whimpering in pain all the way. Everest moves to help me up while Daniel stands, feet planted apart, arms crossed, as if my injury is wasting his time.

"No, no, it's okay," I say to Everest. He has no business picking me up with his bad back. But he insists, half lifting, half dragging me over to my bed like a rag doll.

"I'm very sorry, Miss Mizan," Everest says, wringing his hands once he's ensured I am sufficiently propped up. "I thought you are at work. He promised he was to pick up only one thing. He's been begging me for months! He said it would take no time. I would have stayed with him!"

Daniel doesn't say a word, but his eyes are scanning my bedroom like he's the Terminator. I let out a long breath, trying to push aside the pulsing waves of pain.

"Everest, Everest," I say. "It's okay."

If it had to come to this, Daniel barging in on me, I'm actually glad that Everest is here. It will make the next part pass quicker, like the NyQuil that's become my new best friend does to all my unoccupied time. "It's in there," I say to Daniel, flopping my hand toward my nightstand drawer.

He makes to move but stops himself. "What is?" he says, trying to be all cryptic.

"Daniel, please just take it. It's in the bottom drawer. And don't ask me shit."

He points at the drawer, then swivels his finger to point at Everest. "You want me to open that in front of him?"

I fall back on my bed. "Go nuts."

I hear Daniel yank the drawer open, rummage around, then pull the whole thing out and dump the contents on my bedroom carpet. At the same time, poor Everest lets out a huge gasp, obviously seeing my Womanizer, Magic Bunny, Plunger, feathers, tassels, lubes, cock rings, you name it, sprawled on the floor. "*Santa Maria!*" Everest exclaims, the keys jangling in his hand as he crosses himself. "Miss, I—I—I will be by the hallway," he stammers, then vamooses in a cloud of dust bunnies.

I raise myself up on my elbows and watch Daniel pick the ring out of all that debris. He cradles it in his palms tenderly like a wounded bird, naked joy on his face. I swear his eyes glisten with tears. Wow, he must really love Naomi. And she him, I guess. Age ain't nothing but a number, as they say. Hope she is still in the picture after months of waiting for a ring that he'd probably given her good reason to expect.

"Get that insured, if you want my advice," I say, shimmying my body up to my pillows. "And good luck. Marriage is a fucking beast."

Daniel shakes his head at me, then gets up, first putting the ring in the breast pocket of his shirt and buttoning it carefully. God forbid something should happen to the ring while he's going from kneeling to standing. He turns away, about to leave without another word to me.

What's that thing they say is worse than hate? Indifference. "Are you going to say something or just pretend I'm not even here?" I say, galled by the idea that it could have been this easy: me just giving it back, no questions asked.

He pauses, sighs at the ceiling. "What is there to say to you, Miz? You dicked me around for months and almost cost me my happiness, *purposely*! I've been losing my mind since August, as if my mom's surgery wasn't stressful enough, trying to remember where I could have last seen the ring."

"I didn't take it purposely! I swear! You didn't give back my AirPods and I was looking for them and I found it then I freaked out thinking the ring was for me and I hid it because . . . well, it made sense to do so at the time, but only for a short time, I swear, then—"

But most of what I would say is stopped by Daniel's laughter. He hollers from the very bottom of his pelvic floor. Hell, from the bottoms of his *toes*, even stumbling around, his shoulders slouched for effect. The kind of laughter that would be infectious even if I weren't buzzing on NyQuil. But since I very much am, I join him, little by little, until we're both busting a gut, while somewhere in the far foggy back of my mind, I'm wondering whether I'm laughing *at myself* or *with him*.

"Oh, Miz, you entertain me," Daniel says, cooling down. He starts tossing my toys back in the drawer. "Whoo! See, this is why I never planned to stop seeing you."

"Say what?" I say, wiping the corners of my eyes.

He flips my Magic Bunny in the air like a baton and catches it by the ears. "Marriage doesn't mean monogamy."

"Uh, does Boo Thang Naomi know that?"

"What does Naomi have to do with it?"

Suddenly Kal walks in.

"What's up, man?" Daniel says to Kal, all friendly.

"Hey!" I say happily, as if Daniel and Kal, who know each other only by reputation, being in my bedroom at the same time is totes normal. "You caaaame!" He's carrying a bag of fruit. "With groceries!" Such a sweetie.

It takes Kal dropping the bag to the floor, a whole bunch of lemons and limes going everywhere on my carpet, for me to realize *this looks bad! It's not what it looks like!*

Daniel clocks Kal's wedding ring. His face lights up as if he just found a kindred spirit. "Oh, congrats! When did you get married?"

"Okay, Daniel, bye!" I sing out desperately. "Bye, Daniel!" I even kick my one good foot on the bed for emphasis. Kal, who has been staring at Daniel as if he can't believe his eyes, now trains them on me.

"Him? Still?" he says, scary calm.

"No!" I say, offended. "God no! Not since last summer!"

"So . . . what's going on? Why is he here?"

Daniel throws the Bunny in my drawer and shoves the drawer back in the nightstand. "And I'm out. I just came to get something, man. Peace." He makes a V sign but checks me. "Miz, you good?"

"What are you implying?" Kal says, his eyes sizzling as if he's about to punch Daniel's lights out.

Daniel puffs his chest, his good humour now gone. Kal sneers at that. They take a half step toward each other. How sick am I that I'm kind of turned on right now? It's just . . . I've never seen Kal this angry before.

"Excuse you, Daniel," I say, breaking from my daydream to be the adult here. "You can go now. I'm good. Sorry about . . ." I nod my head at his breast pocket.

He fist-bumps me from afar. "You owe me one, eh? Keep in touch." With a wink, he leaves.

Kal turns to stare at me, stone faced. Is he serious? "Kal, come on," I say playfully. I lean over the edge of the mattress, pick up a lemon, and toss it at him gently. He doesn't react to it bouncing off his chest. "Hello? I'm choosing you. Remember?"

"What was he doing here?" His voice is bone-chillingly flat, but I am determined to have everything be okay again. Enough with the foolishness. There are no innocents here. We've both hurt, and been hurt (some of us literally).

"You heard him. He was grabbing something."

"Care to be more specific?"

That gets my back up. I frown, my playfulness going down a notch. "Care to mind your business?"

He rolls his shoulders back, as if he just got more justification for his victim act. "Must be he left whatever it is more recently. Because otherwise, he's had five months to pick it up, right?"

He's being a total jerk, but for the sake of getting this over with, I waver on the cusp of telling him. *Five months ago, I found a diamond ring, snooping where I had no business. I thought it was for me, and . . .*

And what? I took it?

I took it briefly *and . . .*

And what? I've been giving the owner the runaround since? *Because . . .*

Because I'm . . . fill in the blank with any unflattering adjective.

"Does loyalty mean nothing to you?" he suddenly shouts full blast.

Since when do Kal and I shout at each other? But the brakes are totally snapped now. "Are you really asking me that?" I yell back.

"At the bare minimum, Miz! At the barest minimum, I thought we were enough for each other."

This is why I don't fucking do relationships! "First of all, we *never* had that talk, and even if, that doesn't entitle you to my whole privacy."

"That's how—"

"What?! How *husbands and wives* are supposed to roll? Maybe your perfect mom—"

He turns and leaves. *Shit.* I went too far. Why did I have to go *there?*

"I'm sorry!" I call out, struggling to get off the bed like a bug on its back. "Wait!"

I roll to free myself and land on my face. I squirm my way up, coming first onto my hands and knees, then my good foot and both hands. I hear commotion on my balcony. A second later, Kal carries his bike past the bedroom door.

I hobble out as my front door slams shut. "Would you *fucking* wait!"

Next thing I know, I'm crashing again, falling through citrusy fresh air and slamming into the hardwood. "Waait," I wail pitifully, starfished on the floor, knowing it's hopeless. Out of the corner of my eye, I see the lemon I must have stepped on, destroyed beyond recognition, like my entire life.

39

KAL

When I get home from Miz's place, I go to my bedroom to start packing because there's nothing worth staying for anymore.

40

MIZ

The following week, all I have energy for is dragging myself to work and back in Ubers as if I'm made of money, passing off my injury as the cause of my antisocial miserableness (other than when I'm with clients). I am so glad that Omar doesn't know I know he knows about Kal and me being married, because then I'd have to pretend worse than I already am that everything is copacetic. Since he left me splattered on my floor, I haven't even tried to reach out to Kal. I bailed on him in a bad situation. He bailed on me in a bad situation. Are we even yet? My only excitements in life come from Aimé publishing a new blog post, and planning for when Mom comes home.

"ET 500, right? Or is it 501?" I say to Mom on the phone, sprawled on my couch, scrolling through Netflix. "Unless you have a stopover?" She is due back in seven sleeps! "Mom?"

"Um," she says.

Um? Since when does Mom say *um?* My antennae perk up. "What? Dad?" I say, assuming I'm on speaker phone, because of course every call is a three-way conference now.

"It's just you and I," she says.

"Did something happen?" I sit up, ready to go UFC on Dad from all the way out here.

"Mizu . . ." she says with the drawn-out upward inflection she uses when she wants to ask me to do something for her. I don't realize how bad I've missed that lilt in her voice until now. "I have good news." *Okaay.* "I am going to stay."

"Until?"

"No *until*. I will live here, with my husband, from now on."

Buffering, buffering, buffering. "Eh? Who?"

"Mizu!" Sharp, fast this time.

"Just to be clear, you're talking about . . . Dad?"

"Of course!" she says, shocked.

"You're moving . . . I mean . . . you're staying there? With him? For good?"

"Yes." I can practically see the smile on her face, as if she's accepting a proposal.

"But . . ." *We were supposed to return together.* The thought sounds whiny and childish in my head. Some part of me will always be expecting to take the return leg of our trip, the one we never took when I was two after my heart got fixed.

Dad comes on the line. "Mizan?"

My breathing has become rapid. I think I'm going to cry. *Stop it, girlie. Leave your parents and their Bobby Caldwell playlist alone.* One of my older clients at work had finally put me out of my misery, telling me what that song was that had been nagging me since the hotel room. "Hmm?" I squeak. *Don't cry don't you fucking cry. They deserve to get their vintage romance on.*

"I hope this means now you'll be visiting more often, yes?"

And then it all floods out. I tell Dad everything: that Kal has been in Toronto since 2010, that I signed for him four months ago when his sponsorship fell through, that we had become involved in a real relationship afterward (leaving out the sex part obvs), that we were supposed to have a piggyback *wedding* wedding in Ethiopia, that we are not speaking now.

"Married but not together," I finish off. *Like you guys, once upon and for a long time.*

"Where did this Kalkidan come from?" Mom says. I am briefly mind-blown at how wild it is that she's completely oblivious to a person who is such a huge part of my life.

"Dad?" *Help.*

Long pause. Then I hear Dad lighting a cigarette. *Oh, thank God.* Choosing his words carefully, as if he's building a case for a client who looks very guilty on paper but is actually quite law abiding and innocent, he loops Mom in about *this Kalkidan.* From Mom's intermittent tiny gasps and sounds of surprise, I fear Dad might be landing himself in the doghouse for having allowed a boy to become my guardian of sorts in Addis all these years when a boy was the exact reason that Mom shipped me off to him in the first place.

Everybody caught up, Dad then turns on me. "Mizan," he says. "The signing was not wise."

No shit, Dad. I'm just glad this convo is happening when I'm too old to get in trouble with them. *Where you gonna deport me to now, huh?*

"We could send *astaraki* to the Legesses' house here," Mom says.

Mediators? Oh, hell naw! That's for married *married people!*

"That is the way of our generation," Dad says.

Also that too.

"Mizan, don't be too proud," Dad says. "Don't waste your years like your mother and me. You don't know until the very end of life what was for the good and what was for the bad. The way things seem now is only how things are now. Not how they will be in the future. Only at the end of life do we know what was really bad or good. Understand?"

"Uh-huh," I say. *What?* I don't know why I bothered. Not one piece of what they've said feels helpful. Am I supposed to apologize to Kal? File for divorce? Suggest our own big wedding? Turn myself in to the authorities? Why did I think I could get advice from these two?

I wish them a very belated congrats on their now truly official reunion and get off the call, planning to get in touch with Kal. But I can't bring myself to tap his name on my screen. And I'm not about to barge unannounced into his house either. I put my phone away and continue scrolling through horror film options on Netflix. After the interview. This damn interview that we were supposed to ace in our sleep. Yes. When the admin is over, then we can deal with the personal part. *One thing at a time, girlie.*

"Still nothing from him, huh?" Aimé says on the phone, weeks later, while I am on my way to the interview in an Uber, the red binder on my lap.

"Nope," I say, running my fingers along the tabs on the binder, each like a cut to my soul. "Imagine if I'm the only one there."

"He'll be there. And it'll go fine," she says, her voice choppy from running.

"How are you so sure?"

"Come on. Even when you two weren't together, you looked like you belonged together."

My heart warms at that. "So now you're spitting flat-out lies, huh? Nice."

As my ride pulls into the parking lot of the Service Canada Centre, I see Kal, bundled against the polar vortex, coming from the direction of the subway station. "Let's do this," I say to myself. I put a neutral face on and step out of the car, limping more out of habit than pain, lugging the monster red binder with me. I enter the building without waiting for him, as if he's someone I used to know but hope won't recognize me. We line up at security, show ID and our interview notification letter, pass through the metal detector, sign in and enter the crowded waiting room full of couples, all without exchanging a single word or look. Kal's manner is so detached, his eyes so vacant, as if we have already bombed the interview and he's been given a leave-by date. He sits one chair away from me, so I put the binder on the seat between us.

Thirty minutes later than our appointment time, the interview officer calls us in a dull monotone.

"Mizan Begashaw! Kalkidan Legesse!"

When Kal and I stand up, the officer tilts his head, closely wrapped in a dark indigo turban, just a tiny millimetre in surprise. Oh no. We already messed up. We shouldn't have sat apart. I remembered reading somewhere on the forums that couples arriving for their interview are assessed on CCTV from the moment they enter the building. If there is any truth to that, Kal and I might as well go home now.

In the windowless interrogation room straight out of *Law & Order*, camcorder and all, we stand for the swearing in. Then the officer invites us to take our seats opposite his desk. He takes off the blazer he has on over a black turtleneck and hangs it over the back of his chair.

I hope my face does not show any trace of the resentment I started to feel the moment we entered the room. No one should have to go through this bullshit. Who is this rando to judge whether what Kal and I have is real or not? But I put on my most cooperative smile and angle my body toward Kal, even though my knees are killing me this morning and it makes it worse.

Meanwhile, Kal, Chief Knee-Kisser, is just a few shades short of hostile. Making zero effort to not look as if he'd rather be anywhere but here. What's worse, I wonder, being like dummies or being overly affectionate? Hopefully, the officer will take our formality for cultural modesty, respect for authority. Or hell, for exactly what it is: a couple having a really bad moment . . . if a moment is almost six weeks. That's as much proof of a true relationship as being all lovey, right?

Don't hold it against us, mister, I plead silently. *Believe me, we are in a true relationship.*

The officer adjusts the materials on his desk. Landline phone, biometrics equipment, Bible and our file: the hundred-plus pages of forms, documents and photos we submitted last November. Plus a few printed pages, face down. Those must be the interview questions. The officer picks them up and taps the edges against the desk.

"Congratulations on your marriage," he says flatly. No smile, nothing.

Silence.

"Thank you so much," I say, grinning enough for all three of us. I'm sure I look deranged.

Kal nods, clears his throat unnecessarily.

"As we proceed, please answer only questions directed at you. Do not answer for each other."

I nod, palms flat on my knees to keep me emotionally steady.

Kal nods, legs crossed, arms crossed, like a damn human pretzel.

The initial questions, all directed at Kal, are softball ones about me. My birthday, educational background, when I came to Canada.

Kal mentions only the year of my arrival, not the reason why, answering strictly what he has been asked, not a syllable more. "Oh, when the revolution came," the officer says, assuming, as everyone does, that Mom and I also fled Ethiopia because of the revolution, our big bang that created the universe of diaspora.

"Why did it take you so long to propose to her?"

"*Huh?*" I say, my shock making me forget the rules.

The officer turns cold eyes on me, piercing greenish eyes that I'd decided meant he was kind but now I'm not so sure. "Ma'am. I'm asking him," he says, jabbing his pen in Kal's direction. "Was it *you* who proposed?" he adds condescendingly.

Well, yeah. But I pinch my mouth and shake my head. The officer runs his hand once over his moustache and switches focus back to Kal. "You've known her since childhood. You've been in Canada going on nearly a decade—"

"Actually, eight—" *Shit.*

"Would you be more comfortable to wait outside, ma'am?"

I zip it. *Call me "ma'am" one more time though.*

"I was waiting . . ." Kal says, and exhales deeply.

Oh, sweet Jesus, where's he going with that? After a beat, the officer finishes his thought for him. "To be sure you couldn't get permanent status another way? Was she a backup for you? Mere insurance?"

This motherfucker! Who're you calling an insurance policy?! But Kal keeps his cool. In fact, his face becomes bare, open with sadness.

"I was waiting for my heart to be free of an old pain. It takes as long as it takes."

The officer's breath catches. Oh, so the brother's been there himself. *Ouf*, even I felt all the hurt behind that. For a few moments, nobody moves. Then the officer tugs at his ear and shifts his body toward me, resuming his authority. I sit up. "Meanwhile," he says pointedly. "How long had you been thinking about, hoping for, marriage?"

I pick at my cuticles, twist the wedding ring I shoved back on my finger this morning. I steal a glance at Kal. Now he looks eerily at peace, as if he's given up the fight to stay and is just here to finish the process out of concern for the complications it could cause if he left it hanging. For who? If for me, I'm touched by his thoughtfulness, even in the midst of his anger. He'll make a great husband someday. I so miss the light, the kindness in his eyes that I had instinctively responded to as a sniffly, lonely, heartbroken fourteen-year-old.

Truth is the only way to salvage our relationship. Maybe not the romance but the friendship we had. And this is my only time to say the truth. I may never have another chance.

The truth is I've been thinking about marriage all my life. About *not* being in it. Even when I was in it. "Never," I say.

The officer, who'd been toying with his pen, holds it still. "I beg your pardon?"

"I never thought of marriage."

He jabs his pen in the air toward Kal. "You didn't love him?"

"That's not what I said."

I shuffle up more in my seat, sitting up straighter, and lift my chin. Here goes nothing. "I've always loved him. But what I wanted was to date more."

More like date, period. But no need to barf out all *the truth, girlie.*

"I wanted to take our time, figure out what's developing between us. Not define anything yet. And definitely not become husband and wife when I was just beginning to get comfy as girlfriend and boyfriend." *Comfy* is also a little truth-adjacent but whatevs.

The officer touches his files. "But you said he proposed, by the bird sculptures, in the dog park . . ."

"Yes," I say, affirming the false version of our story. "But there was a time before that . . ."

"Oh, so there *was* an earlier proposal?"

"Uh-huh. You could call it that." Oh god, I don't know how much longer I can keep up this improv. "Which I turned down. Because I wanted to take it slow." I am quivering with the wild thrill of rewriting our history on the spot, to what I wish it had been, in front of an officer of the government no less! I stare at my feet, too scared to look at Kal. What if, back in September, after Nardos and Samri left the café, we had just had a good laugh about my wild idea to find him a sponsor, finished our pastries and gone home? Some part of me believes that we would have got around to seeing each other as more than friends eventually, even if it had to happen long distance. A window of opportunity would have opened up somewhere along the line, one we never had because Kal has been deeply taken, by a real girl or by her phantom, for as long as I've known him.

The officer turns to Kal, expecting him to corroborate this story.

41

KAL

*E*yes on the floor, I observe my breath. I feel the officer's attention on me, but in my mind, Miz and I are alone, at the café beside the Elilly Hotel. Through the officer, and in different words, Miz is saying the same thing she said to me that morning. Except this time, neither of us has the option of walking away from the conversation. Not without serious repercussions. We have to see it through.

"I was so hurt," I say, speaking to the side of Miz's face. She grips her thigh slightly and slowly raises her eyes to meet mine. My anger melts away like butter. "I was so hurt at first," I say softly. "But after a time, I agreed with her. I rescinded my proposal, and we took our time."

I feel as if we are really looking at, not through, each other at last.

"We just dated. Enjoyed being together without pressure."

"I see," the officer says, losing what little interest he had in this behind-the-scenes exclusive, this outtake that was never filmed. To him, it's irrelevant. But to us, this chance we never had to not be forced to rush is everything. *Can we still do it?* we ask each other silently with our eyes. *Can we backtrack and put that part in?* Meanwhile, the officer flips mechanically through the red binder of recent, real mementoes of our short-lived happiness. He opens the envelope that I had put on the desk: photos of the wedding-eve party. I feel my throat tighten. That was the one night where Miz and I had been 100 percent in total sync, body and soul, husband and wife. What I now consider a preview of what may be possible for us, years down the line, I suppose.

"I don't see your mother or father at either of your ceremonies," he says to Miz, presuming the pics to be our second wedding in Ethiopia. "Why?"

"They didn't know I was getting married," she says simply.

The officer sighs. His shoulders sag, and he drops his hands on the table. Too many twists in this case for his speed, perhaps? "And why might that be?"

"They have this very . . . complicated relationship, and I didn't want any of that around mine. What's theirs is theirs, you know, and what's mine is mine. They know about him, of course. And they like him." She smiles at me. My eyes widen at this new information. *They know?* Miz gives me a tiny nod. *We have a lot of catching up to do!* This time, she nods emphatically, eyes wide.

"I noticed you were limping slightly," the officer says to Miz, interrupting our telepathy and trying to return to doing this by the book. He turns to me. "What happened?"

I smile. "Went too fast, too soon."

Miz gives me a thumbs-up. "Ma'am," the officer warns.

Physical contact is prohibited, but I extend my hand to her, as a peace offering. Let's get in trouble together. "Pushed too hard, tried to do too much too quickly," I continue.

Miz accepts my hand, sending a current of warmth spreading through my entire body. The officer slaps his file folder shut and pushes his chair back loudly. "All right, we're done here."

Miz abandons her chair and lands herself on my lap, hugging me tight. I touch her everywhere all at once, as if to confirm it is really her, that she's back in my arms. "Egypt," I say, kissing her palm, surprising myself with a voice from the depths of myself, like Cleopatra is her given name. "Thou knew'st too well my heart was to thy rudder tied by the strings, and thou shouldst tow me after. O'er my spirit thy full supremacy thou knew'st."

"Oh!" The officer gasps. We turn and look at him, almost surprised that he's still there. "My favourite! You know the play?" he says, beaming, his entire demeanour transformed into that of a regular person with emotions and passions.

Miz and I look at each other in wonderment. Unbeknownst to us, we were in the presence of a closet romantic! "He was in it," she says proudly, and adds with a bit of sass, "It's in the files."

"What a small world!" he says, clapping his hands. "I've attended the summer shows in the park ever since I was a boy! It was my life's dream to be on that stage."

"Well, my guy can tell you all about jumping on your dreams," Miz says, cupping my cheeks. "Can't you?" After planting an unabashed, unauthorized kiss on me, she retakes her seat so I can regale the officer with everything he has ever wanted to know about the training, the rehearsals, the productions. In short, the life. Information I would never have guessed might be the key to our success today. After about fifteen minutes of this, the officer reluctantly, but much more pleasantly than earlier, ends the interview.

"I'm very sorry to have missed your performance," he says, extending his hand.

I shake it firmly. "Remember, it's never too late to go for it."

"I'm going to be giving a lot of thought to you two," he says, as he shows us out.

Miz pauses at the door. "Uh, is that a good thing or a bad thing?"

"Thanks for coming in," the officer responds, already dissolving back to his official, unreadable persona. It's a bracing reminder that just because we had a few minutes of friendly informality does not mean that Miz and I are safe from our case being denied.

"Did he just . . . was he just playing us?" Miz says once we are outside, looking just as puzzled as I feel.

"Impossible," I say, snaking my arm around her waist. "No one could play us but us, baby."

She snort-laughs. "Goof!"

42

MIZ

I lead Kal down the aisle, of the Rabba by my workplace, that is, at the far end of which there's only an unoccupied cash register—no priest, no officiant, no vows—and come to a stop three-quarters of the way down, exactly between the toiletries on the one side and breads on the other. "We're here."

Kal squeezes in beside me. "Here where? Aren't you picking something up?"

"Nope. This is where I wanted to come today."

"For our first date?"

"Yup!" In the time since our interview, Kal and I have been busy making up for a lot, mostly within the four walls of my bedroom. But there was one thing I knew I definitely wanted to do that would require us putting on clothes and leaving my apartment: going on our official first date. And I knew exactly where I wanted it to be. Or at least where I wanted it to start. Right here. I had been mostly avoiding this Rabba since before that awkward-as-hell meetup with Khadijah—Ms. Pay-to-Play—and full on steering clear of it since then. But the risk of another awkward encounter was worth it.

"And what's so special here?"

"No, wait." I shuffle a bit to the left. "Right . . . here is exactly where I was when you got in touch for the first time in three years, and on top of that, to tell me that your ass was in Toronto."

"Oh," he says softly, looking around as if we're at the scene of an old accident marked by piles of sun-bleached plastic flowers and laminated photos.

I nod, running my finger down a bottle of baby oil. I had created a space like that in my heart when I had thought our friendship was dead for good. "Yeah."

"I'm sorry."

I wave him off. "Now you know."

"Thank you for bringing me."

"I'd also picked this spot for our fake photos day. But we never got around to it."

"We can do it now . . ."

"Meh. Who for? We can just . . . have our date by . . . shopping!" I say, making it up as I go along. Because when you've been friends with your boyfriend longer than he's been your boyfriend, and you live together, romance just be like that, in the everyday. "For starters, we're out of these," I say, grinning. I knock a few packs of condoms off the shelf and into my basket. Kal reaches over me, coming way more into my personal space than needed, to nudge one more pack off the shelf, which I also catch in my basket. Since he's already all up on me, he takes me by the waist and dips me so far that I see stuff on the bottom shelf I've never noticed.

"May I?" He offers his arm once I'm upright again. I link mine with his, and we stroll the aisles as if we're in a museum on our honeymoon, until our basket is full with the ingredients for a romantic night in: scented candles, strawberries, incense, whipped cream, chocolate, bubble bath and a mixed flower arrangement that, from the looks of it, should be at least 50 percent off.

By the time we finish shopping, who should be at the cash register but Khadijah herself.

Because I'm just lucky like that.

"Eff my life," I murmur to Kal. "It's *her*."

"So?" Kal says, continuing on. He's right. So what? I'm tired of going all the way to the other convenience store ten minutes away in this damn winter. I miss my Subway lunch specials. If she wants to have attitude, that's her potato. I'm a bit impressed though, having never seen any of the women who look like me in charge of the till at any Rabba. *You go, girl.*

"I hope she acts as if she's never seen me before in her life," I hiss to Kal without moving my lips. But she gets right to it while scanning the first item. "You never called," she says. She darts a look at Kal, not sure how much more she should say. I'm so glad I never showed her a photo of him. "Is your friend still looking for someone?"

I scrunch up my face toward Kal, as if I haven't thought about this friend in ages. "You remember what's his name, who needed a sponsor?"

Kal's eyes dance. "Oh, him," he says, playing along. "Hold on. Let me check on him."

When he unlocks his phone, it automatically opens to the last app he was in: his email. Showing there's a new message, which even reading upside down, I can clearly see is from the IRCC. I'd recognize that no-reply@ address anywhere, the one that means there's an update on our case. My heart rate triples. The barcode scanner beeps slowly as Khadijah takes her sweet time with our purchases. Kal swallows, his face becoming serious, his gaze steely. I know he's thinking what I'm thinking. *Already?* It's only been a week and a bit since we (surely) bombed the interview.

I swallow, trying to wet my parched throat while we telepathize over it. *Should I open it? Now? Up to you. You tell me.*

"Do it," I say, my voice low. Why not? Apparently, I am meant to have all my peak life moments in this Rabba. We'll be fine either way. Just, one way, where we get to grow our relationship in the same time zone, will suck less.

Kal taps on the link. I turn away. I can't look. This is like waiting to be jabbed by one of those giant needles for blood donation. I grab a bunch of chocolate bars and put them on the counter.

"Need a bag?" Khadijah says, though of course that's not what she's really asking.

"Yes, please."

I try to concentrate on the total adding on the screen. I don't even bat an eye when she gets to the condoms. Kal is being too quiet. Does it take that long to jump between apps? Maybe the network is down. I take my phone out and look at the bars. Nope, network is fine. Maybe the password didn't preload. We changed it from that marriage proverb to a simple *Wereket*. Paper. Perfect reminder not to ever get ahead of ourselves again—"

"He's good."

I whip around, eyes bugging. Kal is all smiles. "*He is?!*" I leap on Kal so fast he almost doesn't catch me. He spins me around and puts me down with a big kiss. We high-five. "Yes!"

"Yes indeed," Kal says, gathering himself as Khadijah puts our bags on the counter, giving us the withering look of a disapproving aunt. "He found someone," he says to her, then turns to me. "The perfect someone who was there all along."

If I grinned any harder, my smile would go all the way around my head.

"Good for him," Khadijah says, bored. "That'll be seventy-five thirty."

"Give me that," I say, taking Kal's phone. I need my eyeballs on the actual sentence.

This refers to the Application to Sponsor blah blah blah . . . *has been approved.*

ONE YEAR LATER

Me: Guess who's officially landed now!

Aimé: Oh good, they let y'all back in 😄

Me: Yup! 😅

Kiki: Say hello to Canada's newest permanent resident.

Aimé: Was it complicated?

Me: Not at all! The cold was the worst part 🥶

Aimé: Well, it's Niagara Falls in winter sooo.

Me: It took literally 10 min. We crossed the bridge to the US side, K had quick chat with the American border guy, then we U-turned to cross back to Canada's side, got PR stamp at the booth.

Kiki: And bob's your agot.

Me: *uncle

Aimé: I got it 😜 Wow it's finally over!

Kiki: If I never see another form again, it'll be too soon.

Aimé: Until you apply for citizenship.

Me: That's just a test & not for a long while.

Aimé: And by then, u might finally actually be 😌 😌 😌

Me: Be . . . ?

Aimé: MRS. LEGESSE.

Me: Wot that got to do with anything?

Kiki: Our women keep their name, remember?

Me: @Kiki 😗 🌙 Luh ya.

Aimé: Kay C u tmr bright and early! 👍 👍 🏃

I text Kal, who is snuggled under the blanket on the other side of our couch, privately, burrowing my toes deeper into the warm nook of the couch corner and his butt cheek.

Me: Should we tell her?

A mischievous smile comes over his face.

Kiki: No, let's wait. Don't want her getting distracted and coming in over her target time.

"God forbid," I say, widening my eyes. That first race having totally revamped her mojo, Aimé has since progressed steadily to a full marathon and is fast becoming a "rocking it toward midlife" coach-influencer. All my projects a resounding success, if I do say so myself. Including Project Miz. As usual, Aimé's hunch isn't totally off. When Kal and I were coming back over the Rainbow Bridge, he'd wanted to make a brief stop to take a photo with Niagara Falls in the background so that we'd have something more personal than paperwork to mark the big day. Little did he know though that I had something much more special in mind. Maybe it was the romantic, two-hour number 12 GO Bus ride we'd just been on, or the memory of how things had been between us the last time we re-entered Canada. Or maybe it was the past year of simple, pressure-free dating, but I felt ready.

I didn't get down on bended knee or send my people to Kal's people. Though jewellery was involved. I just used my words, peering at him through my faux fur–lined hood, squinting against the biting wind. "Hey." I squeezed hard to feel his fingers through the thick padding of our thermal gloves.

"I think it's time to order those custom-made rings from Teklu Desta."

I could only see his eyes over his extra-thick scarf and parka zipped up past his nose, but those pools of hot chocolate syrup told me all I needed to know even before he responded.

"I thought you'd never ask."

ACKNOWLEDGEMENTS

For sponsoring my entry into this life and being unwavering sources of love and encouragement, I would like to thank my parents first and foremost. Also much love and thanks to my extended family far and wide, for always cheering me on and for being interested in how it's going with the writing thing. Sorry I never give a coherent answer! Milu and Lina, your Gen Z fandom warms my heart and keeps me going.

Serkie and Mesi, my tireless, relentless, smart, generous and tough readers, who not only read an untold number of drafts, but have also hung on with me during every rise and fall and spin and inversion on the emotional roller coaster of the writing life. Thank you from the bottom of my temperamental insecure paranoid heart.

Special thanks also to Els, for the many idea-workshopping and life-anecdote-sharing sessions, the playlists, and for keeping me well fed. To Tamara for your friendship, your faith in me as a writer, and your very honest feedback! And cousins and friends of mine who answered my invasive questions about your experiences with United States Citizenship and Immigration Services (you know who you are!), thank you for sharing, especially about the spousal sponsorship and interview process.

Thank you to my agent Marilyn Biderman, for always being there to address all my concerns, founded and unfounded, and for being the best advocate, counselor, coach, you name it! I am so reassured by having you in my corner. Thank you to my editor Bhavna Chauhan, for taking on my pseudo-romcom manuscript, despite my zero track record, and guiding me with so much patience and expertise through the painstakingly slow process of shaping it into the best actual romcom it could be. And thank you to my editor Megan Kwan for your concise and insightful edits and chats, and for all the books! I am very lucky to have worked with you both.

Funny thing about writing—you take up hours of people's time interviewing them about a given topic in the name of research, only to barely end up using any of the information, or only a fraction of it. So, an apologetic thank-you to these generous folks: Professor Timkehet Teferra, for answering my questions about traditional Ethiopian music; Asmeron Desta and Phaedra Kennedy, for in-depth talks about long-distance running; Aws Waham, for sharing about the backstage area at the High Park Amphitheatre; Jean Meltzer, for sharing your romcom-structure cheat sheet; Virginia and Fiona of the Toronto City Hall Wedding Chambers, for giving me a tour and chatting about officiating ceremonies.

For inspiration across time and space, thank you to the late Asnaketch Worku (Asni), who was a true original ahead of her time. (*Asni: Courage, Passion & Glamor in Ethiopia* is a must-see!)

Thank you to Talia Abramson for such an eye-grabbing cover design, and Maggie Morris and Chandra Wohleber for your meticulous copyediting and proofreading. A heartfelt thank-you to everyone on the Doubleday Canada team for your hard behind-the-scenes work getting this book into readers' hands.

I acknowledge the financial support of the Ontario Arts Council Works for Publication grant, and of Invisible Publishing, Inanna Publications, Second Story Press, Wolsak & Wynn and Book*hug Press, through the OAC's Writers Reserve program.

QUESTIONS AND TOPICS
FOR DISCUSSION

1. Miz jokes that Kal is a dead ringer for the actor John David Washington. If you were to cast the screen adaptation of *Only Because It's You*, who would you envision playing the roles of Miz and Kal? Aimé, Silvio and Daniel?

2. Would you rather spend a week exploring Toronto or Addis Ababa? What's the first thing you would do when there?

3. Miz's parents' separation had a huge impact on her view of marriage. What are your thoughts on the tradition? Has reading *Only Because It's You* changed them at all?

4. They say opposites attract and, in many ways, Miz and Kal fit that stereotype: Miz tends to be bold and carefree, whereas Kal is more contemplative and reserved. Whose personality is

more in line with your own? Who do you think you'd be better friends with? Would you date or marry someone who is your opposite?

5. The way in which Kal's father keeps his mother's memory alive could be described as unconventional. What do you think?

6. Put yourself in Miz's shoes at the start of the book. How would you have reacted to finding the engagement ring in Daniel's gym bag?

7. Kal thought long and hard about what to get Miz as a thank-you gift for her sponsorship help. Were you surprised by what he chose? How would you have reacted if you'd received that as a gift?

8. Running is Miz's go-to activity when she needs to destress or ruminate. What do you like to do when stressed?

9. Miz went full throttle on her mission to keep Kal in Toronto—he didn't even have to ask her to. Is there someone in your life who you'd do just about anything for, no questions asked, only because it's them? And vice versa?

10. Do you think Miz and Kal's marriage will stand the test of time? Why or why not?

© Tom Lai

REBECCA FISSEHA is an Ethiopian Canadian writer based in Toronto. She is the author of the novel *Daughters of Silence*, as well as short stories, creative non-fiction and personal essays that appear in various publications, including the anthologies *Addis Ababa Noir* and *Tongues: On Longing and Belonging Through Language*. Rebecca is a graduate of the Humber School for Writers and the Vancouver Film School, and an alumnus of the TIFF Writers' Studio.